APR - - 2022

MURDER MOST VILE

*The Langham and Dupré mysteries by
Eric Brown from Severn House*

MURDER BY THE BOOK
MURDER AT THE CHASE
MURDER AT THE LOCH
MURDER TAKE THREE
MURDER TAKES A TURN
MURDER SERVED COLD
MURDER BY NUMBERS
MURDER AT STANDING STONE MANOR

MURDER MOST VILE

Eric Brown

SEVERN
HOUSE

First world edition published in Great Britain and the USA in 2022
by Severn House, an imprint of Canongate Books Ltd,
14 High Street, Edinburgh EH1 1TE.

Trade paperback edition first published in Great Britain and the USA in 2022
by Severn House, an imprint of Canongate Books Ltd.

severnhouse.com

British Library Cataloguing-in-Publication Data
A CIP catalogue record for this title is available from the British Library.

ISBN-13: 978-0-7278-5099-7 (cased)
ISBN-13: 978-1-4483-0835-4 (trade paper)
ISBN-13: 978-1-4483-0834-7 (e-book)

All Severn House titles are printed on acid-free paper.

Typeset by Palimpsest Book Production Ltd.,
Falkirk, Stirlingshire, Scotland.
Printed and bound in Great Britain by
TJ Books, Padstow, Cornwall.

ONE

Langham pushed open the door of the detective agency and was stopped in his tracks by the overpowering reek of naphthalene. He stared enquiringly across at Pamela who sat behind her desk.

'I know,' she said, pulling a comical face. 'Fair stinks, doesn't it?'

'Mothballs?' He hung up his hat and coat and sniffed again. 'And there's something else – something sharper.'

'Ah, that'll be the snuff.'

'Snuff? You haven't taken to using the stuff, have you?'

'Not me,' she said, pointing a polished fingernail at the door of the inner office. 'An old chap was waiting at the top of the steps when I opened up at eight thirty. First thing he did when I let him in was take a great noseful. Then he goes and sneezes all over the place, doesn't he, and blows his hooter on a handkerchief. You should have seen the state of it!'

'His hooter?'

'His handkerchief. Looked as if he'd dipped it in tar. Sopping, it was.'

'Delightful.'

'He sat in here for a while,' Pamela went on, indicating a straight-backed chair against the wall, 'but he was getting on my nerves with his constant sniffing, so I asked if he'd like to wait in your office. You don't mind, do you?'

'Of course not.' Langham moved to the office door. 'Did he say who he was and what he wanted?'

Pamela referred to her notes. 'A Mr Vernon Lombard of twelve, Saddler's Lane, Highgate. He mumbled something about a missing person, but I didn't get everything he said.'

When Langham opened the door and stepped into the inner office, the aroma of naphthalene and snuff intensified. He walked around his desk and sat down.

Vernon Lombard sat hunched in the chair before the desk.

He appeared to be in his seventies or eighties and wore a heavy Harris tweed overcoat from which the scent of mothballs radiated in waves. His arthritic fingers clutched the knob of a white cane.

'Mr Lombard? I'm Donald Langham. How can I be of help?'

The man's eyes were sealed with a milky film, the result, presumably, of cataracts, and he stared sightlessly over Langham's right shoulder. His face was thin and grey, with a small, drooping mouth and a straggling white moustache stained a vivid rust colour from his habitual use of snuff.

'Ah, Mr Langham,' Lombard said in slow, refined tones. 'I take it that Mr Ryland is not available?'

'My colleague is busy on a case at the moment.'

'He comes highly recommended, you see. He once performed a service for a friend of mine, before the war. But no matter.'

'I understand you're here about a missing person?' Langham said.

'I have two sons,' Lombard said. 'They are in their late thirties now. They were born two years apart and received identical upbringings, with a nanny, and then a governess, followed by excellent educations at day schools.'

Lombard hesitated, and Langham took the opportunity to say, 'And it's one of your sons who is missing?'

'If you would be so good as to hear me out,' Lombard admonished. 'As I was saying . . . They had the very best educations, and later they were boarders at one of the finest public schools in the country. They wanted for nothing; the only blot on their childhoods was the death of their dear mother when they were four and six respectively.' He leaned forward. 'I stress that they were treated equally, with neither Christopher nor Nigel receiving any preference. My quandary, given this, is why did they turn out to be so different in their essential characters?'

Feeling that this was a rhetorical question, Langham leaned back and remained silent.

Lombard went on, 'I suspect the rot set in when they were away at school. My younger son, Nigel, was wayward, and I had more than one letter from the headmaster reporting on his misbehaviour. Nigel scraped into Oxford, but from then on led a dissolute lifestyle which culminated in his being sent down for circumstances which we need not go into here. I saw him rarely in his twenties, and then only when he needed bailing out of trouble, or when he was in need of financial assistance. I am a rich man, Mr Langham, but I resented Nigel's assumption that the family wealth might be employed to sustain his indolence. Though I inherited a certain wealth from my father, I invested it wisely and sank it into manufacturing. I made provisions for my sons, and while Christopher used his annuity to better himself, Nigel did not. He frittered away his allowance and came back shamelessly for more. The last time I saw him must have been two years ago.'

'And it's your younger son, Nigel, whom you wish me to locate, I take it?'

'I would ask you not to anticipate the reason for my presence here, Mr Langham.'

'Quite,' Langham said, duly reprimanded. 'If you'd care to continue.'

Lombard cleared his throat. 'Nigel never held down any one job for longer than a few weeks,' he said, 'and nor was he at any one address for more than a month or two. In 1950 I discovered, through Christopher, that my son had married – though, of course, neither of us was invited to the nuptials. Christopher described Nigel's wife as a ne'er-do-well who, like Nigel, drank too much. I believe that the marriage lasted no more than a year, and that Nigel left his wife for another woman.'

The old man reported the details of his youngest son's life with concision, rarely letting his emotions show, although his choice of words betrayed his rancour and disappointment.

'Now, whereas Nigel has been nothing but a thorn in my side since his early teens,' Lombard said, 'the same cannot be said of Christopher. Even though he passed through school without distinguishing himself academically, I had no cause for concern as far as his behaviour went. He was a model pupil and applied himself, to the best of his ability, to every subject. He was never academic, but showed an aptitude for art, which I can only assume he inherited from his mother, as

Ada did like to dabble in watercolours. During the war he was employed at the Ministry of Information, and in '46 he set himself up in a studio in Chelsea and began selling his oil paintings. It might not have been the profession that I had had in mind for Christopher – I had rather hoped he would take on the directorship of the company – but to his credit he managed to earn a decent living. He lived in London until the early fifties, then moved to a place outside Hereford – I understand it was some kind of artistic commune. While he was resident in London, we saw each other regularly, perhaps every other week. Since he moved to Herefordshire, our meetings have occurred somewhat more sparsely – perhaps every couple of months. Until, that is, a little under four months ago.'

'Ah,' Langham said to himself.

'I last saw him at Christmas. I had him up for a little get-together at my place in Highgate. He seemed in good spirits – a gallery in Mayfair had just sold a number of his paintings. On leaving, he said he would be up again in late February, and we made a casual arrangement to meet at the In and Out for lunch.'

Langham said, 'And I take it he hasn't been in touch?'

'That is correct,' the old man said, 'and I don't mind admitting that I am more than a little concerned.'

'And you've tried contacting him at his Hereford address?'

'Of course. Although I never had his phone number, I do have the address – from time to time we'd correspond with each other. In March I wrote to ask why he hadn't been in touch, but I heard nothing in return.'

'I take it that this is unusual – he's never gone so long without contacting you in the past?'

'Never,' the old man said. 'He was most punctilious in ensuring he kept in contact.'

'You haven't gone down to Hereford yourself?'

'My health precludes such a journey, Mr Langham.'

'I wonder if I could ask you for his Hereford address and the name of the gallery in Mayfair?'

'The gallery is Weatherby and Lascelles on Cork Street, and I have Christopher's address here.' He reached into the folds of his overcoat and produced a tiny, dog-eared address book, which he passed across to Langham.

'There was a time, a few years ago, when I could just make out my feeble scribbles, but no more.'

Langham failed to find the elder son's name under the letter L, but located him under C: Christopher Lombard, Henderson's Farm, Swavesy, Herefordshire.

He made a note of the details and returned the address book.

'I wonder . . . It might help if you could supply me with a recent photograph of Christopher.'

Lombard smiled. 'I'm afraid we're not a sentimental family, Mr Langham. We don't go in for photographs, though I daresay Ada might have had some, from when the children were little. Not that those would help in any way.'

Langham agreed, then said, 'Very well. I'll look into this over the course of the next couple of days, sir, and get back to you. In my experience, there's often a simple explanation in cases like this. I wouldn't worry yourself unduly.'

The old man gave a thin smile below his snuff-stained moustache. 'Alas, as the years proceed, Mr Langham, I find myself assailed by anxieties I am unable to assuage. And . . .' He hesitated. 'And in this case, I have a pressing need to find Christopher.'

Langham leaned forward. 'You have?'

Lombard gazed sightlessly into the sunlight cascading through the window. 'I was diagnosed with incurable heart disease just after Christmas,' he said. 'My physician gave me six months. I made out my will as soon as I was given the diagnosis, leaving everything to Christopher. And naturally, of course, I would like to speak with him before I die.'

'I will do everything in my power to find your son,' Langham said.

Again the old man reached into an inside pocket and this time produced a cheque book and a gold ballpoint pen. Langham watched as he expertly measured the open cheque book with the fingers of his left hand and, using the position of his fingertips to guide him, made out a cheque for twenty-five pounds.

He carefully tore out the cheque and passed it to Langham. 'I hope that might be sufficient to keep you going for a few days at least.'

'If I locate Christopher within the next week,' Langham said, 'this will more than cover everything.'

'Thank you, Mr Langham; you have been more than kind.' Lombard rose slowly and tapped his cane towards the door. 'If you would convey my regards to Mr Ryland.'

'I'll do that.' Langham escorted the old man from the office and opened the outer door. 'I'll see you down the stairs—'

'That won't be necessary, Mr Langham,' Lombard said curtly, then made his laborious, questing way down the staircase to the busy Earl's Court street.

When Langham returned, Pamela said, 'Who's missing, Donald?'

He perched himself on the corner of the desk and gave her the bare bones of the case.

'That's a coincidence, isn't it? Ralph looking for a missing greyhound, and you a missing artist.'

'How's he getting on with it?' Langham asked.

'He rang in first thing and said he almost had it wrapped up.' Pamela crossed to the sink in the corner and put the kettle on. 'Cuppa?'

'Love one.'

He moved to the window and stared down into the street. It was mid-April and London was enjoying wonderful spring weather; Langham felt his spirits lifting in response. The road grumbled with traffic and pedestrians were out in force, men in shirtsleeves and women in summer dresses.

She passed him a mug of tea – black, no sugar – and stood beside him at the window.

'So, will you be working on The Case of the Missing Artist?' The way she accented the last half dozen words made it sound like the title of a bad mystery novel.

'I'll say. Old Mr Lombard's paid upfront, and paid well.' He took a sip of tea. 'Chances are, though, that it'll come to nothing.'

She raised her eyebrows. 'You think?'

'Nine times out of ten, it turns out that the "missing" person isn't missing at all.'

Pamela nodded, biting her lip. 'So you'll talk to the gallery where he sold his stuff, and visit the people at this farm in the sticks?' She hankered after working on a case herself and never lost an opportunity to pick his brain about procedure.

'I'll give the farm a ring,' he said, 'and see what I can learn there. Then I might tootle along to the gallery. It would be a good idea to track down this black sheep of a brother, too.'

The phone rang, and Pamela answered it with her poshest accent. 'Hello, you're through to the Ryland and Langham Detective Agency. How might I help?'

She listened, her head on one side.

Langham nursed his tea and stared down at the busy street. Old Alf, taking his dog for its morning walk, stopped to buy an *Express* from the vendor on the corner, and a delivery van pulled up outside the Lyon's tea room situated below the office.

'I see,' Pamela said. 'That's correct, yes. Actually, it was Mr Langham who spoke to your father. Very well, I'll put you through. One moment, please.'

She flicked a switch on the intercom, and the phone rang in the inner office.

Pamela covered the mouthpiece with her palm and murmured, 'Victoria Lombard, about her father's visit.'

Langham moved to his office and picked up the phone. 'Hello, Miss Lombard?' he said, lowering himself into his chair and sitting back.

'Mr Langham? I understand you spoke earlier with my father, Mr Vernon Lombard?'

'That's correct, yes.'

'I wonder if I might discuss the situation with you, Mr Langham?'

'The situation?'

'That is . . . I wonder if I might see you, face-to-face?'

'You can't speak over the phone?'

'Ah, I'd rather not. The servants, you see.'

'I understand.'

'I'll be free this afternoon at one o'clock,' she said, 'if you could possibly find the time to see me.'

He glanced at his watch. It was just after eleven. 'I am rather busy at the moment, but I could squeeze you in. You're in London, I take it?'

'That's correct. Twelve, Saddler's Lane, Highgate.'

'You live with your father?'

'I have a separate flat in the same building. Please don't ring at the front door,' she went on hurriedly. 'I don't want my father knowing I called you. You'll find a flight of steps to the right of the building, leading up to the top floor.'

'I wonder if I might ask what this is about?'

The woman hesitated. 'I really can't speak at the moment, Mr Langham.'

'Very well. I'll see you at one.'

She thanked him and cut the connection.

Pamela appeared at the door and leaned against the frame. 'What did she want, Donald?'

Langham relayed the conversation.

She raised her plucked eyebrows. 'Curiouser and curiouser. The plot thickens. The game's afoot.'

Langham laughed. 'Any more clichés up your sleeve?'

'How about "the beautiful, mysterious daughter desires an enigmatic meeting with the gumshoe"?'

'You've been reading too many hard-boiled shockers,' he said. 'Mark my word, Pamela, when all's said and done, it'll be a very mundane reason she wants to see me. She probably fears her pater's going loopy and her brother won't be missing after all.'

TWO

Ralph Ryland left his Morris Minor outside the old greyhound stadium at Shadwell and pushed open the mesh gate to the compound, his entrance greeted by the yapping of what sounded like a hundred dogs.

The kennels were ranged around the concrete yard in the shade of a dilapidated grandstand. A timber lean-to, built as an extension to the stadium, housed the office of Grayson's Greyhounds. A silver-grey Bentley stood outside the office, and through the window Ryland could see Arnold Grayson striding back and forth as he dictated something to his secretary.

Half a dozen dog handlers stood at the far end of the compound, taking a cigarette break and chatting in the sunlight. They saw Ryland approaching and fell silent.

He stopped before the group. 'Young Len Turner around?'

A middle-aged man, as thin as a greyhound himself, indicated the stadium with a nod. 'In there with a dog,' he said. 'What're you wanting with Len?'

Ignoring him, Ryland crossed to the stand and passed through what had been a turnstile entrance, now without the turnstile. He climbed into the stand and sat on a hard bench overlooking the cinder oval of the racecourse.

Three young men stood by the traps down below, one of them consulting a stopwatch. The mechanical hare shot past the traps along an outer rail and the greyhounds were released to chase the lure, something beautifully elemental in their stretching, animal grace as they sprinted around the curve of the track.

Ryland kept an eye on his wristwatch and estimated that the first dog completed the circuit in a little over forty seconds, the second and third dogs just seconds behind it.

That's what he liked about this job, he thought as he settled back in the sunlight. For all the routine cases that brought in the bread and butter, from time to time others came along to provide a bit of variety. He often took Annie to watch the dogs at White City, and this case was providing him with an insight into what went on behind the scenes.

As soon as he'd interviewed young Len the previous day, he suspected that all was not as it appeared, and his subsequent investigations had proved him correct. Now he was back to wrap up the case and have a quiet word in Len's shell-like.

Down on the track, the handlers gathered their respective dogs and Len looked up and saw Ryland. He passed the leash of his dog to another handler, nodding towards the stand, and made his way up the concrete steps to where Ryland was sitting.

'Take a pew, Len,' Ryland said. 'Forty-two seconds, I made it. Happy with that?'

'It'll do for a training run,' Len said.

Len Turner was a scrawny, underfed youth, with a rash of

acne on his jaw and cheeks that emphasized the pallor of his face. He sat down nervously, exuding perspiration that had nothing to do with the heat of the day.

'Didn't think I'd see you here again, Mr Ryland.'

'No? You thought I'd jack the case in when I couldn't find the dog and admit defeat to Mr Grayson?'

'Something like that.' The youth shrugged miserably. 'I mean, Neb could be anywhere now, couldn't he?'

Ryland sat back and contemplated the young man. 'So . . . what do you think happened to the dog?'

'Stands to reason, don't it? One of Billson's yobs took him. I mean, Neb was odds-on for the Gold Cup, wasn't he? We had it won. No other dog could come near him, not even Billson's best.'

'So you reckon Billson sent one of the boys round the other night to break in and take Neb?'

The youth shrugged. 'Reckon so.'

'And did what with him?'

Len shrugged his slope-shoulders again. 'I reckon they did him in, like the bastards they are.'

'That's one possibility, I suppose. But it's not the one I fancy.'

The young man shuffled on his bony backside and avoided Ryland's gaze. 'No?'

'No, Len. Do you want to hear what I think happened?'

Len looked away. 'Go on, then.'

'I reckon on Thursday morning you took Neb out for his regular run on the heath, only you didn't go there that day. You took a bus up to Dalston, taking the dog with you, and popped in to see your bird for a bit of the old how's-your-father. That's what I reckon happened, Len.'

The young man turned bright red and stared down at his soiled fingers.

Ryland went on, 'Only, on your way back, your attention was elsewhere – still thinking about little Mavis, no doubt, and her obvious charms. And when Neb saw a cat across the road and bolted, he caught you by surprise. He yanked the lead from your grip and went right under the front wheels of a double-decker bus.'

Len hung his head and drew a long breath.

'You were in a right pickle, then, weren't you? If Mr Grayson found out what'd happened, that you'd taken his best dog on a jaunt up to Dalston so you could have it off with your bird, then let Neb get run over . . . well, your life wouldn't be worth living, would it? So you had a bright idea.'

Ryland paused, watching the youth squirm.

'Luckily for you, you'd set off before the other handlers got in, so no one saw you leave. When you got back here, you jemmied the lock on his kennel to make it look as if someone had broken in and taken the dog.'

Len stared into the distance. 'Don't know what you're talking about.'

'No?' Ryland said. He pulled a chisel from his jacket pocket and showed it to the youth. 'You used this to force the hasp – there's still flakes of blue on it, see? – and then hid the chisel under Neb's bedding, where I found it yesterday.' He shook his head. 'What puzzles me, Len, is why you were daft enough to leave it there in the first place, and then why you didn't go back and shift it.'

The youth swallowed. 'One of the other handlers was coming across the yard, see, so I had to ditch the chisel sharpish. Then' – he shrugged – 'I never got the chance to go back and get it, did I?'

Ryland nodded. 'So after you jemmied the lock, you went to Mr Grayson and reported Neb missing. Christ, you must have been fair sweating, eh?'

Len hesitated, then nodded. 'I was, Mr Ryland. No word of a lie.'

'But you stuck to your guns and said you knew nothing about the break-in. That must've taken some nerve. I know what an evil bastard Grayson is.'

Len looked up quickly, giving Ryland a complicit smile. 'Don't mind telling you, Mr Ryland – I felt like shitting bricks and building myself a barricade.'

Ryland laughed. 'So Grayson gets me in to investigate, as he can't decide whether some competitor's done it to stop Neb taking the Gold Cup, or whether you're in on the little game for a back-hander.'

Len swallowed. 'Grayson said that?' He sounded terrified.

'That's what he told me, Len. Those were his exact words.'

The youth sat in silence, hanging his head.

At last Len said, almost inaudibly, 'So . . . so what're you going to do now?'

Ryland was silent as he regarded the youth. He was a pathetic sight, sitting there sweating bullets and massaging his knuckles.

Len glanced up, a pleading look in his eyes. 'Don't shop me, Mr Ryland! You don't know what Grayson's like. If he found out what happened . . . Jesus, he'd—'

'Have you beaten to a pulp?'

'Worse! I'd be lucky to live, I would.'

Ryland stared at the youth. He'd made a stupid mistake, that was all. *And we all make mistakes*, he thought. *Christ Almighty, I did things I regret – things far worse than letting a dog run under a bus . . .*

Impulsively, Len reached out and grabbed Ryland's hand. 'Please, don't tell Grayson what happened!'

Ryland stared down at the youth's grubby paw, and Len removed it quickly.

'I was young, once,' Ryland said. 'And Mavis is a pretty little thing – I wouldn't like her shedding tears over you when Grayson's had his fun. So I'm going to tell the old bastard that some out-of-town outfit took Neb and got rid of him, and I wasn't able to find out who it was. The case will be closed. Grayson can claim on his insurance, and you're in the clear.'

Len looked up, tears streaming down his cheeks. 'Straight up, Mr Ryland? You won't shop me?'

'What happened to Neb was a nasty accident. And I don't particularly like Mr Grayson, truth be told. So let's leave it at that, OK? Only, be a bit more careful in future, eh?'

'I owe you one, Mr Ryland!' Len said, pathetically grateful. 'Tell you what, I'm due a break, so how about I buy you a pint down the Lion?'

Ryland thought about it. Why not? A job well done, and ten guineas earned. And he could do with wetting his whistle.

'I'll just pop in to see Grayson, then I'll meet you at the Lion.'

'Thanks again, Mr Ryland!'

Ryland left the stadium and crossed the compound to the lean-to.

Arnold Grayson sat behind a desk piled with papers, the butt end of a cigar plugged between his liverish lips – a fat, red-faced geezer in his fifties. He was an East End boy made good, and he radiated an arrogance built on the sure knowledge that he was invincible. As well as owning fifty racing greyhounds and a local brewery, he ran a protection racket that stretched along the river from Chelsea to Purfleet. Word on the street was that Grayson was close to making his first million.

He looked up and scowled. 'Ryland. You've found the dog, I take it?'

'I'm not a magician, Mr Grayson. I did what I could, but some things . . .' He shrugged. 'Well, let's just say that, in this case, I couldn't perform miracles. Rumour is some mob out Essex way wanted Neb dead – betting syndicate, so I understand, who're piling the lolly on another dog in the Gold Cup.'

Grayson swore and leaned forward, staring at Ryland with tiny, porcine eyes. 'And young Turner?'

'Len is just as cut up about losing Neb as you are, Mr Grayson. He loved that dog. You've got a good lad there. He had nothing to do with it.'

Grayson grunted. 'If you say so.'

Ryland made to go.

'One thing,' Grayson said. 'These Essex scum – you get any names?'

Ryland shrugged. 'Sorry, Mr Grayson,' he said, moving to the door. 'My invoice will be in the post.'

He left Grayson muttering to himself and made his way back to the car.

The Lion and Unicorn was situated half a mile along the river from the greyhound track, a small, red-brick ale house adjoining Grayson's brewery. Ryland parked outside and waited until he saw Len Turner, the youth hunched forward with his hands in his pockets and his thin legs taking long strides.

Ryland joined him and they entered the public bar.

'This your local?'

'Could say that.' Len thumbed towards the ceiling. 'I lodge here. What'll it be, Mr Ryland? They serve bitter and mild, but the mild tastes like witch's piss.'

'Then I'll have the bitter.'

While the bartender pulled their drinks, Ryland leaned against the bar. At a table at the far end of the room, half a dozen men sat clutching their pints and talking with the hushed air of conspirators. A huge, bald-headed bruiser in the dungarees of the brewery dominated the conversation, repeatedly ramming a fat finger down on to the tabletop and staring around the group as if inviting disagreement.

Ryland recognized one of the men and turned away quickly, hoping he hadn't been seen. Christ, the sight of the disfigured face and the eyepatch brought back memories – and unpleasant ones at that. Fancy seeing Alf Bentley here! He'd last seen the little spiv back in the late thirties.

He dropped that line of thought and turned to Len, who was passing him his beer. 'Ignore that lot,' the youth murmured. 'Big Horace – the bald chap – he's a right bastard, and the others aren't much better.' He hesitated, then went on in an even lower tone, 'They're Grayson's men.'

'Enough said,' Ryland grunted, raising his glass. 'So how did you find yourself working for Grayson, then?'

'My dad had greyhounds and I was brought up with 'em. Dad said I was a natural with dogs, and he knew Grayson. He had a quiet word with him and got me in at the track. I thought I'd landed on my feet back then, but . . .'

The youth stared into his beer. 'Mr Ryland,' he went on, 'things are going on there.'

Ryland lowered his pint. 'What do you mean, *things*?'

Len looked supremely uncomfortable, as if he wished he'd never opened his mouth.

'I'm not sure I should—' he began, only to be interrupted by one of the drinkers.

'Ralph!' Alf Bentley cried, reeling up to the bar. 'If it ain't old Ralph Ryland, as I live and breathe!'

Len looked alarmed and rapidly necked his pint. 'I'd better

be getting back, Mr Ryland. And thanks again.' The youth pushed his empty glass across the bar and hurried off.

Ryland turned to Bentley, forcing himself to smile. 'Alf, long time no see,' he said, and a slew of unwelcome memories came flooding back, images he thought he'd succeeded in forgetting. With them came emotions he'd long held in check, uppermost among them a corrosive sense of guilt.

The years had not treated Alf Bentley well: ugly in youth – his face had been carved to ribbons and his right eye gouged out in a street fight – age had added wrinkles to his injuries and he looked like an old man. In fact, Ryland calculated, he was not a day over forty, five years younger than Ryland himself.

He was also as pissed as a newt.

'Ralph Ryland! Those were good times. What're you doing with yourself these days?'

'This and that, Alf. Dodging and diving. What about you?'

'Cushy number at the brewery, in the office. And some of the tarts in there . . .' Bentley described curves in the air with an unsteady hand. 'But . . .' he leaned closer, dousing Ryland with beery halitosis, '. . . but more important, why not come back and join us, eh? It'll be just like the old days.'

Ryland winced and took a swig of ale.

'Listen,' Bentley went on, 'I've been promoted. Area convener for the union now, under Grayson—'

'The trade union?' Ryland quipped. 'Didn't have you down as a socialist, Alf.'

'Sod that,' Bentley spat. 'I mean the British Union . . . Listen.' He reached out and clutched Ryland's lapel, then went on in lowered tones, 'It's about to kick off again. Just like the good old days. Remember them? Remember Cable Street? Christ, those were the days!'

'I've moved on since then, pal. Settled down, married—'

Bentley went on as if he hadn't heard a word. 'Grayson's got it all planned. The twentieth. Know what that is? The great man's birthday, that's what—'

'I said I've grown up!' Ryland snapped. 'The war taught me something—'

'The war!' Bentley waved drunkenly. 'We were on the wrong bleedin' side, matey! The wrong side.'

Someone called out from the far table, 'Alf, shut it, for Christ's sake!'

Bentley went on, 'Well, like I say – Mr Grayson's got it all planned. You gotta join us, pal.'

Someone loomed above them – the bald-headed thug Len had called Horace. He clamped a meaty hand on Bentley's shoulder and boomed, 'I said *shut it!*'

'But this is Ralph Ryland,' Bentley whimpered. 'He's one of us, a good bloke.'

Horace glared at Ryland, a look that froze the blood in his veins, and leaned in close to him. 'Don't know what the little bastard told you, Mr Ryland, but if I were you, I'd keep schtum, or else.' Then he dragged a protesting Bentley back to the corner table.

Ryland downed his pint, wiped his mouth with the back of his hand and hurried from the pub.

He sat in his car for five minutes, clutching the apex of the steering wheel and cursing quietly to himself.

A little later, calmer now, he started the engine and drove to Earl's Court.

THREE

Langham was enjoying a cup of tea and a ham sandwich when the door opened and Ralph breezed in, tossing his trilby at the hatstand and missing.

He took a seat, leaned back and lodged his feet on the desk. 'Greyhounds!'

'What happened?'

'Turns out one of the handlers took the animal on a jaunt up Dalston way . . .'

Langham listened while Ralph gave him the details of the case, then finished with a description of the greyhound's grisly demise.

'So young Len's off the hook,' Langham said, 'and Grayson thinks the dog was taken by some Essex mob?'

Ralph nodded. 'I'll invoice Grayson for my time, but ten to one the bastard won't cough up.'

Langham indicated the cheque on the desk. 'I shouldn't worry if I were you.' He finished his sandwich and washed it down with the last of his tea.

Ralph picked up the cheque and whistled. 'Nice.' He read the name on the cheque and his face clouded. 'Just a sec – Vernon Lombard?'

'He asked me to pass on his regards. He said you'd done a friend of his a good turn, back before the war.'

Ralph looked uneasy and muttered, 'That's right. They were both mates of my father.'

Langham looked at his partner. 'Ah, I see. Am I right in thinking . . .?'

Before Christmas, Ralph had let slip that his father had been involved with Oswald Mosley's Blackshirts back in the thirties. It was something he wasn't proud of and didn't want to discuss. Since then, when three or four beers had loosened his tongue, he'd mentioned that his father had been the area convener for the Brixton branch of the British Union of Fascists, reporting directly to Mosley himself.

Ralph nodded. 'Lombard and this other chap were high-ups in the union. Just before the war, Lombard's pal wanted me to look into a theft from the local branch. Turns out the secretary had his mitts in the till. I only met Lombard once, and I didn't much like him.'

'He wants us to locate his missing son, but there have been developments on that front.' He told Ralph about the telephone call from Lombard's daughter, Victoria.

'When are you seeing her?' Ralph asked.

'One o'clock,' Langham said. 'I might be wrong, but it struck me as odd that she said she couldn't speak over the phone because of the servants.'

'You think there's more to the case than meets the eye?'

'I'll find out when I meet her,' Langham said.

'Lombard was stinking rich,' Ralph said. 'Had a big place in Highgate.'

'He owns his own business. Do you happen to know what it is?'

'Can't rightly recall. Something shady, I bet. What did you make of him?'

'He was decrepit and blind, or as near blind as makes no difference.'

'How the mighty have fallen,' Ralph said. 'I recall he was a natty dresser and moved in all the right circles back in the thirties.'

'How the mighty have fallen, indeed. He stank something shocking of mothballs.' Langham glanced at his watch. 'I'd better be cutting along.'

'You don't mind if I hitch a ride?' Ralph asked. 'I'm curious to meet this daughter of his.'

Langham took his hat and coat from the outer office and led the way down to his car.

They found a parking space on Saddler's Lane and walked along the cobbled way, counting off the houses. Number twelve proved to be a Georgian mansion on three floors with an unkempt front garden swamped by ivy and miscellaneous shrubbery.

'Strewth!' Ralph exclaimed as he took in the rusting gate and tangle of vegetation beyond. 'I wonder what the neighbours have to say.'

'I should think that a man like Lombard wouldn't give two hoots,' Langham said, trying the gate. It opened with a squeal of hinges and they made their way along the path, batting aside overhanging fronds and branches.

'If I had all Lombard's brass, Don, I'd employ someone to keep up with the place, wouldn't you?'

'I received the distinct impression that Lombard is well past keeping up appearances. He has a bad heart and won't last much longer.'

Ralph grunted. 'But this little lot's been left to go to seed for years. Probably a case of what the eyes don't see, eh?'

'You might be right at that,' Langham said as they reached the house.

Ralph made for the front steps, but Langham stopped him and pointed to a flight of metal stairs bolted to the side wall of the building.

They climbed the staircase to a door on the top floor, and Langham utilized the *fleur-de-lis* knocker.

The door was opened promptly by a small, dark-haired, attractive woman in her mid-thirties.

'Ah, Mr Langham. It's so good of you to come.'

Her glance moved across to Ralph, and Langham made the introductions.

Ralph touched the brim of his trilby, and they followed the woman into a spacious open-plan apartment with a big picture window at the far end of the room looking out across the rooftops of Highgate.

Victoria Lombard wore a navy-blue dress with a white lace collar, flaring from her waist and cinched with a wide white belt. Her poise, along with her raven-black hair, gave her the appearance of an Italian countess. It occurred to Langham that Vernon Lombard had said nothing about having a daughter.

The room was impeccably furnished with a green velvet three-piece suite, a beige pile carpet, and jade-and-cream striped wallpaper. Oils, for the most part rural landscapes, occupied the walls. He wondered if any of the canvases were the work of her brother, Christopher.

'Can I get you a drink, gentlemen? Tea or coffee, or perhaps something stronger?'

'Not for me,' Langham said, but Ralph asked for tea with milk and three sugars.

While she stepped into an adjoining kitchen, Langham took the opportunity to look around the room.

A small bookcase stood beside an art deco fireplace. Novels by Ayn Rand and Louis-Ferdinand Céline sat beside volumes by Arthur Koestler and George Orwell – a collection suggesting that Victoria Lombard's reading spanned the political spectrum.

She returned with a tray bearing a china teapot and two delicate cups, sat down on a settee and indicated that they should occupy the armchairs. She poured two cups of tea and passed one to Ralph.

'About your father's meeting with me this morning . . .' Langham said.

'I understand he's concerned that he hasn't heard from my brother, Christopher, for a while?'

'That's right. He mentioned that he hadn't seen him since Christmas. They had arranged to meet again in February, but Christopher failed to show up, or to contact your father either to postpone the meeting or to apologize. Your father wrote to his son – apparently, he didn't have his phone number – but heard nothing in reply.'

Victoria replaced her teacup on its saucer on the coffee table. 'Did my father describe the state of his relations with his sons, Mr Langham?'

'He gave a somewhat partial account of what he thought of them,' Langham temporized.

Victoria smiled thinly. 'I bet he did. Now let me guess. I suspect he painted Nigel as a dissolute wastrel without an ounce of moral fibre, who never did a day's work in his life and hounded my father for money. Am I correct?'

'Something along those lines.'

'And no doubt he had only paeans of praise to heap on Christopher, his golden boy who could do no wrong, the talented artist who, through his own hard-fought endeavours, succeeded in the cut and thrust of the art world?'

'He didn't go that far,' Langham said, 'but it was obvious that Christopher was his favourite.'

'And tell me truthfully, Mr Langham: did he so much as once mention that he had a daughter?'

He shook his head. 'He didn't.'

Victoria stood quickly and moved to the window, staring out for a time with her back to the men.

She turned, her dark figure silhouetted in the sunlight, and looked from Ralph to Langham. 'If I were to say nothing to correct what my father told you, Mr Langham, then you would embark upon your investigations with a completely erroneous view of the situation.'

She resumed her seat and crossed her stockinged legs. 'My father installed me in this apartment just after the war,' she began, 'and granted me an allowance of five hundred pounds per annum. At the time, against my better judgement, I took it as an act of altruism. I had recently lost my fiancé and had hardly a penny to my name. I should have been more cynical and realized that he wanted me to be at his beck and call – to act as his eyes, as it were. He was already ninety per cent blind even then, and the fact that I drove a car suited him very well. I could also manage the household situation, the hiring and dismissing of staff, et cetera. At the time I was more than a little grateful to him. Only as the years wore on and his demands increased . . . well, I came to resent my virtual imprisonment.'

Ralph finished his tea and, not one to beat about the bush, said, 'I don't see what all that has to do with his missing son.'

'I was merely endeavouring to describe the situation here – to make you understand that my father is a self-centred, manipulative bully whose view of people is coloured not by any objectivity but by the subjective assessment of his own narrow-minded ego and selfish desires.'

Langham ventured, 'And his description of his sons this morning . . .?'

'Bears no relation to reality. Far from being a feckless wastrel, my younger brother, Nigel, is a caring, gentle soul – too gentle, in my opinion. But how could he be anything other, bullied as he was by Christopher throughout his childhood and derided by my father for what he called his "namby-pamby" ways? It's something of a miracle that Nigel survived to be the quiet, considerate man he is now.'

'And Christopher?' Ralph asked.

Victoria sighed in exasperation. 'He's a product of his upbringing. Spoilt rotten as he was by my father after my mother's death, how could he have turned out to be anything other than a narcissist with an overweening ego and an innate sense of his own superiority?'

'That's all very well,' Langham said, 'but as to how it influences the fact that your father hasn't seen Christopher for almost four months, and considers him missing—'

She interrupted. 'My father treats Christopher like the prodigal son, and even Christopher – prone though his ego is to lapping up the praise of others – even he finds it too much at times.'

'You're suggesting that Christopher had had enough of your father, needed some time away from him and simply neglected to make contact?'

'Exactly,' she said. 'In fact, Christopher rang me not two weeks ago. He said that father's attention was wearing him down and that he needed some space.'

'But you didn't mention this to your father?'

'Even though my father and I don't see eye to eye,' she said, 'I didn't want to hurt him with the truth about Christopher's feelings.'

'Your brother didn't happen to say where he was at the time, did he?'

The woman shook her head. 'He didn't say, but I assumed he was at the farm.'

'I see,' Langham said. 'Thank you for putting us in the picture.'

'Over breakfast this morning, my father mentioned you, Mr Ryland. I saw my father leave the house and take a taxi, and on questioning his manservant learned that he intended to hire a private detective to look for Christopher.' She hesitated. 'I thought it might be best if I were to apprise you of the true state of affairs.'

'You did right,' Ralph said. 'Saved us a lot of useless footwork, you have.'

'Before we go,' Langham said, 'I wonder if I might ask how *you* get on with Christopher?'

'As you've no doubt worked out for yourself, Mr Langham, I resent him. And I assure you that it has nothing to do with the fact that my father is leaving everything to Christopher when he dies, and has made no bones about the fact.'

She bit her lip, as if considering something. At last she said, surprising both men, 'Please, come with me.' She stood swiftly and strode across the room.

Exchanging a glance, Langham and Ralph followed her through a door and down a narrow flight of stairs.

At the bottom of the staircase, she opened a door upon a gloomy corridor, then found a light switch. 'My father phoned just before you arrived,' she said, 'and told me he intended to spend the rest of the day at his club. He won't be back until well after six.'

She led them along the corridor to a darkened living room. The curtains were drawn, shutting out the sunlight, and she switched on a standard lamp, revealing a room full of heavy Victorian furniture.

She crossed to a door, opened it and stepped into another darkened room, switching on a light and gesturing with an air of triumph. 'Look!'

They entered after her and stared around in wonder.

Ralph whistled.

Langham guessed that the room was stocked with at least fifty paintings stacked against each other five deep; those he could see were studies of nude women.

Victoria explained. 'I always wondered how it was that Christopher managed to make a living by his painting. Oh, he had a modest talent; he could catch a likeness, but he was no better than your average Sunday painter. I only found out about the contents of this room last year when Wilkins, my father's manservant, let slip something about the "art room", as he called it. Imagine my anger when I discovered . . .' She gestured around her at the massed canvases.

Langham said, 'Your father buys up Christopher's work?'

'And all without Christopher's knowledge,' she said. 'Oh, how I fantasize, when Christopher is at his most arrogant and overbearing, about telling him of this room. But even I am not that cruel, gentlemen.'

'Well, what do you make of that?' Ralph asked as they drove from Highgate back to Earl's Court.

'Poor woman,' Langham said. 'When old Lombard shuffles off, he's leaving everything to the prodigal son. I just hope he's made adequate provision for Victoria.'

'Surely he'd leave her the flat and her annuity?'

'I'd like to think so,' Langham said as he pulled up outside the Lyon's tea room.

'One thing,' Ralph said. 'Why did you ask for the phone number of Henderson's Farm before we left?'

'Old Lombard left us a cheque for twenty-five quid,' he said. 'I might as well be conscientious and dot all the i's and cross the t's.'

Ralph looked at him. 'Just to make sure that what Victoria told us is on the level, right?'

'Well, we've only got her word for it that Christopher *is* avoiding his father,' Langham said. 'It's possible that her subjective judgement is somewhat clouded by her prejudices. I'd like to make sure, just to be on the safe side.'

He climbed from the car and took the stairs to the office two at a time.

Pamela looked up as they entered. 'I've just had a call from Maria. She can get off early and suggested meeting at the cinema bar at five instead of six. She said to give her a ring.'

'Will do.'

While Ralph discussed the greyhound case with Pamela, Langham moved to the inner office and picked up the phone. He dialled the operator, asked for Mr Christopher Lombard of Henderson's Farm, Swavesy, and gave the number.

'Putting you through now, sir.'

He sat back and listened to the dial tone.

Just as he was giving up hope of his call being answered, a woman's deep voice said, 'Hello, Henderson's. Who's calling?'

Langham gave his name and asked if he might speak with Mr Christopher Lombard.

His request was greeted with silence.

'Hello – are you there? Hello?'

The sultry voice said, 'Did you say Christopher? You want to speak to Christopher?'

'That's right. I'm calling on behalf of—'

'We don't know where he is,' the woman interrupted. 'He hasn't been seen here for over a month. If you don't mind my asking, who are you?'

Langham gave his name again and said he was a private investigator working on behalf of Christopher Lombard's father. 'And you are?'

'Dorothea Marston. I run the show up here.'

He hesitated, then said, 'I'm thinking of driving up this weekend. Would you and the other residents be around if I did so?'

'I will be,' she said brusquely. 'Can't vouch for the others.'

He thanked her, replaced the receiver and wandered into the outer office.

'Curiouser and curiouser,' he said.

'What?' Pamela asked.

He told them that the artist Christopher Lombard was indeed missing, despite his sister's assurances otherwise.

'Well, stone the crows,' Ralph said.

Langham phoned Maria at the literary agency and arranged to meet her at the cinema at five. 'We could go for a bite to eat before the film, instead of after, if that suits.'

'Wonderful,' Maria said. 'I'm famished.'

'Oh, and how would you care to spend a couple of days in Hereford?'

'Donald,' she said with a smile in her tone, 'am I right in thinking this might be a working holiday, *mon cher*?'

'How on earth did you guess?' he asked. 'I'll tell you all about it over dinner.'

FOUR

They left their Kensington flat after breakfast on Saturday morning and three hours later were motoring through the undulating countryside towards Hereford; before setting off that morning, he'd phoned and booked a room for the night at the Mulberry Hotel.

He pulled into the side of the lane at the crest of a hill and admired the view. Farmland rolled away to the distant, sun-hazed horizon, alternating with darker patches of woodland. Far off, a wood pigeon gave a muffled coo.

'I've never been to this part of the country before,' Langham said.

'Isn't it lovely?' Maria said. 'I remember going to Hereford and visiting the cathedral on a school trip. We had the most wonderful picnic on the way back.'

'Housman country – well, almost,' he said, and quoted: *"That was a land of lost content, I see it shining plain."*

"The happy highways where I went," she finished, *"and cannot come again."* She smiled at him. 'I'm not

sure that applies to me, though. I've never been happier than I am now.'

He smiled. 'Country living suiting you?'

'I'll say!'

In January they'd moved to Ingoldby-over-Water in Suffolk, and Langham had enjoyed immersing himself in village life. Only the fact that Maria had meetings with several authors next week had forced their return to London for a few days.

He slipped the Rover into first gear and set off down the hill.

'It was a good idea of yours to take a short break,' she said a little later.

He glanced at her. 'Even though it'll be a working holiday?'

'I'm intrigued,' she said. 'The Lombards seem *quite* a family.'

'Indeed. I suspect they have an entire cupboard-full of skeletons. Reading between the lines, the father seems an unpleasant piece of work. A pal of Mosley back in the thirties.'

She wound down the side window to let in a freshening breeze. 'Isn't it strange that he's hired you to locate Christopher, and yet Victoria spoke to her brother just a couple of weeks ago? Didn't she tell her father about this?'

'She said she didn't want to upset him by inferring that Christopher didn't mind speaking to her, and not to his father.'

'What did you make of Christopher Lombard's paintings?'

'I couldn't see much of them in the half-light. They seemed competent enough, but I'm no expert. Female nudes, for the most part.'

'If his father had to resort to buying up his son's work, that can't speak very highly of their quality, can it?'

'I suspect you're right.'

'I feel sorry for him,' Maria said after a while.

'Christopher? Spare your sympathy. From what Victoria said about him, he's an overbearing egotist. It's her I feel sorry for, to tell the truth.' He grunted a laugh.

'What?' she asked.

'Hearing about that nest of vipers – the Lombard siblings – I'm glad I'm an only child.'

'Me, too,' she agreed. 'I did wish I had a sister when I was younger, but I don't regret it now. I suppose it made me more resourceful and confident in my own abilities. I've had to be.'

He reached out and patted her knee. 'How about a spot of lunch before we set off for Swavesy? Hungry?'

'Famished. What is it that Ralph says? "I could chew the hind leg off a donkey."'

'I doubt we'll find anywhere with mule baguette on the menu. I'll settle for sandwiches and Earl Grey, myself.'

They came to a crossroads, and he leaned forward to read the fingerpost. 'Here we are. Hereford, five miles.'

He turned left and accelerated along the road.

Ten minutes later they pulled up before the Mulberry Hotel near the cathedral. They left their luggage in the bedroom and enjoyed a lunch of tongue and tomato sandwiches at a nearby café.

At two o'clock, after a pleasant stroll around the cathedral, they made the five-mile drive west to the village of Swavesy. With the gazetteer open on her lap, Maria directed Langham along the narrow winding lanes.

'Wouldn't it be nice if we found that it's all a storm in a teacup?' he said. 'Christopher's returned to the farm and, what's more, turns out to be a thoroughly decent chap. The artists invite us to stay for tea, and we can enjoy tomorrow exploring Hereford.'

She reached out and tweaked his ear. 'I'm discovering a romantic, optimistic streak in you that I never suspected, Mr Langham.' She sighed. 'No, we'll find an artists' commune seething with resentment, and an errant Christopher who's every bit as vile as his sister claims.'

'And I'm discovering a cynicism in you that I never dreamed of,' he said.

'I much prefer the term "realism", Donald. Turn right here! Well done – I thought you'd missed it.'

He made a swift turn and they motored past the nameplate of the village bolted on to a massive rock on the grass verge: *Swavesy*.

They approached the village green where half a dozen children were playing French cricket. Langham rolled to a halt and wound down the window. 'We're looking for Henderson's Farm,' he called out. 'Do you happen to know the way?'

The children wandered towards the car, conferring noisily among themselves.

'You looking for the Bohs?' a lanky, tousle-haired youth asked.

'Well, we're looking for a chap called Christopher Lombard. He lives at the farm.'

'That's Big Chris,' a little girl said. 'He's a Boh.'

'A Boh?' Langham enquired.

'That's what my dad calls 'em,' the boy said. 'Go through the village and turn left at the fork. Then turn right when you see the big cherry tree. The farm's along the track.'

Maria leaned forward and asked the girl, 'Have you seen Big Chris lately?'

The child looked at the ground and shook her head shyly.

'He ain't been around for weeks,' the young lad said.

Langham thanked them and drove off.

'Bohs?' he said wonderingly.

Maria tapped his knee. 'Of course, Bohs. *Bohemians.*'

Langham smiled. 'I suppose a bunch of artists would gain a reputation in the back of beyond.'

'So much for your hope of finding Christopher returned and all's well with the world,' Maria said.

'We haven't found out otherwise for certain yet, my girl.'

They came to the fork and took the left-hand lane, then arrived at the blossoming cherry tree and turned right along a bumpy track. Half a mile away, across a field of barley and partially shielded by a stand of beech trees, he made out a series of low farm buildings.

He drove slowly along the track and came to a stop in a cobbled farmyard.

'How lovely,' Maria said.

Planters bearing daffodils were arranged before the honey-stoned facade of the building, and the window frames and front door had been painted canary yellow. A barn adjoined the house, with a small inset door above which a sign read: *Studio Open.*

'What a singular place,' he said.

A young woman in khaki shorts and a man's white shirt, her peroxide-blonde hair caught up in a knotted red headscarf, appeared at the kitchen door and waved at them. 'Hello there!' she called out, smiling. She indicated the entrance to the studio. 'Go right in – I'll be with you in a minute.' She disappeared back into the house.

'She thinks we're customers,' Maria murmured.

'Well, we could have a gander,' Langham said. 'If you like something, we could always make a purchase and get off on a good footing with the Bohs.'

She laughed. 'Come on!' she said excitedly, and Langham followed her from the car.

Artists' studios and galleries, he had learned in nine months of marriage, exerted an hypnotic attraction on his wife: she rarely left one without having purchased an artwork.

The studio was a big room with a flag-stoned floor and rough whitewashed walls. Sculptures stood on timber pallets ranged around the space, Giacometti-like human figures in polished wood.

Burned into a length of planking nailed to the wall was the artist's name: *Dorothea Marston* – the woman he'd spoken to on the phone yesterday.

'What do you think?' he asked Maria.

'Incredible!'

'You like them?' he asked, surprised.

'I . . .' She pondered, a crimson fingernail pressed to her lips. 'I find them . . . interesting,' she said.

'Disturbing?'

'Ye-es. Yes, they are. But then what do you expect?' She indicated folded cards beside each piece. 'Look at the titles.'

'*Grief,*' he read, referring to a two-foot-tall, asexual figure holding its head, its ribcage prominent. *Earthly Torment*, read another, describing a female figure rolled into a foetal ball, as if in agony.

He indicated the artist's name on the wall. 'They're by the woman I spoke to yesterday,' he said. He recalled her low, sultry voice and went on, 'And she sounded just the kind of person who might create such pieces.'

Maria pointed to a low doorway which led to another room.

He followed her through, and the melancholic atmosphere changed immediately. The space was hung with big, bright, breezy canvases depicting sunlit fields and meadows, strewn with sunflowers and poppies. A sign on the wall read: *Penny Archer*.

'This is more like it,' he said.

Maria laughed. 'I thought you might like these, Donald.'

'Do you?'

'They're accomplished, and benefit from being seen after the sculptures.'

'Would you buy one?'

'No,' she said. 'They're too brash for my liking. I prefer my paintings to be a little more subtle and understated.'

'Hmm,' he said.

A doorway in the far wall led through to another gallery, and Langham made out a further room beyond.

They passed into the third room.

'Now these I like,' Maria said, strolling across to a series of pale, washed-out seascapes on the far wall, almost abstract in their representation of foreshore, sea and sky.

'They're wonderful,' she said, and looked at him. 'What do you think?'

'Yes, I like them. Especially the one with the lighthouse.'

She gripped his hand. 'Me, too. I wonder . . .'

She was interrupted when the young woman entered the gallery and called out, 'Ah, there you are. Simon's good, isn't he? So subtle. Quite a contrast to the man himself!'

She indicated the name on the wall: *Simon Lipscombe*. 'Simon's work is exhibited in some very good galleries in London. These are his latest. I'm Penny, by the way,' she went on, advancing and shaking their hands. 'I'll let you browse, and if there's anything you especially like, just give me a shout. I'll be in the kitchen next door.'

'If Mr Lipscombe is big in the city, he's probably out of our price range,' Maria said.

Penny Archer smiled, and Langham winced in anticipation.

'These small canvases are quite competitively priced,' she said. 'It's the bigger pieces the London places prefer. These' – she pointed to the seascapes – 'are just ten guineas each.'

Maria flashed Langham a look which he interpreted as meaning 'Let's!'

Penny said, 'But Simon should be back any time soon. Perhaps you'd like a chat with him about his work?'

'We really like this one,' Maria said, indicating the lighthouse scene. 'In fact, I like it so much I'd like to buy it. It will go really well in the cottage hallway, don't you think, darling?'

Langham agreed that indeed it would, then turned to the young woman. 'I wonder, is Dorothea Marston around?'

'Dorothea? Why, yes – that is, she went out for a walk a little while ago, but she should be back pretty soonish.'

'You see, we spoke on the phone yesterday.'

The young woman raised paint-spattered fingers to her cheek. 'Oh, I see. Then you must be . . . I'm sorry, Dorothea told us your name, but I've quite forgotten. You're the detective enquiring about Chris.'

'That's right,' he said. 'Donald Langham, and my wife, Maria. I'd just like a few words with Dorothea – and whoever else lives here. Christopher's father is naturally concerned about his whereabouts, you see.'

'Of course, yes; I quite understand. Look,' Penny said, as if coming to a sudden decision, 'would you care for a cup of tea in the kitchen? We can wait there until the others get back. They shouldn't be long.'

'If it's no trouble,' Maria said.

'Not at all. This way. We'll go through Chris's studio and you can see his work.'

She led the way through a low-lintelled doorway into another whitewashed outbuilding. A series of big canvases depicted a dozen naked women, all in graphic postures. Langham found the paintings unpleasant, not so much in the flagrant poses of the models, but in how the subjects seemed depersonalized, almost as if they represented nothing more in the eyes of the artist than slabs of meat.

Penny read his expression. 'Yes, I don't care for them, either. But I'm afraid that's how Chris regards the fairer sex.'

They moved into a low farmhouse kitchen, with an Aga cooker at one end and a scrubbed-pine table in the middle of the stone-flagged floor.

'Take a seat while I put the kettle on,' she said, busying herself at the sink.

'I like the way you've decorated the front of the farmhouse,' Maria said.

'Oh, that. Yes, it's a joint effort – under Dorothea's direction, I must admit. Anything to smarten the place up, give it a little life. You should have seen it when we moved in here. It was a ruin!'

She asked them how they took their tea, poured out three cups, then sat down with them at the table.

'How long have you been here?' Langham asked.

'I moved in almost five years ago, just after Dorothea decided to rent the place. Old farmer Henderson who owns it had a son in the war – he was a war artist. But he died in '45, you see – a freak accident in Germany, something to do with an unexploded bomb or a mine or something. The farmer was too old to manage the farm – I think he hoped his son would take it on – and when Dorothea expressed an interest in turning the place into an artists' commune, the idea appealed to him. Dorothea knew Chris and asked him if we'd like to work here – so we came, back in '52.'

Langham looked at her. '"We"? You mean, you and Christopher Lombard . . .?'

She coloured, looking down at her cup. 'We were together back then, yes.'

He said, 'But not now?'

She shook her head. 'No. After a couple of years here, things between Chris and me became . . . well, fractious, let's say. He wasn't the easiest person to live with. He's very egocentric. I knew he'd had the odd fling with other women while we were together, but this was different. He ditched me and took up with Dorothea.'

Maria winced. 'Ouch.'

'Are Christopher and Dorothea still together?' Langham asked.

'Well, until a few weeks ago, they were.'

'That must have been a bit difficult,' Maria said. 'Living all together here?'

Penny smiled. 'Not in the slightest. I simply ignored Chris

and got on with my work. And anyway, Simon and I got together a year ago.' She shrugged. 'So all's well that ends well.'

'You weren't at all resentful of Dorothea?' Maria asked.

The young woman frowned. 'I suppose I was, a little, in the early days. But Dorothea's a lovely person. We've become very close, over the years. Let bygones be bygones, I say.'

Langham sipped his tea. 'Were you surprised when Christopher left?'

Penny considered the question. 'I suppose I was, really. I mean, he and Dorothea – their relationship was tempestuous at best. They had blazing rows as often as other couples had cups of tea, but they always seemed to make up afterwards.'

'But not this time?'

'I wasn't aware that things had been especially acrimonious between them,' she said. 'In fact, I'm sure they weren't, because Dorothea was just as shocked as the rest of us when she woke up one morning and found that Chris had vanished. He'd taken a few clothes and his old van, and off he went. We didn't even hear him go.'

'And none of you have heard from him since?'

'No, not a word.'

'How has Dorothea taken it?'

Penny frowned, staring down at her cup. 'I think, deep down, she's very hurt. But she's prideful and perhaps wouldn't admit it.'

'Does she or anyone else know where he might be?' he asked.

'If Dorothea does, she hasn't said anything to us.' Penny hesitated.

'And you?'

She shook her head. 'I don't know specifically, but I assumed he'd headed for London.'

'Do you know if he has an address there?'

'Not that I'm aware of,' she said. 'We had a few mutual friends, back when we were together. I rang them, on Dorothea's behalf, just after Chris walked out. But those I did manage to contact knew nothing about where he might be.' She shrugged. 'I'm sorry.'

Maria indicated the studio through the open door. 'Isn't it
odd that he didn't take his canvases with him?' she said. 'They
must represent a considerable sum of money, if he sold them?'

'Oh, he could sell them, all right. He never had any trouble
in that respect, though I have no idea who might want such
things. But yes, you're right. Simon and I were discussing it
just the other day. I said it was very unlike him to leave his
latest work behind like that. Oh,' she said, jumping up at the
sound of a car engine and moving to the window, 'that must
be Simon.'

A car door slammed and a voice called out, 'Pen! Give me
a hand, would you?'

'Excuse me,' Penny said and dashed outside.

She returned a little later hugging a big brown paper bag
of groceries, closely followed by a tall, hatchet-faced young
man bearing another bag. He had hair as dark as Indian ink,
worn unfashionably long, blue eyes and a pleasant smile.

He deposited the bag on a chair and shook their hands. 'You
must be Langham, the detective. Thea mentioned you might
drop by. I hope Penny's been looking after you?'

Langham smiled and raised his cup, then introduced Maria.

She said, 'I very much like your work, Mr Lipscombe. In
fact, we'd like to buy the lighthouse scene.'

He smiled. 'Simon, please. Let's not stand on ceremony.
The lighthouse? Well, it's not one of my best.'

'Simon!' Penny admonished. 'He's always doing that,' she
said in an aside to Maria. 'I wish you wouldn't deride your
work, Simon.'

'Well, it's better than thinking it the best thing since
Augustus John,' he said, helping himself to a cup of tea. 'As
our friend Mr Lombard is wont to do.'

He joined them at the table, scraped out a chair and sat
down.

Langham said, 'No love lost between you and Lombard,
then?'

'To be perfectly frank, I dislike the fellow intensely.'

Penny put in, 'Simon's too honest by half.'

The young man shrugged. 'It must be said. And I'd say as
much to his face, too, Mr Langham.'

'Penny was saying that you were all surprised when he left, and you've no idea where he might be now.'

'I was surprised that he left so much work,' Lipscombe said. 'We don't have a clue where he might be – not that I'm in the slightest bit bothered. Good riddance, as far as I'm concerned.' Penny explained, 'Simon found Chris's arrogance insufferable.'

'Not only his arrogance – everything about him,' the young man said. 'For starters, we didn't see eye to eye politically. Lombard was so far right of centre he was almost off the scale. Before the war, he was one of Mosley's lackeys. But what would you expect, with his father in the line of business he's in—'

'Which is?' Langham asked.

'Lombard senior is an arms manufacturer, and not just a small-time dabbler – one of the big cheeses. He bought a small munitions manufacturer in the late twenties, then moved on to produce artillery pieces in the thirties and wangled a contract with Franco. Would you believe it! While good Englishmen went out there to fight with the Republicans, they were mown down with arms made in their own ruddy cities!'

He clutched his mug, visibly shaking, and calmed down by degrees. 'The arguments we've had on the subject! And what galls me, Donald, is that Lombard tried to justify the Franco deal. He said that if Lombard and Co. didn't supply these people with arms, then someone else would simply step in to fill the breach. I've never heard such a lily-livered, self-serving argument! I'm sorry. You've hit a raw nerve.' He shook his head. 'Lombard called me a simple-minded Commie, would you believe? That's the trouble with people like him, Donald; they categorize everyone on the Left as died-in-the-wool, card-carrying Stalinists. I call myself a Labour-voting socialist, and I'm proud of it.'

Langham smiled. 'The more I hear of Lombard junior – and senior, come to that – the less I like. Perhaps I should donate the cheque Lombard senior gave me to the Labour Party?'

Lipscombe laughed. 'My word, that'd enrage father and son alike.'

Maria said, 'What do you think of Christopher Lombard's paintings, Simon?'

Penny rolled her eyes. 'Don't get him started on that!' she pleaded.

'I promise not to get angry,' Lipscombe said. 'Or not *as* angry.' He shook his head. 'They're fifth-rate daubs without much technical or aesthetic merit. He treats his subjects with contempt – just as he treats the women in his life – so, on reflection, perhaps his views and his art can be seen as faithful to the man himself: his art successfully communicates his misogyny. But quite apart from that, he lacks technique. Just study his human figures if you don't believe me. His sense of bodily scale is way out. I once put this to him, and he had the effrontery to claim that it was deliberate – that his distortions of the female form were his way of representing his subject's psychological failings. Baloney! It's merely the result of his technical deficiency. In fact,' he went on, 'I'd go so far as to say that his brother, Nigel, has more ability than him.'

'Nigel?' Langham said. 'Do you know him?'

'He's invited himself here a few times over the years.'

'He paints?'

Lipscombe shook his head. 'He draws, sketches. He has a minor talent. If he applied himself, he could make a go at being a commercial illustrator. But he's too shiftless to bother himself with anything like hard work.'

'How does Nigel get on with his brother?'

'When Nigel comes to stay here, they always end up arguing.'

Maria asked, 'What about, do you know?'

The young man shrugged. 'I don't. I've kept well away from both of them when they're at daggers drawn.'

'What do you make of Nigel?' Langham asked.

'I don't like him one bit.' He nodded across the table at the young woman. 'And Penny detests him, too.'

'I'll say. Nigel resents his older brother's way with women, and tries too hard, in my opinion.' She looked uncomfortable. 'He's come on a bit strong with me once or twice, trying it on. Some men just can't take no for an answer.'

Lipscombe said, 'The last time he was here, a couple of years back, he had Penny up against the wall just there, and

I swear if I hadn't come in at that second . . . My God, I could have knocked his block off! What is it about that family? One brother's so inadequate he tries to compensate by coming on strong to defenceless girls, and the other thinks he's the next best thing after Picasso. But in the end I saw sense and gave Nigel a dressing down.'

'You're getting angry again, Simon!' Penny said in a sing-song voice.

He reached across the table and squeezed her hand, smiling. 'I'm sorry, Pen. I'll shut my big mouth.'

Langham recalled the roomful of Lombard's paintings in his father's house – and wondered if Lombard senior did indeed buy up everything that his son painted. He said, 'And yet Christopher manages to sell his work through a gallery in Mayfair, doesn't he?'

'Would you like to hear my theory on that?' Lipscombe said.

'Go on,' Langham said, catching Maria's amused glance.

'I think it's something to do with his father,' the young man said. 'They're all alike, these big knobs. They swim in the same foul, polluted waters and only understand one thing – filthy lucre. Mark my word, Lombard senior is probably subsidising his son's success, either by bribing galleries to take on his work or persuading his cronies to buy the stuff.'

Langham smiled. 'All that to one side, it doesn't really get us any closer to working out where Christopher Lombard might have vanished to, does it? Do you have any ideas on that front?'

The young man shrugged. 'He's probably met some woman or other and decided to kick poor Thea into touch. It'd be just like him. He has a proven track record when it comes to treating women like that.'

Across the table, Penny coloured to the roots of her blonde hair and fingered the grain of the table.

'And the paintings he's left in there?' Langham said.

Lipscombe shrugged. 'It isn't as if he needs to sell them,' he said. 'He's rolling in it as it is. But knowing him, he'll hire someone to come in the dead of night and take them away.' He grinned around the table. 'Perhaps we should burn them before he does that.'

Penny stared at him, wide-eyed. 'Simon Lipscombe! I never thought I'd hear you say such a thing!'

The young man laughed. 'I'm joking, my sweet. I'd never desecrate art – not even the execrable Lombard's. Even though, on second thoughts—'

He was interrupted by a sound issuing from the nether regions of the farmhouse, the banging of a door followed by a stentorian cry that echoed throughout the building.

'I don't believe it!' bellowed a woman's voice. 'I'll murder the bastard! I swear, I'll murder him!'

FIVE

A red-haired woman burst into the kitchen brandishing a sheet of notepaper.

'Dorothea!' Penny exclaimed. 'What on earth . . .?'

Dorothea Marston was a big, blowsy woman in a voluminous canary-coloured shirt and brown dungarees. In her youth she might have possessed a certain masculine handsomeness, but now her face had hardened with experience and the passage of time. She had a broad forehead and a rather square jaw, with a big, sensuous mouth outlined with crimson lipstick.

Langham judged she was in her late forties – older than he'd expected.

She paused when she saw Langham. 'Oh,' she said, 'you must be . . .'

Langham introduced himself and Maria, and the woman swept on, waving the letter at Penny.

'When did this arrive?'

'About an hour ago,' Penny replied. 'Just after you left. I slipped it under your door.'

'I don't hear a bloody peep from him for a month,' Dorothea said, 'and then this!'

'It's from Lombard, I presume?' Langham said.

'I'll say it is!' Dorothea said. She leaned back against the

Belfast sink. 'The infernal cheek of the man,' she raged. 'He has the effrontery to say he's had enough of life at the farm – and, indirectly, enough of me! – and would I be good enough to package his bloody paintings for collection!'

'He's coming for them?' Lipscombe asked.

'No fear! He wouldn't have the guts to come back to the place with me on the warpath! No, he's sending someone up for them this coming Tuesday, around midday.'

Langham indicated the letter. 'Does he give his address?'

'No, nothing. He doesn't say where the hell he is.'

Lipscombe asked, 'Does he mention who he's getting to collect the paintings?'

'Not a dicky bird. Some cheap-jack haulier, I expect. But if he expects me to go to the trouble of packaging his paintings all nice and neat, he can think again. The bloody hauliers can take them as they are.'

Langham indicated the letter. 'Do you have the envelope?'

She fished about in the pocket of her dungarees and pulled out a crumpled envelope. Langham smoothed it out on the tabletop and examined the postmark. He frowned. 'Smudged, but I can just make out "London S.W." Not that it helps us much.'

He looked around the table. 'Do you know if he had a place in London? Somewhere he rented, perhaps?'

Dorothea shrugged. 'He never said anything to me. He rented an old place by the river, but that was years ago. Penny, be an absolute darling and make me a cup of tea, would you?'

'Of course.' The young woman jumped up and put the kettle on the Aga.

Dorothea read the letter again, swore under her breath, then looked up at Langham. 'You said you're working for old Lombard?'

'That's right. He hasn't seen Christopher since Christmas. They were due to meet in February, but Christopher never showed up.'

'That's Christopher all over. He'd hare off at the drop of a hat without a word of explanation. Could be gone for a few days at a time. A month ago . . . well, I thought it was just another one of his unexplained excursions. But as the weeks went by, I suspected he wasn't coming back.'

'I wonder if you have the time to answer a few questions about him?' Langham asked.

Dorothea sighed. 'I don't see why not. But not here. Come out to my garden. I designed it myself – it's my escape after a hard day's work.' She accepted a mug of tea from Penny. 'You're an angel, my dear.'

She led the way through the farmhouse to the rear of the building; Lipscombe and Penny remained in the kitchen.

They emerged into bright sunlight. An area in the crook of the L-shaped building had been turned into a cottage garden, with forsythia and laburnum providing shade around a small pond. The artist led the way to a couple of benches and they sat down.

'I hope you'll excuse that outburst,' Dorothea said. 'I suppose it's been building in me for weeks. The letter was the final straw.'

'That's entirely understandable,' Maria said. 'I probably would have broken crockery into the bargain.'

Dorothea laughed. 'Men!' she cried. 'Present company excepted, of course.'

Langham smiled. 'Of course,' he said.

'I hope you didn't mind my dragging you away from Penny and Simon,' Dorothea said, 'but if you're going to quiz me about the bastard, I'd rather it not be in Penny's presence. You see, Penny and Christopher were a couple when they moved here five years ago.'

'Penny said as much,' Langham said.

'You've probably gained a picture of the kind of person Christopher is, from speaking to various people, no doubt?'

'We have, though I must admit the picture is rather one-sided. No one has a good word to say about him.'

'He has a maddening ability to rub people up the wrong way. Nine out of ten people hate him. You're probably wondering what I saw in him?'

Langham smiled diplomatically.

'He has many good qualities,' she said. 'He could be generous, compassionate and loving.' She gave a wintry smile.

'It's a pity he couldn't be faithful for more than a few months at a time.'

Langham glanced at Maria, who pulled a distasteful expression.

Dorothea went on, 'I suppose the more I got to know him, the more I came to realize that he was deeply damaged – and perhaps that increased the . . . the compassion I felt for him. I was fool enough to think that the love I showed him might effect some kind of cure. If so, I was bloody well wrong, wasn't I?'

'You say he's damaged? In what way?'

'I blame his childhood – how his father treated him. Lombard senior was a nasty disciplinarian, the product himself of a stern Victorian upbringing. He packed his sons off to some God-awful Jesuit boarding school just as soon as he could, and Christopher especially suffered at the hands of the Fathers there. He was always something of a non-conformist, and he just couldn't buckle down and accept discipline. Therefore, the Fathers rather took exception to him and beat the living daylights out of the little chap. Scarred him for life, in my opinion. It didn't help that his mother died when he was young – I think in some twisted way he blamed her for deserting him, and his grief, combined with his schooling, gave him a somewhat jaundiced view of women. One need only examine his paintings to see that.'

'How would you describe his relationship with his father latterly?'

She thought about it. 'Superficially cordial, I'd say. I think his father, in his old age, regretted his earlier coldness towards Christopher and tried to make amends. He certainly favoured Christopher over Nigel, whom he detested – he saw his younger son as a wastrel, and Nigel certainly disliked his father.'

'Lombard senior tried to make amends?'

'He was instrumental in Christopher's recent success on that front,' she said. 'He introduced Christopher to a gallery owner, who took on his work. And' – she hesitated – 'between you and me, I think it went further than that.'

Maria leaned forward. 'In what way?'

'I'm pretty certain that many of Christopher's more important sales were bankrolled by his father.'

'You're "pretty certain"?' Langham said.

'Christopher himself was suspicious. When his canvases started selling like hotcakes, he asked the gallery owner who the purchasers were and the chap was evasive. And then, as Christopher was passing through Highgate one day a couple of years ago, he happened to see a delivery van parked outside his father's place, and a couple of workmen delivering a canvas. When he asked his father about it, the old man blustered and said something about a Minton he'd bought as a gift for an old friend.'

She hesitated. 'You see, for all his arrogance, his defensiveness about his work, I think Christopher understands in his heart of hearts that he isn't very gifted.' She smiled without humour. 'That's another of his hang-ups – his natural ego battles with his paranoia. Oh, he's certainly a damaged man, Mr Langham.'

'I'll say he is. You paint a comprehensive picture—'

'I've had plenty of time to study him,' she said. 'Too long, perhaps. For all that I miss him, to tell the truth I think I'm well shot of the bastard.'

Langham watched a wren dart from branch to branch in the laburnum. A koi carp broke the surface of the pond with a sudden plop. The sun was warm, although the garden was cooled by a pleasant southerly breeze.

'How did Christopher get on with his siblings, Nigel and Victoria?' he asked.

The woman crossed her legs. 'Not well at all. He called Victoria a stuck-up bitch, which I thought rather harsh. I rather liked her – and felt sorry for her. You see, her father could never forgive the girl for what he saw as her part in his wife's death.'

'But I understand she died when Victoria was just a toddler?' Langham said.

Dorothea nodded. 'That's right, but Ada went through hell giving birth to her, and was never the same afterwards. She suffered some kind of depression and would have nothing to do with the girl. Now, Lombard senior treats her as nothing better than a glorified maid. Victoria, quite naturally, resents what she sees as her father's pampering of Christopher. It's all very sad.'

'I understand Christopher's brother, Nigel, stays here from time to time. Are they close?'

Dorothea laughed. 'Close? No, they hate each other.'

'Well, well.'

'Nigel has stayed here a handful of times over the past few years, but it's always as a last resort – because he has nowhere else to go, or he's on the run from creditors. He sponges off his brother something shocking – again, like Victoria, he resents Christopher for being his father's golden boy. Christopher tolerated Nigel in the early days, but as Nigel has done nothing with his life, Christopher's forbearance has turned to active enmity. And I must admit I always found Nigel a shifty, untrustworthy character.'

She smiled at them. 'Well, I feel better for getting all that off my chest. But I suppose it hasn't helped one bit in tracking him down, has it?'

Langham smiled. 'Perhaps not, but I have an idea.'

'The hauliers?' Maria asked.

'You read my mind. They're probably under strict instructions from Christopher not to divulge where they're taking his paintings – so they'd give us short shrift if we asked them straight.'

'What do you intend, Donald?' Maria asked.

'I'll come up here on Tuesday morning and follow them back to London – if that's where he is – and track Lombard to his lair.'

Dorothea smiled. 'It sounds like something from a film.'

'In my experience, trailing subjects is always pretty dull, but needs must in this case.'

'If you do locate him, could you give me his address? I'd like to send him a blistering letter.'

'I'll do that,' he promised.

She thanked him, then asked if they'd care for another cup of tea.

An hour later, having bought the lighthouse seascape from Simon Lipscombe, they said their goodbyes and left Henderson's Farm.

* * *

That night they dined at the Mulberry Hotel, and on Sunday morning explored the city and took a tour of the cathedral. They set off back to London after lunch and arrived at Kensington a little after five o'clock.

Rather than cook something that evening, Maria suggested they pop round the corner to the Buono Napoli, a cheerful Italian bistro they frequented from time to time.

After the meal, over a bottle of chianti, they discussed the Lombard brothers and Christopher's treatment of Dorothea Marston.

'I like her,' Maria said. 'She's a strong, independent woman who knows her own mind.'

'Yet she fell for the charlatan.'

Maria gave an exaggerated Gallic shrug. 'It is easy to be wise in retrospect, *non*? How was she to know what he would be like? Men have a way of concealing their true natures in the opening moves with women.'

He laughed. 'You make it sound like a game of chess!'

'Well, to some men it is a game, Donald. With Christopher, I'd say that is certainly so. As Dorothea said, he has an ambivalent attitude towards women. A love–hate relationship.'

Langham took a sip of wine. 'In the morning, I'll bring Ralph up to speed with what we learned at Swavesy – then how about we meet for a drink at the Bull at three-ish? We could ask Pamela and Ralph to join us.'

They walked home, arm in arm, through the balmy spring night, and it was almost eleven by the time they let themselves into the apartment.

'That's the phone!' Maria said, and hurried through the hall to the living room. Langham followed her.

'Yes,' Maria said into the receiver. 'Yes, that's right. Who is calling, please?'

She listened, frowning in concentration as if it were a poor line.

'Yes, he is here,' she said, and passed Langham the receiver, mouthing, 'Victoria Lombard.'

'Hello, Langham speaking.'

'Mr Langham. I'm sorry for phoning so late, but you did

say to contact you, if . . .' She trailed off; it was evident from her slurred voice that she was more than a little tipsy.

'How can I help?' he asked. Maria leaned against the doorpost, watching him.

'I . . . I had a thought, over dinner. I was dining alone, you see, and . . . and my thoughts were going round and round.'

Langham raised his eyebrows at Maria and mouthed, '*Sozzled*.'

'I was enjoying a little brandy, you see, and I find brandy always makes me . . . makes me . . . Anyway, I realized something.'

'And what was that?' he asked patiently.

'I realized that I might be able to find out where Christopher is hiding—'

'You might?'

'You see . . .' She gave a muffled hiccup, then went on, 'You see, my father keeps an address book in his living room, and I know that he'll have Christopher's old addresses in it.'

'*Old* addresses,' he pointed out, wishing the woman would hurry up so that he could get to bed. 'That might not be so useful.'

'Yes, but you see . . . it might have one of Christopher's London addresses that he might still be using.'

'In that case, I suggest you take a quick look and get back to me if you find anything.'

'Yes, but . . . but it's not as easy as that. You see, my father keeps his desk locked, and it's in the living room. He's not planning to go out for another week, and he sits in the room all day listening to his damned Wagner.'

'Very well. In that case, why don't you simply wait until he goes to bed and look in the desk then?'

He rolled his eyes at Maria.

'Yes, but you see . . .' Victoria slurred. 'It's his manservant. He might hear me.'

Langham sighed. 'Very well. So what do you suggest?'

'What . . . what I suggest is that you pop around tomorrow morning – say, eleven – to see my father. You could say you're bringing him up to . . . to speed with your investigations. I'll serve you tea on the patio, and while he's occupied with you, I could take a little peek at the address book in his desk.'

'I see,' he said. 'And what about the manservant?'

'Ah, but Wilkins . . . he goes to Harrods every Monday morning to do Father's weekly grocery shopping.'

Langham sighed. It seemed an overly elaborate charade to go through on the off-chance of finding an old address.

Victoria said, 'You *will* come at eleven, Mr Langham, won't you?'

Reluctantly, he gave in to her wheedling tone. 'Very well,' he said. 'I'll see you at eleven.'

The woman hiccupped again, thanked him profusely and rang off.

'What was all that about, Donald?'

'Lord, save me from drunken women, *please.*' He gave her the gist of Victoria Lombard's convoluted plan, which Maria seemed to find inordinately funny.

'Mark my word, my girl,' he said, 'it will come to naught.'

'My poor dear.'

'And so to bed.' He yawned.

SIX

On Monday morning, Langham dropped into the office and filled Ralph in on his weekend in Herefordshire, the situation at Henderson's Farm and Christopher Lombard's plan to send hauliers to collect his canvases on Tuesday.

'If we don't locate Lombard today,' he said, 'I'll motor up tomorrow morning and follow the hauliers, and I'll charge Lombard senior an excess for petrol fees.'

'I'm popping along to that Mayfair gallery this morning,' Ralph said. 'They might have Christopher Lombard's address. I've just phoned them, but the snooty chap I spoke to was reluctant to cough up.'

As he was about to leave, Langham paused in the outer

office. 'By the way, how about we all knock off early today and meet at the Bull at three?'

Pamela looked up from her typewriter. 'That would be lovely.'

'Suits me,' Ralph said. 'I haven't had a decent pint for almost a week.'

'What about your Thursday-night darts session?'

'Annie was sick, so I stayed in and put the nippers to bed.'

'That's devotion for you,' Langham said, and left the office.

He drove to Highgate and parked outside the mansion at a little before eleven o'clock. He made his way down the overgrown garden path, climbed the metal staircase to the top floor and rapped the knocker.

Victoria opened it immediately and smiled at him rather sheepishly.

'I hope you didn't mind my calling so late last night,' she said as she led him into the apartment. 'I must admit that I'd had a little bit to drink and . . . Well, the best-laid plans seem not so good in the cold light of day.'

'I take it we're no longer going ahead with it?'

'On the contrary, I told my father that you'd like to see him this morning.' She hesitated. 'I wanted to talk to you about something else, as it happens.'

At her invitation, he sat down in an armchair and waited.

Instead of telling him what was on her mind, she asked, 'I take it you learned nothing in Herefordshire?'

'Only that your brother left about a month ago.' He gave her the details of his visit to the farm.

'He walked out on poor Dorothea without an explanation?'

'Just vanished,' he said. 'Oh, and he had the temerity to write and ask her to package the paintings he was arranging to have collected.'

'That's just typical of Christopher – but do you know where he wants them delivered?'

He told her about the letter and his plan to follow the hauliers.

'Do you know,' Victoria said, 'I can't say I'm that surprised, about his leaving Dorothea that way. He treats women abominably. I like Dorothea.'

'Did you know her well?'

'I met her a few times,' she replied. 'She wasn't Christopher's usual type: she was older than him, for one thing. And not the usual floozy. But she was dependable, and I thought she'd be good for him. He needed someone a little older and sensible.'

'What sort of women does he usually go for?'

'Actresses, chorus girls. That type. Good-time girls, in short. They're attracted to his good looks and money, and Christopher usually gets what he wants and then dumps them.'

'You mentioned you were in telephone contact with him a couple of weeks ago—'

'That,' she interrupted, 'was what I wanted to talk to you about. Aside from his saying that he needed time away from Father, there was something else. I just recalled it last night, as I sat here brooding. He said he'd been in contact with Nigel – or, rather, Nigel had been in contact with him.'

'Don't tell me,' Langham said. 'He wanted to tap Christopher for a loan?'

'It was a little more serious than that, I'm afraid. Nigel had rather got himself into some hot water.'

'In what way?'

'Christopher said it was a gambling debt. Nigel told him that he owed some people a lot of money. And they were nasty people.'

'How much?'

'A little over two thousand pounds.'

Langham whistled. 'That's some gambling debt.'

'I'll say.' She pulled a pained face. 'The people he owed the money to . . . Well, they were insisting he pay it back rather quickly, or he'd suffer the consequences.'

'Did Christopher agree to bail him out?'

Victoria bit her lip. 'He said he was considering it. But it was a huge amount, and he couldn't raise so much immediately. He said that he'd got Nigel out of more than one hole in the past, and he always managed to climb into another.'

'Do you think he might have refused, this time?'

She shook her head. 'I honestly don't know. Two thousand pounds . . . It was a lot of money to find, even for Christopher.'

'Do you know if Nigel approached your father for the money?'

'I did consider that, but I don't think he had – not for that much. At least, Father never mentioned it.'

'Did Christopher know where Nigel was living? If we could locate Nigel—'

Victoria shook her head. 'I asked Christopher that, and he didn't know. Apparently, they met in a pub.'

'And this was two weeks ago?' Langham mused. 'Did he mention whether this was in London?'

'He didn't say.'

'When was the last time you heard from Nigel?'

She thought about it. 'Perhaps six months ago. He dropped in here out of the blue but didn't stay for long. He said he was going to Bristol to stay with friends, borrowed ten pounds from me, and away he went. I say "borrowed" . . .' she finished with a wry smile.

'Very well,' Langham said, and glanced at the carriage clock on the mantelshelf: it was ten past eleven.

'I'll show you down,' she said. 'I'll make some coffee – or tea, if you'd prefer.'

'Earl Grey for me, if you have it. Black, no sugar.'

He followed her down the narrow staircase to the ground floor, just as dark and sepulchral as it had been on his previous visit. From far off, the strains of classical music could be heard. Langham recognized Mahler's fifth symphony.

They moved along the corridor to the darkened living room, and the volume intensified. Victoria said something, but the music was so loud that Langham was unable to make out her words.

The old man sat upright in an armchair, his claw-like hands clutching the knob of his white cane.

Victoria marched across to the curtains and tugged them aside, flooding the room with dazzling sunlight. 'Father, a Mr Langham is here to see you.'

She lifted the needle carelessly from the rotating record, sending out a piercing smear of acoustics.

The old man looked up, the sunlight emphasizing the pallor of his thin face. 'Ah, Langham.'

'It's a lovely day,' Victoria went on, 'so I'll arrange a table on the patio.'

She opened the French windows that gave on to a paved area at the back of the house. She stepped out and placed two garden chairs before a wrought-iron table, then returned and assisted the old man from his armchair.

He shuffled out beside her, muttering to himself.

She came back and murmured to Langham, 'I'll make the tea and coffee, and then . . .' She pointed to a roll-top desk in the corner of the room.

Langham stepped into the sunlight, removed his coat and took a seat at the table.

'Mr Lombard, it's good to see you again.'

The old man's head twitched in Langham's direction and he held out a frail hand. Langham shook it; the flesh was cold, almost lifeless.

'I trust you've been busy, Mr Langham?'

'That's right, I drove up to—'

Lombard held up a hand. 'Not until our drinks have been served and Victoria has gone,' he said. 'I don't want her over-hearing our conversation.'

The old man fumbled in a pocket for his snuff, produced a tiny silver box and proceeded to nip a pinch on to the back of his hand. He raised it to his left nostril, inhaled noisily, then repeated the process and applied the snuff to his right nostril. He sneezed shortly thereafter, and blew his nose on a voluminous handkerchief.

'That's better,' he said, smiling in Langham's general direction. 'Do you like Mahler?' he asked.

'A little heavy for me,' Langham admitted.

'Then you won't like Wagner,' the old man said. 'I cannot imagine a life without the accompaniment of Wagner. Such a consolation, I find.'

'Is that so?'

Lombard sighed. 'So many regrets,' he said, apropos of nothing. 'The older one gets, Langham, the more there is for one to regret. And do you have any idea what I regret most?'

Victoria stepped from the house, bearing a tray. 'Here we

are, Father. Your coffee, just as you like it, strong and sweet. And your favourite Rich Tea biscuits. Black Earl Grey for you, Mr Langham.'

He thanked her and she poured the tea and coffee. 'Now I'll leave you to get on with it,' she said, returning inside and closing the French windows after her.

Despite the sunlight reflecting on the glass, Langham could see Victoria cross the living room to the desk.

'Where were we?' Lombard asked, taking a biscuit and lodging it on the saucer beside his cup.

Langham said, 'You were talking about regrets.'

'Ah, yes, *those*.'

He fell silent, and Langham wondered if the old man was having second thoughts about broaching the subject of his lifetime's regrets.

Langham sipped his tea. 'You were saying . . .?'

The old man stirred himself. 'I haven't treated my children as well as I should have,' he murmured. 'One only becomes aware of one's failings in retrospect. At the time' – he gestured absently – 'at the time, one is too taken up with one's selfish preoccupations. I should have given them more time, more affection. But that's the domain of women, isn't it, and with Ada not there to . . .'

He looked up – or, rather, his head lifted – and he stared sightlessly above and beyond where Langham was sitting. 'Is it little wonder they've turned out as they have?'

Langham said, 'But Victoria is a credit to you, and—'

The old man interrupted irritably. 'But it's Christopher I wish would be here for me, Langham! He said we would meet again in February! What happened to him? What have I done to drive him away?' He shook his head. 'I've helped him in every way I could.'

'Ah, speaking of Christopher,' Langham said, 'I spent the weekend up in Hereford.'

'And?' Lombard asked with eagerness.

Forgetting that the old man could not see him, he shook his head. Then he remembered himself and said, 'Your son left the farm a month ago.'

'Left? With . . . with that woman? The artist?'

'Dorothea. No, not with her,' he said.

'The young idiot! I like her. Forthright woman, head screwed on the right way. Down to earth.' He sniffed noisily and wiped his nose on his handkerchief.

Stuffing it back into his trouser pocket, he said, 'You said he left, but where the bally hell did he go?'

'I have a lead, and I'll be able to tell you more, I hope, in a day or two.'

Behind the French windows, Victoria appeared and held up a tiny black book. She indicated the upper floor with a fore-finger and moved towards the far door.

'Good show,' Lombard said. 'Do you need further funds? How much did I give you the other day?'

'Twenty-five pounds. That's sufficient for the time being.'

Lombard was silent for a time, then said, 'I enjoy my conversations with Christopher. What he doesn't know about art isn't worth knowing, and I admit to my vast ignorance in that area.' Belatedly, he remembered the biscuit and chewed it ruminatively. 'He's a highly successful artist, you know. His stuff hangs in the very best galleries, and he has exhibitions all over London.'

'Yes, I've seen some of his paintings,' Langham murmured, feeling an inordinate sympathy for the old man.

He let Lombard ramble on, only having to interject the odd monosyllable to assure him of his presence. He sat back in the sunlight, thought of Maria and their cottage in Suffolk, and thanked his lucky stars.

'But here I am, bending your ear,' Lombard said after a while, rousing Langham from his reverie. 'I'll keep you no longer, young sir.'

'It's been pleasant to catch up,' Langham said. 'Can I assist you inside?'

'No need, no need. In fact, I think I'll stay out here and enjoy the sun. Oh, if you'd be so kind as to put some music on when you go back inside. Damned woman turned it off.'

'Of course.'

'You'll find some Wagner on a pile beside the gramophone,' Lombard said. 'Be so good as to put that on, would you?'

Langham thanked him for his time and stepped inside.

He found a heavy shellac record of Wagner's *Träume*, slipped it from its brown cardboard sleeve and placed it on the turntable, carefully lowering the needle on to the outer edge of the disc. A series of crackles filled the room, followed by the opening bars of the piece. He increased the volume, then turned and looked through the French windows.

The old man leaned forward in the sunlight, clutching his cane in both hands, his head cocked as he listened to the music.

Langham made his way upstairs and found Victoria in the living room, examining the address book on the coffee table.

'Don't tell me,' he said as he joined her. 'A hundred and one old addresses, all crossed out?'

'Well, a lot of Christopher's old addresses have been scored out, Mr Langham' – she tapped the open book triumphantly – 'but this one hasn't. I recall that he still rented the place, a year or two ago.'

He took the book and examined the address, written in Lombard senior's spidery hand: The Loft, Madras Wharf, Wapping.

'Would you mind if I took this with me? Even the old addresses might prove useful.'

'By all means.' Victoria hesitated, then asked, 'I wonder . . . Would you mind terribly if I came with you? If Christopher is there, I'd like to persuade him to see Father before he vanishes again.'

'If it's all the same,' he said, searching for an excuse as he didn't want the woman dogging his steps, 'I'd like to see Christopher alone – if I do find him, that is. But I promise to contact you immediately, and, of course, I'll pass on your request that he should see his father.'

Victoria frowned, clearly put out at the rebuff.

He pocketed the address book, thanked her for the tea and took his leave.

SEVEN

Weatherby & Lascelles Fine Arts was a plush, double-fronted establishment on Cork Street. The window display to the right of the front door was draped in mauve velvet, with a landscape set on an easel for passers-by to enjoy and envy.

Ralph Ryland pulled up outside the gallery and sat for a while, thinking back to meeting Alf Bentley in the Lion and Unicorn on Friday. The encounter had shaken him – he didn't mind admitting that – and stirred up unpleasant memories.

Don hadn't noticed anything amiss with him, but there had been no pulling the wool over Annie's eyes. She'd come straight out with it last night: 'Ralphy, something's bothering you and I won't shut up till you've told me what it is.'

So he'd told her about bumping into Bentley and the guilt it had provoked. She knew all about his past and had said, 'You were young, Ralphy. Young and foolish. You're a different person now.'

'You know that, Annie – but it's Don's reaction that worries me. He doesn't know, you see, and if he finds out . . .'

'Donald's no fool, my love. And you're close to him, aren't you? We all make mistakes. Don will understand that.'

Ryland had let the matter drop, but it had kept him awake all night.

He swore to himself and climbed from the car.

The gallery was the kind of place that made him feel inadequate merely looking at the posh frontage with its navy-blue livery and brass nameplate. He pushed through the door and pretended an interest in the contemporary landscapes that decorated the wall to the left of the entrance.

He was approached by a woman who reminded him of his old school headmistress. 'And how might I be of assistance?' she asked in an icy tone entirely at odds with the content of her enquiry.

'I understand you represent an artist called Christopher Lombard?' he said.

'Mr Lombard is on our books; that is correct. And you are?'

She was one of those superior types he liked to wind up, so he flashed his PI accreditation for about half a second and said, 'Detective Inspector Ryland from Scotland Yard.'

She blinked, which was the extent of her discomfiture. 'And how might I be of assistance, Inspector?'

'Do you deal directly with Lombard?' he asked.

'I don't; you would need to speak to Mr Timothy,' she said. 'But as today is Mr Timothy's day off . . . I suppose I could enquire as to whether his deputy, Mr Hector, is available.'

'If you could, that'd be grand,' he said, and gave her a dazzling smile.

He watched her bustle off and disappear through a door at the back of the gallery.

She returned a minute later. 'If you would care to follow me.'

She led the way through the door into a long room stacked with paintings. An ancient, balding man, almost bent double, stood behind a desk consulting a thick ledger.

The woman introduced them and departed.

The old man proffered a palsied hand and smiled. 'We don't often get police inspectors in the gallery, sir,' he said in a marked Cockney accent. 'Mrs Dolores mentioned that you were asking after Mr Lombard?'

Ryland seated himself on the corner of the desk, side-saddle. 'Fact is, Mr Hector, we're trying to trace him. Seems he's vanished into thin air. I was wondering, do you have Mr Lombard's contact address, other than his place up in Herefordshire, that is?'

'Let me see, let me see,' the old man carolled, pulling another fat book from a drawer in the desk. He turned the alphabetized pages until he came to one marked L, and ran a finger down a column.

'Henderson's Farm, Swavesy,' he burbled to himself, 'and . . . here we are . . . care of twelve, Saddler's Lane, Highgate.'

'Which is his old man's address,' Ryland said. 'Back to square one.'

Mr Hector closed the book and appeared sympathetic to Ryland's plight. 'I'm sorry, Inspector.'

'When was the last time you saw Christopher Lombard?'

'As a matter of fact, we rarely see Mr Lombard in person. He prefers to conduct business by letter, and very occasionally over the phone – and then always with Mr Timothy.'

'So you don't, personally, know the artist?'

'Oh, no, no, Inspector!' Mr Hector laughed as if at a good joke. 'Truth be told, I am merely a dogsbody in this place, though I have worked here for nigh on forty years, man and boy.'

'I see,' Ryland said, nodding. 'And Mr Timothy, your boss – how long's he been here?'

'Well . . . let me see . . . Not long, now that you come to mention it. Perhaps five years, since leaving university.'

'There you have it,' Ryland said. 'These educated toffs lap up all the cream, as my old mum used to say.'

'But you seem to have done well for yourself, Inspector, if you don't mind my being so bold.'

Ryland winked and leaned forward. 'Between you and me, I told a porky-pie to old Mother Superior out there.'

Mr Hector snorted. 'Oh! I know I shouldn't laugh, Mr Ryland.'

'We've got to stick together, Mr Hector!'

'Indeed we have!'

'Now, I don't suppose I could have a quick shufti at some of Lombard's daubs, could I, seeing as I'm here?'

'Strictly speaking, access is only allowed to prospective customers, but I'm sure Mrs Dolores wouldn't mind an *inspector* from Scotland Yard having a quick look, would she?'

'I'm sure she wouldn't,' Ryland chuckled, following Mr Hector to a long back room stocked with dozens of canvases leaning against the walls.

'Here we are, Mr Ryland,' the old man said, indicating half a dozen large nudes.

Ryland blinked. He moved closer to the paintings and inspected the brushstrokes, then stepped back and shook his head. The women depicted were huge, fleshy and quite misshapen. He did wonder whether Christopher Lombard might be afflicted with the same ocular malady as Lombard senior.

'And people buy these, Mr Hector?'

'For figures in the high hundreds, Mr Ryland.'

'Well, I never. But . . . not that I'd call myself a critic . . . but that looks like no woman I've ever seen, dressed or undressed. Looks more like a side of beef, it does.'

'I must concur,' the old man said. 'But don't tell Mrs Dolores that I told you so!'

'Your secret's safe with me,' Ryland said.

He returned to the gallery showroom and gave the old man his business card. 'If Christopher Lombard should be in touch, I wonder if you could give me a quick bell?'

'I'll do that, *Inspector*,' Mr Hector said, chuckling to himself.

Ryland thanked the old man for his time and took his leave.

As he stepped from the gallery, Ryland mused that while he might have learned nothing from the interlude in Weatherby & Lascelles – other than the fact that the fine art world was the scam he'd long suspected – it had taken his mind off things for a short while.

Rather than return to the car, he decided that a strong cuppa and a sandwich might be in order and made his way along the street and around the corner to a little caff he'd used once or twice in the past. On the way, he saw a display of bagels in a Jewish bakery and winced at the name above the shop-front: Spiegelman & Sons. He stopped and stared at the sign, experiencing an involuntary wave of despair.

But all that was over twenty years ago, he told himself. What had Annie said last night? '*You were young, Ralphy. Young and foolish. You're a different person now.*'

As he was about to walk on, he looked back and saw a tall figure duck into a shop entrance about fifty feet away. He turned and continued along the street.

He crossed the road and casually examined the shop windows. Outside Brown & Muffs, he lit up a Capstan and, turning to cup the match from the breeze, glanced covertly back along the street.

There was no doubt about it: the tall chap in drainpipe trousers was following him.

He threw the spent match in the gutter and hurried along the street.

Twenty yards further on, he ducked smartly into a side alley and ran, turning right along a deserted cutting between a church and the back of a row of shops. He ducked into the rear doorway of a bakery, pressed himself to the brickwork and waited.

He wondered if it might be Christopher Lombard who was taking exception to his enquiries, or someone else linked to another ongoing investigation. He thought back to the last few cases but dismissed them as not being important enough to warrant a tail.

He slipped a hand into an inside pocket and clutched the butt of his revolver.

He heard hurried footsteps approaching along the alley and the tall form of the man flashed by. He stepped quickly after him and caught up.

'Hold it right there,' he called out, 'and turn around *very* slowly.'

The man stopped in his tracks. Ryland drew his revolver and directed it at the man as he turned.

Ryland didn't recognize him. Thin-faced and down at heel, he had the desperate cast of a cut-price hoodlum, a thug-for-hire who might be able to handle himself in a scrap but who was, essentially, a nobody.

'Hands up,' Ryland said.

The thug raised his hands, licking his lips nervously as he glanced at the weapon.

'Who the hell are you and what do you want?' Ryland said.

'Put that thing away and I'll tell you.'

'And have you jump me, chum? Do I look like a mug? Out with it, or I'll make you regret the day you were born.'

The man licked his lips again, calculating.

'Who the hell are you?' Ryland pressed.

'Jones,' the man said.

Ryland stepped forward, prodding the air with his gun. 'OK, Mr Jones. Who sent you?'

'Mr Grayson,' Jones said. 'He wants to know something.'

'Grayson?' Ryland said. 'I get it. Who the Essex boys are, right? The betting syndicate?'

The man blinked, nonplussed. 'Mr Grayson wants to know what Alf Bentley told you in the pub the other day.'

Now it was Ryland's turn to be nonplussed. 'Alf Bentley?'

'He blabbed to you,' Jones went on.

Ryland thought back to the encounter, shaking his head. 'He told me nothing. He was bladdered, could hardly string two words together. Said something about the twentieth.'

Jones stepped forward, his expression hardening. 'What did he say?'

Ryland raised the gun. 'Like I said, he was drunk and didn't make sense.'

'That's not what Horace told Mr Grayson,' Jones said. 'Horace said Bentley blabbed about what he shouldn't've.'

'Look, Bentley was yapping about the good old days, and to be honest I wasn't listening. Why don't you tell your Mr Grayson that if he wants to know what Bentley said, he should ask him?'

Jones smiled, and Ryland liked nothing about the leer, or its implications.

'Oh, he did that,' Jones said. 'He questioned the bastard good and proper, but Bentley claimed he told you nothing. Only Grayson didn't believe him, so he made sure Bentley wouldn't blab again in a hurry.'

Ryland tried not to wince. 'Go on.'

Jones laughed. 'Just had Horace cut the bastard's tongue from his head, is all.'

Ryland tried to work out if this was a lie but, going by the tales he'd heard of Arnold Grayson's excesses in the past, Alf Bentley was probably now minus a tongue.

'So what did Bentley tell you, Ryland?' Jones went on. 'Grayson wants to know – or you'll be next.'

'I've told you everything I remember. Tell Grayson—'

Jones sprang, surprising him. The punch caught him on the side of the head, but Ryland recovered, ducked and came up behind his assailant, bringing the butt of his revolver down on the back of the man's head. Jones hit the flagstones, grunting with pain. Ryland turned him over with a foot. Jones stared up at him, groaning, his nose a bloody mess.

'A message for Mr Grayson,' Ryland said. 'Next time, don't send a boy to do a man's job. Get it?'

As Jones lay groaning, Ryland pocketed his revolver and hurried off.

Arnold Grayson was up to something – that much was obvious. Something he didn't want people knowing about.

Scratch that tea and a sandwich, he thought. Now he was in need of a pint or three.

EIGHT

Madras Wharf was less than half a mile from a pub Langham had frequented on a case a couple of years ago, Turner's Old Star on Watts Street. As it was approaching lunchtime, he popped in for half a pint of bitter – limiting himself as he was meeting Maria and the others for a session later that day – and a couple of pork pies. He sat at a corner table and leafed through a copy of the *Daily Herald* obligingly left by a previous customer. He read an article detailing the government's agreement to grant Singapore limited self-rule, then skipped over the report of Arsenal's one-nil defeat at the hands of Sunderland at the weekend.

He finished the second pie and laid the paper aside, thinking not about the news or Christopher Lombard's whereabouts, but mulling over the rewrite of his latest novel. He could improve the penultimate chapter with a small cut and extend the action scene towards the end.

The atmosphere of the quiet snug, with sunlight slanting in through the frosted window, was soporific and conducive to daydreaming. Sounds retreated into the background: the murmur of conversation between the publican and a customer, and the occasional wheeze of the hand-pulled beer pump. Half an hour slipped by in no time at all.

It was almost one o'clock when he emerged from his reverie, drained his beer and left the pub. He returned to his car and drove down to Madras Wharf on the Thames.

The red-brick warehouse had suffered considerable damage thanks to the Luftwaffe, and, more than twelve years on, brickwork and broken beams scattered across waste ground indicated that the building had once extended for half a mile along the river front. He climbed from his car and stared at the warehouse, inhaling the heady scent on the warm spring air: the aroma of spices from the Far East that the building once stocked.

What remained of the warehouse had been converted into workshops. He approached what had once been a loading bay, now pressed into service as a garage. A hand-painted sign hung above the open entrance: *Cohen Brothers, Vehicle Repairs.*

He paused outside the garage and asked a thin, lean-faced mechanic if he knew how to get to the loft, Madras Wharf.

The man wiped his hands on a rag and nodded towards a narrow alleyway, ten yards away. 'Down there.'

Langham thanked him, then asked, 'I don't suppose you've seen anyone up there recently?'

The mechanic thought about it. 'There was a bloke knocking about there last week. I saw him coming and going a few times.'

'Could you describe him?' Langham asked. 'Was he young, old?'

'Hard to say. Maybe late thirties. Tallish, dark-haired. Can't say I took much notice.'

Langham nodded his thanks and made his way to the corner. The alleyway between the warehouses led down to the bank of the river, and a metal staircase zigzagged up the side of the building.

When he reached the foot of the steps, he stopped and peered up, shielding his eyes from the glare of the sun. Several treads had rusted through, and in more than one place the handrail was missing.

He climbed the steps cautiously, marvelling that anyone with money to their name would voluntarily elect to live in such a place.

He came to the first rusted tread and stepped over it gingerly, turned and climbed the next run of steps, thankful that the rusted treads did not coincide with the sections where the handrail was absent.

He came to the top and stood facing a black-painted door. He tried the handle and the door swung open to reveal bare floorboards receding in the perspective of a cavernous loft space.

Christopher Lombard had evidently used the place as a studio in the recent past. The floorboards were splattered with multi-coloured daubs of paint, and a broken easel was propped against the whitewashed wall to his right.

At the far end of the loft, a battered green brocade sofa stood before the open double door of a loading hatch. In the corner of the room, to the right of the sofa, was an old mattress and a nest of soiled bedding.

Beside the mattress a leather valise lay on its side, open and spilling clothes. On the far wall, beyond the mattress, was a filthy china basin and a single tap.

He called out, his 'Hello?' echoing through the overhead girders.

He approached the sofa, then saw the decoration on the wall to its left. He wondered if Lombard had moved on from depicting the female form to something more abstract. The whitewashed wall was covered in a spray of vivid crimson embedded with what looked like small white pebbles.

No, not pebbles, he thought as he looked more closely.

Teeth and shards of bone . . .

He turned and stared at the sofa, and wished he'd spared himself the sight.

His vision blurred and he felt a hot wave of nausea rise through his chest as he tried to make sense of what he was looking at.

The body lay on its back, clutching a double-barrelled shotgun as a knight on a catafalque might hold a sword, the barrel lodged beneath what had been the corpse's chin. The jaw, along with the entire face, was missing, and what remained of the skull was brimful with a mess of coagulated blood and brain.

The body wore a pair of old baggy trousers and a white shirt. A big square-faced watch was strapped to its right wrist.

On the floorboards before the sofa was an empty bottle of whisky and an old briar pipe.

Langham crossed to the mattress and knelt beside the open valise. He made out some soiled clothing, a paperback book and a small toilet bag. He searched the rest of the loft but, other than a dirty glass beside the basin, found nothing.

He returned to the sofa and stared down at the shotgun, noting the way it was gripped in the corpse's right hand.

Then he moved to the door, made his way back down the zigzag staircase and returned to the open-fronted garage. Proffering the mechanic a sixpenny piece, he asked if he could use the phone. The man indicated a telephone bolted to the back wall.

Langham considered dialling 999, thought better of it and called Scotland Yard, giving his name and asking to speak to Detective Inspector Jeff Mallory.

'One moment, sir,' a desk sergeant said.

It seemed an age before he heard the breezy tones of the South African detective. 'You've just caught me, Don. I was about to pop out for a spot of lunch.'

'I'm sorry to interrupt, but I need your help.'

Briefly, he gave Mallory the details of the missing artist and the discovery of the body.

Mallory swore. 'So you think the corpse might be this Lombard chap?'

'It's a possibility. I think he was renting the loft.'

'And it looks like suicide?'

Langham hesitated. 'I'm not at all sure about that. It appears that way, but there's something I'm not happy about.'

'Right-o, I'll be with you in fifteen minutes,' Mallory said. 'I'll grab a sandwich on the way.'

'Not a wise move, Jeff. It's not a pretty sight.'

He gave Mallory the address and replaced the receiver.

On the way out, he asked the mechanic about the man he'd seen 'knocking about' the warehouse last week.

'This chap you saw, I don't suppose you noticed him here over the weekend?'

The mechanic shrugged. 'I don't work Saturdays or Sundays, but my brother was in yesterday – you'll have to ask him.'

'Is he around?'

'Taken the day off, but he'll be in tomorrow.'

Langham nodded and stepped out into the sunlight.

He walked back down the alleyway, sat on the bottom step and waited for Jeff Mallory.

NINE

The detective inspector's Humber turned into the alley, quickly followed by another unmarked car and a squad car.

Mallory climbed from behind the wheel, taking a last bite from a sandwich and tossing the crust to the ground. He was joined by his colleague, an officer whom Langham recognized from a previous case as Detective Sergeant Venables.

'Hunger overruled your warning,' the South African said. 'I've yet to see a corpse that turned my stomach.'

'You haven't seen this one yet,' Langham said.

'Lead the way.'

A police surgeon emerged from the second car and followed them up the staircase. Two constables climbed from the squad car, one ascending after them while the other stationed himself at the foot of the stairs.

'The forensics boys are on their way,' Mallory said. 'They were settling down for a game of cards when I dropped by, and weren't best pleased at being interrupted.'

Langham told him that he'd got the address from Christopher Lombard's sister, and at the top of the steps paused to let Mallory enter before him. They crossed the echoing floorboards and stopped before the sofa.

Mallory stared down at the corpse with his hands lodged on his hips, his broad face expressionless. His eyes moved along the length of the body, taking in the remains of the skull, the shotgun, the man's old corduroy trousers, then the empty whisky bottle and pipe lying on the floorboards.

Langham admired his friend's composure: he'd seen Mallory

at crime scenes before and noted his professional dispassion. He supposed it came with repeated exposure to such situations, an ability to detach oneself from the macabre physicality of the scene and concentrate on the evidence.

Mallory turned and stared at the mess on the wall. He took a step towards the spray of blood and bone and peered more closely.

The police surgeon, a portly man in a gabardine coat and trilby, pulled on a pair of rubber gloves and knelt beside the sofa to examine the corpse.

Across the room, Detective Sergeant Venables was crouching beside the mattress, carefully extracting the contents from the valise.

Mallory watched the surgeon at work.

'I see why you doubt he topped himself,' Mallory said, indicating the weapon. 'The recoil from one of those things would be significant. It wouldn't be lying there on his chest, would it, with his forefinger neatly inserted in the trigger guard? The gun would be somewhere near his feet. It looks to me as if it's been arranged.'

Langham nodded. 'Also, Christopher Lombard lived up in Herefordshire until a month ago. He took off suddenly, leaving a lot of his work up there, then arranged to have the paintings collected tomorrow. Why would he do that if he intended to kill himself?'

Mallory indicated the empty bottle. 'How about he got himself drunk and this was a spur-of-the-moment thing?'

'And he just happened to have a shotgun with him?' Langham pointed out. 'His arranging to have his work collected, and the position of the shotgun . . . That doesn't add up to suicide, as I see it.'

'You say he was a successful artist?'

'To all appearances, yes – but it wasn't all as it seemed.' He told Mallory about the roomful of paintings that Lombard senior had stashed away at his Highgate mansion.

'Do you have any idea why he left this place in Hereford?'

Langham shook his head. 'None at all. He was prone to up and off at the drop of a hat, apparently, but there seems to have been something more permanent about this move, given that he'd arranged to have his work collected.'

'Enemies?'

'Hard to say. He wasn't much liked by a couple of the artists up at the farm, and he'd just left his lover up there. According to his sister, he was a prickly customer.'

'Were they close, he and his sister?'

'There was no love lost between them. There was a younger brother, too – and he didn't see eye to eye with Christopher, either.'

'And his father? Don't tell me he detested his elder son, too? But no – he can't have, if he bought up his son's art works.'

'That's right. Lombard senior doted on him – the apple of his eye – though according to his sister, Christopher found his father's attentions somewhat wearing.'

Mallory nodded. 'And what do you make of the father?'

'He's blind, half deaf and dislikes his younger son intensely. He begged me to find his elder son, and evidently feels nothing for his daughter who runs after him like a skivvy.'

'I've come across him,' Mallory said. 'He was a high up in the British Union of Fascists in the thirties and worked with Oswald Mosley on various committees, all very hush-hush.'

'Does he have a police record?'

'Not him. He was very careful to keep his hands clean. He was a money man, funding the union and assisting behind the scenes. He left the dirty work to the thugs.'

'How do you know about him?'

'His name's cropped up in various investigations over the years. You'd be surprised how many of his associates have criminal records – or, then again, you might not be. He's big pals with the gang boss, Arnold Grayson.'

Langham nodded. 'I know of the chap.'

Beside the sofa, the surgeon confirmed what Mallory had already surmised.

'The kick-back would have left the gun anywhere but where it is now, and the hand placement is all wrong. The forefinger is in the trigger guard, but he would have found it awkward to pull the trigger with his finger. He would have used his thumb.'

'So in your opinion?' Mallory said.

'It appears to me that someone else was responsible and arranged the gun like this after the event.' He shook his head. 'But I won't swear to that until I've spoken to the fingerprint boys and forensics.'

Mallory looked at his watch. 'What the hell's taking them so long?'

'Maybe they decided to finish that game of cards, after all,' Langham said.

Mallory asked the surgeon, 'Can you estimate the time of death?'

'Approximately. I'd put it between around five and midnight last night.'

Langham moved across to the loading hatch. He lit his pipe and stared down at the river sparkling in the sunlight. Mallory joined him. A dozen boats moved back and forth, small tugs on their way to and from the docks further along the Thames, and larger flatiron ships burdened with loads of coal.

He glanced at the detective. 'So how's married life suiting you?'

'It's the one thing that keeps me sane,' Mallory grunted. 'Crikey, I sometimes wonder how I managed to get through life before Caroline.'

'How is she?' Langham asked. 'Maria met her for coffee a month ago, and Carrie said something about an audition.'

'She got it. A decent part in a BBC TV play, shooting this summer, and at the moment she's in a comedy at the Lyric.'

'The comeback continues,' Langham said.

'It's very strange; we're sometimes stopped in the street by people who recognize her from her Hollywood days. I'm not sure I like it, to be honest. They think that because she appeared on the silver screen, she belongs to them. But Carrie doesn't seem to mind, which is all that matters.'

'Give her my love, Jeff.'

'Will do. We'll have to get together for a meal at some point—'

He was interrupted by Venables, who had taken the contents from the valise and laid them side by side on the floorboards. 'Sir, here!'

He held a navy-blue passport aloft in a rubber-gloved hand. 'It was hidden in the lining of the valise, sir.'

Mallory borrowed a pair of gloves from the surgeon and they joined Venables beside the mattress. Mallory took the passport and leafed through it, swearing to himself from time to time.

'What is it?' Langham asked.

Mallory held out the document so that Langham could read the name printed on the front.

Langham swore. '*Nigel* Lombard?'

Mallory turned to the photograph and showed it to Langham: a lean-faced, dark-haired man in his late thirties.

The detective read out. 'Height five foot ten, eyes grey, hair black. Special peculiarities' – he looked at Langham, his eyebrows raised – 'a nine-inch scar on his left arm running from wrist to elbow.'

He nodded to the surgeon, who unfastened the corpse's cufflink and carefully rolled up the shirtsleeve to reveal an old scar cross-hatched with stitch marks.

'Well, there we are. Right-ho,' Mallory said to the surgeon, 'do you have a tape-measure in your bag of tricks?'

The surgeon nodded, opened his bag and rummaged through its contents.

'Venables,' Mallory said, 'on your hands and knees. There's a chance that his peepers might have survived the blast. Get Travers to help you.'

'Sir,' Venables said, failing to hide his displeasure at the idea.

While he and the constable combed the floorboards, Mallory and the surgeon ran the length of the tape from the soles of the corpse's brogues to the remains of its skull.

Mallory grunted. 'Well, that's approximately five feet and ten inches, though it's hard to be accurate with the top of the skull missing. And the hair on the back of the head is certainly black.'

'Sir,' Venables said from where he crouched six feet away. He was staring with extreme distaste at something that had fetched up against the base of the whitewashed wall, a gelatinous mass that reminded Langham, at this distance, of an oyster.

'Well?' Mallory snapped.

'It's far bigger than I thought it would be,' the detective sergeant offered.

'Very interesting,' Mallory said, his tone heavy with sarcasm, 'but is it grey?'

Venables nodded. 'It is, sir.'

'Well,' the South African said, 'this puts the cat among the bloody pigeons.' He stared down at the corpse. 'I'd like to get someone in to have a gander at the corpse. You said Lombard senior was blind?'

Langham nodded. 'As near as makes no difference.'

'What about this sister? You mentioned she was close to Nigel?'

'That's right.'

'Once I get the corpse to the morgue, I'll have her in to take a look.' He grimaced. 'She'll be able to identify him by the scar, if nothing else. Do you have her address?'

Langham gave him the woman's details.

'What do you know about Nigel Lombard?' Mallory asked.

'Not that much – but he was in financial trouble,' Langham said, and told Mallory about Nigel's debt to the tune of two thousand pounds.

'This isn't a gangland killing,' Mallory said categorically. 'Thugs wouldn't make it look like suicide. They'd shoot the poor bastard in the back of the head and dump the body in the river. This was done by cack-handed amateurs.'

The detective lit a cigarette and gestured with it to the corpse. 'I wonder what Nigel Lombard was doing here. You said it was Christopher who rented the place?'

'According to Victoria, Nigel approached Christopher for a loan, to clear his debt. This was a couple of weeks back. Perhaps he came here to try again?'

Mallory nodded. 'I suppose that's a possibility.'

'We need to locate Christopher Lombard, Jeff, and I have a lead on that.' He told Mallory about the hauliers and the collection at noon the following day.

'I'll go up there in the morning,' Langham said, 'then follow the hauliers when they head off. I'll be in contact if we run Christopher Lombard to earth.'

'Do that. I'd like to haul this Christopher chap in for an interview.'

The detective took one last look at the corpse, then sighed. 'Right, I think I've seen enough here, Don. I'll be in touch.'

They made their way from the loft and down the treacherous stairway.

TEN

L angham drove to Highgate, ordered a pot of coffee and a toasted teacake in a café on the main street, and considered his imminent meeting with Vernon Lombard.

Forty-five minutes later he parked outside the mansion on Saddler's Lane, batted his way through the tangled vegetation and climbed the steps to the front door.

He knocked, waited a minute and tried again. Presently, he made out the shuffling figure of the manservant through the stained-glass panels.

A white-haired old man pulled open the door and peered out myopically. 'Yes?'

Langham gave his name and said he'd like to see Mr Vernon Lombard.

'Are you from the police?' the man asked. 'A constable came just ten minutes ago and left with Miss Victoria.'

'I'm working on the case,' Langham said non-committally. 'Is Mr Lombard in?'

'This way, sir.'

He led Langham down a gloomy hallway, as funereal as the rest of Lombard senior's abode. Langham expected to hear the strains of Wagner or Mahler booming forth, but a deathly silence greeted him as he was shown into the living room.

'Mr Langham, sir,' said the manservant.

The curtains were drawn. In the gloom, Langham could just make out an armchair and seated in it the marmoreal figure of Vernon Lombard, illuminated by a chink of sunlight penetrating the room like a rapier.

'Thank you, Wilkins,' Lombard said.

The manservant shuffled back down the corridor.

Langham crossed the room. 'Would you mind if I opened the curtains?'

'Do as you please,' Lombard said.

Langham tugged the curtains open, squinting at the sudden assault of sunlight. A storm of dust motes danced in the air as he turned and looked at the old man.

Lombard said, 'Victoria was with me when the constable called. I heard him say something about identifying a body, but she hurried off before I could question her.' He clutched the arms of the chair and leaned forward suddenly, his expression fearful. 'Well, was it Christopher?'

Langham found a seat and sat down. 'It wasn't Christopher,' he said.

Lombard's face sagged with obvious relief. 'Thank God,' he murmured under his breath. 'Then who—?'

'I'm afraid it would appear that the body was Nigel's, sir.'

The blind eyes widened fractionally, showing even more of the milky orbs. 'Nigel? How did he . . .?' He evidently could not bring himself to say 'die' and fell silent as he waited for Langham to speak.

'He was found at the Thames-side warehouse where Christopher once lived. Nigel was shot. I'm sorry, sir.'

'Shot dead? You mean murdered?'

Langham gestured. 'That remains to be seen. The police are investigating. I'm sorry to bring you such bad news.'

'Nigel . . .' Lombard said, his gaze staring past Langham at the sunlight. 'He was a wastrel, Langham. A damned, ungrateful little . . . I tried to help him. I did, in the early days. I tried to put work his way. I opened doors, gave him plenty of opportunities.' He shook his head. 'But he was lazy, feckless. He always thought he knew best.'

Langham hesitated, then said, 'I hope you don't mind if I ask a few questions? I need to find out more about Nigel, his lifestyle, his friends. Every little I learn might go some way to—'

'If you led the kind of life that Nigel did,' Lombard interrupted, 'then what can you expect? He must have made enemies along the way.'

'I know you said you hadn't seen him for a couple of years,' Langham said, 'but you must have heard things about him during that time. Did he write to you? Did Christopher or Victoria mention him – or might you have heard something from friends of his?'

The old man was shaking his head. 'Christopher had very little to do with his brother. He knew him for the wastrel he was. He never mentioned him in my presence, loath to get me going on that subject! And though Victoria was close to him, for some reason, she knew better than to bring him up in conversation.'

'He never wrote to you?'

Lombard gave an irritable wave. 'Oh, the occasional begging letter, which I always binned. And I never replied or gave in to his demands.'

'Did you ever notice a return address? I'd like to know where he might have been living so I can trace people who knew him—'

The old man cut him off. 'I never gave a damn where he was living, Langham. I don't think you appreciate how much Nigel's conduct pained me. I wanted nothing to do with the scoundrel.'

'He mentioned he was going to see friends in Bristol. Do you happen to know who these people were?'

Lombard sighed. 'Do you really expect that Nigel and I might have acquaintances in common? I have no idea who they were – rascals as low as Nigel, I've no doubt.'

Langham sat back. 'You see, if I know more about Nigel and his lifestyle, it might assist me in my investigation into Christopher's whereabouts.'

Lombard considered that, his head held to one side. 'I very much doubt that, Langham. They moved in completely different circles and had very little to do with each other.'

Langham tried a different tack. 'Could you tell me something about Nigel's politics, sir?'

Lombard snorted.

'Well?' Langham prompted.

'Nigel was a political fool,' he said at last.

'A fool? In what way?'

'What do you think? I did my best, with both of them. I gave them books, talked to them, introduced them to people. I should have realized that Nigel would repudiate everything I stood for – but I didn't think he'd . . .' He fell silent, his right hand making an ineffectual scrabbling gesture as words failed him.

'What?' Langham asked. 'You didn't think he'd . . . *what*?'

Lombard sighed. 'I didn't think he'd purposely and vindictively take up a cause diametrically opposed to my own, expressly to get at me.'

'He had socialist sympathies?'

The old man leaned forward, shaking with rage. 'Just after the war he joined the blasted Communist Party, the young idiot! Can you believe that? A son of mine!'

'I see,' Langham said, beginning to understand the root cause of Lombard senior's antipathy towards his younger son. 'You said you last saw Nigel a couple of years ago – can you recall anything about the meeting?'

Lombard waved vaguely. 'I can't recall. No doubt he was begging, as usual.'

Langham hesitated, then asked, 'And Christopher's politics?'

'Now there, Langham, I was more successful. Christopher is intelligent and can see the truth when it's set out before him. We saw eye to eye on political matters from when Christopher was a young man.'

'He's a member of the British Union of Fascists?' Langham asked.

'That's correct.'

'And Victoria?' Langham said. 'Could you tell me what your daughter's politics might be?'

Lombard waved dismissively. 'I never talk politics with Victoria,' he said. 'What's the point? A waste of time. What do women know about such things?'

A silence came between the two men as Lombard gazed blindly into space, his expression unreadable.

'I think I've learned all I can for the moment,' Langham said a little later. 'You have my telephone number. If you recall anything, anything at all regarding Nigel, please don't hesitate to contact me. As I said, it might help me to locate Christopher.'

Absently, his thoughts elsewhere, Lombard nodded.

'I'll let myself out,' Langham said, climbing to his feet.

'Oh, before you go.' The old man gestured towards the silent gramophone. 'If you would be so good as to put a little Wagner on the turntable. I'm feeling much better now.'

Suppressing his sudden revulsion, Langham did as instructed, then moved towards the door. There, he turned and stared at the old man. Lombard, head raised, was smiling as if in appreciation of the stirring strains.

Langham turned and left the room.

It was three thirty by the time Langham arrived at the Bull.

A few drinkers were standing outside on the pavement, taking advantage of the fine spring weather, but the public bar was quiet. Maria and Pamela sat at a table in the far corner, small glasses of sherry before them. Absorbed in conversation, they didn't look up as he entered and made his way to the bar.

He ordered a pint of Fuller's bitter, leaned against the bar and watched them. What was it about two women in conversation that exhibited an intimacy never matched by men in a similar situation? They had known each other less than a year, met once a fortnight for lunch in Chelsea and were fast friends. And all this despite the age difference – Maria was thirty-five, Pamela in her mid-twenties – and the fact that Maria was from upper-middle-class stock and Pamela working-class. Come to that, he thought, they were even of different nationalities.

Maria looked up and smiled. He raised his eyebrows and mimed lifting an invisible drink to his lips, and she responded with a shake of her head and a hand placed over her glass.

He carried his pint across to the corner table.

Pamela looked at the tiny gold watch on her wrist. 'You're late, Donald.'

Maria narrowed her eyes, peering at him as he sat down and took a mouthful of ale. 'Something is wrong. I know it.'

Beginning with his meeting with Victoria that morning, he

told them about finding the address of the warehouse and the subsequent discovery of the body.

'I assumed it was Christopher at first, but it appears it was his brother, Nigel.' He went on to tell them about the passport.

'It seems he was murdered, though the killer tried to make it look as if he'd taken his own life.'

They discussed the discovery for a while, and then Pamela glanced up. 'Look what the cat's dragged in,' she said.

Ralph sank into the seat next to Langham, mopping his brow with a handkerchief. 'I've been stuck in roadworks on the King's Road,' he said. 'I could murder a pint.'

'Coming right up,' Langham said.

'You're a gentleman and a scholar.'

When Langham returned from the bar, Ralph took a long drink and licked his lips, then stared across the room in silence. Langham glanced at him; his friend appeared preoccupied.

'Everything OK?'

'Why shouldn't it be?' Ralph said. 'Just been along to that gallery on Cork Street,' he said hurriedly, and went on to detail his meeting with Mr Hector at Weatherby & Lascelles.

'So no joy on that front,' Langham said.

Pamela leaned forward. 'Tell Ralph what happened, Donald.'

For the second time, Langham recounted his discovery of Nigel Lombard's body in the warehouse.

'Let's get this straight,' Ralph said. 'Nigel Lombard was shot dead, his older brother is still missing, and there's no love lost between the brothers?'

'Also,' Langham added, 'Nigel was in debt to a person or persons unknown to the tune of over two grand.'

Pamela said, 'So perhaps it was either his brother or whoever he owed the money to?'

'If someone owed you two grand,' Ralph said, 'what would you do – kill the chap or do your damnedest to get what's owed to you?'

'Put like that . . .' Pamela murmured, sipping her drink.

Langham said, 'Still, we need to find Christopher Lombard – to eliminate him from our enquiries if nothing else. Fancy a trip up to Herefordshire tomorrow, Ralph?'

'I'm game. I need a change of scenery.'

'We'll get up there early and talk to the artists.'

'When are the hauliers due to arrive?'

'Around midday,' Langham said, 'which will give us time to talk to Dorothea and company. What I suggest is that I make myself scarce before the hauliers arrive. I'll conceal my car in a lane near the farm while you help them load up. Try to find out exactly where they're delivering the paintings – though no doubt Christopher's told them to keep schtum on that score. When they leave, I'll follow them and you bring up the rear.'

Pamela shivered. 'It's like something from a film,' she said.

'I remember the last time I had to follow someone by car,' Ralph said.

Pamela leaned forward, wide-eyed. 'What happened?'

'Lost 'em in a traffic jam in Bow, didn't I?' he said. 'They got clean away. Turned out they were diamond thieves and I would've been in for a nice cut of the reward money – but I got sweet bugger all. Story of my life.'

'Well, there'll be two of us following them tomorrow,' Langham said. 'They won't get away.'

Ralph downed the rest of his pint.

Langham said, 'One for the road?'

Ralph looked at his watch. 'I'd better be pushing off, or Annie'll have my guts for garters. I said I'd be back by five with some fish and chips.'

'I'll meet you at the office in the morning, seven sharp,' Langham said.

Ralph tipped his trilby to the women and hurried off.

Pamela finished her drink; Langham offered to buy her another, but Maria said, 'Pamela has a date with a certain young policeman.'

'Ah,' Langham said, smiling, 'so how are things going with Sergeant Wilson?'

'Ladies don't tell,' Pamela said. 'But between you, me and the garden fence, I think he's smitten.'

'And you?'

She smiled with a certain self-satisfaction. 'I think Dennis is a charming young man,' she said. 'He's taking me to the flicks at seven, so I'd better get home and change. See you tomorrow, Donald, for the next thrilling instalment.'

They watched her leave the bar, and Maria took his hand. 'Are you all right?'

He finished his pint and described his meeting that afternoon with Vernon Lombard, and the old man's reaction to the death of his son.

'He was frankly relieved that it wasn't Christopher, and went on to criticize Nigel for his political leanings. His son was lying in the warehouse with his head blown to bits, and all Lombard could do was revile him. Yesterday I found myself feeling sorry for the old blighter. Now I realize that I detest the man – and I don't say that about many people.'

Maria tipped her head to one side. 'I've never heard you say it about *anyone*.'

'He's a malign influence, Maria. The damage he's done to Victoria and Nigel . . . And because of him, Christopher Lombard took up fascism at an early age.'

'You don't think . . .?' she began.

'What, that Lombard senior had a hand in Nigel's death?' He shook his head. 'I'd like to think not, though I suppose anything's possible. But enough of the Lombards!'

He pointed through the window to the Lyon's Corner House across the road. 'Ralph's mention of fish and chips has made me hungry. How about another drink, then supper at the Corner House?'

Maria squeezed his hand. 'You're so romantic, my darling.'

ELEVEN

Langham was in the office a little before seven the following morning when Jeff Mallory rang.

'Don, I called your place but Maria said you'd already left,' the detective said. 'I've got more on the identification of Nigel Lombard.'

'Go on.'

'I had Victoria Lombard join me at the morgue yesterday. Poor woman was beside herself. Anyway, she formally identified him. The scar was the clincher. She said Nigel almost bled to death in his teens when he put his arm through a window.'

'So there we are.'

'The poor woman was in a state. The surgeon sedated her and thought it best if she was hospitalized. He suggested she book into a private place in St John's Wood for a day or two.'

'It's looking all the more imperative that we locate Christopher Lombard,' Langham said. 'I'll be in touch if we hit the jackpot in Herefordshire.'

'Good luck with that, Don.'

Langham thanked him and rang off.

Ralph arrived five minutes later and they set off in their respective cars, making good progress on the busy road out of London and reaching the outskirts of Hereford a little after ten.

Langham skirted the city and headed for Swavesy, pulling up outside Henderson's Farm at ten thirty.

'Nice place,' Ralph commented as he climbed from his Morris Minor, 'if you like this sort of thing.'

'We'll never make a country boy of you,' Langham said.

'I think I'd miss my local too much.'

'There's a pub a mile away in the village,' Langham pointed out.

A belligerent goose waddled up to Ralph and took exception to the appearance of his winklepickers, extending its neck and hissing like a faulty soda syphon. Ralph kicked ineffectually at his attacker and hurried after Langham.

They found Dorothea and Penny in the kitchen, sitting at the table with big mugs of tea. Langham introduced Ralph as his senior partner in the agency, then faltered as he sensed the somewhat subdued atmosphere.

'Everything OK?' he ventured.

Dorothea looked at Penny; the young woman regarded her cup for a few seconds, then murmured, 'Simon's laid up in bed with a broken arm.'

'My word,' Langham said, 'what on earth happened?'

He expected to hear that the artist had injured himself while working around the farm, but what Penny said surprised him. 'He was in London on Sunday, and he got himself into a bit of trouble.' She seemed reluctant to elucidate.

Dorothea stood up. 'I'll put the kettle on. Would you like a cup of tea, Donald, Mr Ryland?'

Ralph accepted the offer, but Langham declined. He said, 'Do you think Simon's up to having a visitor?'

'I'm sure he'd like to see you,' Penny said. 'He's bored rigid.' She pointed through the door. 'Up the stairs, the first door on the left.'

Dorothea gave him a mug of milky tea. 'If you could take this up to Simon . . .'

'You've got yourself a very nice place here,' Ralph was saying as Langham left the kitchen and climbed the creaking staircase to a narrow corridor.

He knocked on the bedroom door, and Simon's voice called out, 'Hello?'

Langham opened the door and ducked under the low lintel. 'Room service,' he said, crossing the room and placing the mug on a bedside cabinet.

'Donald,' the artist said. 'I thought I heard a car. It's good to see you.'

Simon Lipscombe sat up in bed, supported by fat pillows. He wore a blue-and-white-striped pyjama top and his right arm was encased in a plaster cast. The broken arm was not his only injury. The flesh around his right eye was a lurid combination of sulphurous yellow and cobalt blue.

He gestured at a duffel coat draped across a chair. 'Just hang it on the back of the door and pull up a seat.'

Langham did so, then nodded at the artist's arm. 'Penny said you've been in the wars.'

Lipscombe hesitated, then said, 'There was a fascist march in the East End on Sunday. We got to know about it last week—'

'We?'

'Some friends of mine in the Socialist Action Front. They invited me down.'

'To stage a counter demonstration?'

Lipscombe avoided his eyes. 'Something like that,' he said. 'You can't counter fascist ideology with mere rhetoric. They don't understand dialectic.'

'So you and a few friends . . .?'

'Let's just say that the fascists came out second best.'

Langham pointed at the young man's arm. 'It'll curb your painting for a while.'

'Do you know something, Donald? I think it was worth it. I mean, it's all very well my holing myself up here, painting seascapes, but does that really help the cause? Sometimes I think I should be working on more political paintings – but the fact is, social commentary doesn't sell. Pretty little landscapes do.'

'Ah, there's the rub,' Langham said.

The young man lifted his mug with his left hand and drank. 'Anyway, what brings you to this neck of the woods? Still searching for Christopher Lombard?'

'Well, as it happens . . .' Langham began, and went on to tell the artist about Nigel Lombard's murder.

Lipscombe swallowed, staring at Langham. 'He was *murdered*?' He sounded incredulous. 'You don't think . . .?' He stared through the window, his gaze far away.

'Go on.'

'Well, seeing as Christopher Lombard did a bunk, and the brothers were continually at loggerheads . . .'

'The possibility that Christopher might be implicated hasn't been overlooked,' Langham said equivocally.

The artist nodded.

Langham regarded the young man. 'Were you aware that Nigel Lombard had communist sympathies? In fact, according to his father, he was a card-carrying member of the British Communist Party.'

Lipscombe frowned. 'Nigel Lombard?'

'You didn't talk about his political leanings when he was up here?' Langham asked.

'We . . . we hardly spoke – not seriously, that is. The only occasion we really said anything meaningful to each other was that time he came on strong to Penny and I warned him off.'

'He never said anything about his political beliefs?'

Lipscombe stared through the window. 'He didn't. I just assumed he shared his brother's reactionary views.'

'Did he ever say anything about his friends in London or elsewhere, or indeed his enemies?'

'Not that I remember. As I said, I disliked the chap and kept out of his way. He tended not to socialize with us.'

Langham nodded. 'Well, if you do recall anything you think might have some bearing on his death, don't hesitate to contact me.'

He fished a business card from his jacket pocket and placed it on the bedside cabinet. 'There's a good chance that the police might contact you about the case, so don't be surprised if you get a call.'

Leaning back against the pillows, Lipscombe nodded.

Langham moved to the door, then indicated the young man's arm. 'I hope you're back painting sooner rather than later.'

He slipped from the room and returned to the kitchen.

He found Penny Archer sitting alone at the long table, disconsolately spinning her empty mug.

She looked up and smiled. 'Dorothea and Ralph are in Christopher's studio,' she said, 'packing the canvases.'

'So she relented?' he said, recalling Dorothea's indignation the other day at Christopher Lombard's request to prepare his paintings for collection.

'I think she's at a loose end, and she sees this as a way of saying good riddance to the man.' She looked up from her mug. 'Did Simon tell you about what happened at the march on Sunday?'

Langham nodded.

She sighed. 'The trouble with Simon,' she said, 'is that he's naive and lacks any intellectual thoroughness.'

He sat down across the table from her. 'Meaning?'

'Please don't misunderstand me. I love Simon. He's a kind, caring man, but he can't see the bigger picture. He's unable to see that you can't achieve any kind of victory over these people – the Christopher Lombards of this world – by bashing their brains out. You must win their minds; you must show them the mistake in their thinking. No amount of violence will change their views.'

He stared at the woman across the table with sudden respect and realized that, until now, he'd underestimated her.

She went on, 'It was the same with how he reacted to Nigel Lombard that time.'

'Go on.'

Rolling the mug between her palms, she said quietly, 'Instead of talking to him, reasoning with him, trying to understand the man, he just stormed in and threatened him.' She shook her head. 'He didn't have the first inkling of who or what Nigel Lombard was.'

Intrigued, he said, 'And you did?'

'That day when Simon came in and saw Nigel with me – there was more to it than that. We were arguing about politics.' She hesitated. 'It wasn't our first real conversation on the subject. I'd broached it with him a few days earlier. Nigel was arrogant, and he had a massive insecurity complex – something to do with his father, no doubt. It resulted in him continually having to prove himself. To brag. And when I accused him of being a political lightweight, of being a mindless lackey of Moscow, he told me something.'

She hesitated, then went on, 'He said he was in the pay of the KGB.'

Pole-axed, Langham opened his mouth to say something. At last he managed, 'He was lying, of course?'

Penny shrugged. 'That's what I assumed, at first. I must admit that I laughed in his face. What would Russia see in him? I asked.'

'What did he say?'

'He told me that in reaction to the political views of his father and his brother, just after the war he joined the Communist Party and made contact with someone at the Russian embassy. He bragged to me that he was quite a catch for the Soviets – Nigel Lombard, son of the arms dealer Vernon Lombard. Apparently, an attaché at the embassy started offering inducements, a few pounds here and there, help with his rent. In return, the Soviets wanted to know all about Vernon Lombard.'

Langham shook his head, aware that this might cast a wholly new light on Nigel Lombard's death. 'Did he say why the Russians wanted information about his father?'

'That's the first thing I asked him,' she said. 'He assumed, initially, that it was because of his father's contact with Oswald Mosley – but it wasn't. Moscow knows that the fascists in Britain are a spent force, politically. They have nothing to fear from that quarter.'

'So their interest in Lombard was . . .?'

'Nigel said that the Soviets wanted him to introduce his father to an African politician.'

'Even though Nigel wasn't on speaking terms with his father?'

'That's just what *I* said, and Nigel said that the Russians didn't know that. Apparently, Russia was fomenting unrest in this African state, and couldn't be discovered exporting arms there. But if they could persuade Lombard to ship them in via an intermediary through the back door, as it were . . .'

'But Lombard wouldn't agree to supply communist rebels—' He stopped. 'Of course,' he said, 'he wouldn't know they were Reds, would he?'

She was smiling at him. 'No, of course not. As far as he was concerned, this African dictator came to him, via the intermediary, promising wads of American dollars gained from his country's gold mines – so Lombard was given to understand – and all he saw was the profit for himself.'

'My word, I bet Nigel Lombard was laughing up his sleeve at duping his father like that.'

'I'll say.'

'And the deal took place?'

'He told me that the consignment was signed, sealed and delivered a couple of years ago, and that his father was none the wiser.' She shrugged. 'I think Nigel wanted to tell someone, to brag about his part in the deception, and when the opportunity arose to put me right, he took it.'

'Did you tell Simon about this?'

Penny shook her head. 'Good God, no.'

'Do you mind my asking why not?'

She hesitated, considering the question. 'It was nothing to do with the politics of it,' she said. 'It was more personal than that. Simon can be jealous, and I didn't want him thinking that there was anything between Nigel and me.'

'And you thought that if he knew Nigel had confided in you, he might suspect something that had never happened?'

'I didn't want to jeopardize what I've got with Simon. In many ways he's still very immature. I just didn't want him to know that Nigel had confided in me.' She faltered, staring at him. 'What is it?' she asked, as if alerted by something in his manner.

Langham said, 'Well . . . speaking of Nigel' – he took a breath – 'I'm afraid I have something to tell you about young Mr Lombard.' He went on to recount his discovery of Lombard's body at the warehouse.

She stared at him, pale-faced. 'He's . . . *dead?*'

'It would appear that he was murdered.'

He watched her as she took this in.

She stared at him, her expression frozen. 'He was murdered? My God. Have . . . have the police any idea who might have . . .?'

'No concrete leads,' he said. 'But they'll certainly be interested to hear about his Soviet connections.'

She swallowed. 'Do you think that might have something to do with his murder?'

'It can't be ruled out.'

Penny sat in silence for a while, staring down at her mug. 'I never liked Nigel Lombard,' she said, 'but it's awful to think that . . .'

'Did Nigel ever say anything to you about friends, fellow travellers, people he stayed with up and down the country?'

'Not by name, no. We didn't have much contact, as I said. He certainly didn't discuss his friends with me.'

Langham glanced at his wristwatch. It was almost eleven thirty.

He pushed back his chair and climbed to his feet. 'I'd better go and find Ralph and Dorothea,' he said.

Penny nodded absently, lost in thought.

He left the kitchen and headed for Christopher Lombard's studio, considering everything Penny Archer had told him.

TWELVE

He found Ralph and Dorothea in Christopher Lombard's studio, removing paintings from a small storeroom and stacking them with others by the doorway that led through to the other studios.

Dorothea looked up as he entered the room. 'I know, I know,' she said. 'The last time I saw you, I swore blind I wouldn't help the bastard in any way.'

'So why the change of heart?'

She leaned a big canvas up against half a dozen others and mopped her brow. It was hot in the studio, and wearing a pair of brown dungarees, with her hair tied up in a headscarf, she looked the very image of a Second World War Land Girl.

'In the early days, Chris did a photographic study of my head and shoulders and said he'd like to do a painting from them one day.'

'And you're trying to find this painting?'

'I don't even know for certain that he did it. But if he did, I don't want him profiting from it.'

Ralph emerged from the storeroom, almost hidden behind a big canvas. He set it down with the others and said, 'Just half a dozen more to go.'

'Ralph told me about Nigel,' Dorothea said. 'I can't believe it.'

'Did Nigel say anything to you about his having enemies?' Langham asked.

'We didn't have much to do with each other. He certainly never mentioned anyone who might have . . .'

'How do you think Christopher will take the news?'

She regarded him calculatingly. 'I know they weren't close, but I assure you that Christopher didn't dislike Nigel to that extent.'

She returned to the storeroom and Ralph followed her. Langham was about to step outside when he heard her swear out loud. He moved to the storeroom and found Dorothea standing arms akimbo, a sour expression on her face as she stared at a canvas.

It showed a naked woman reclining on a divan. The painting was quite clearly of Dorothea, but she appeared bloated, her flesh rendered in impasto smears of pink, pale green and mauve. Her breasts were splayed, and her sex appeared mutilated, raw. Whereas in reality Dorothea was handsome, Lombard had given her face a hard, sneering expression.

Langham glanced at Ralph, who looked red-faced and uncomfortable.

'I didn't pose for this, if that's what you're thinking,' Dorothea said. 'He often asked me, but I refused point-blank to pose nude.'

She dashed tears from her eyes with the back of her hand and tried to laugh. 'It's bad, isn't it? And I don't mean that it doesn't show me in a good light.' She gestured at the canvas. 'The proportions are all wrong, as well as the perspective.' She fell silent, then spat, 'The bastard!' She looked at Langham. 'And do you know what I find *most* upsetting?'

He shook his head.

'Those,' she said, pointing.

Arranged around the reclining figure was an assortment of fungi and other vegetation.

'Belladonna, deadly nightshade and hemlock,' Dorothea said. 'How's that for symbolism? If I was ever in any doubt as to what he felt about me . . .'

She hurried from the storeroom, across the studio and into the kitchen.

Ralph stared at the canvas. 'It's bloody awful, isn't it?' he said. 'He's made her look like an overfed witch.'

'I think that might have been Lombard's intention, I'm afraid.'

Dorothea returned clutching a big pair of pinking shears. 'This is one work by Christopher Lombard no one will ever see again!'

As they looked on, she attacked the painting with the scissors, slicing the canvas from top to bottom and grunting in satisfaction as she did so. The image of the naked woman flapped and rolled under her assault, and soon all that was left of the painting was a pile of paint-smeared fragments on the floor and an empty, gaping frame.

She stood back and lodged her hands on her hips. 'Well, I feel much better for that, gentlemen.'

'Hear, hear,' Ralph said. 'You did right, if you ask me.'

'But do you know something?' she went on. 'That's not enough.'

'Perhaps if you were to burn the remains?' Langham suggested, half-jokingly.

'I might do just that,' she said. 'But I don't think even that would be enough. No, I want to confront the bastard, look him in the eye and ask him outright why he painted this.' She turned to look at him. 'Donald, when you run him to earth, promise you'll let me know where he's hiding.'

'Are you sure?' he asked.

'Of course I'm sure. There's nothing I want more than to watch him squirm when I ask him why he painted the bloody thing. Then I'll get a great deal of satisfaction from telling him that I destroyed it.' She regarded him. '*Promise* me, Donald!'

'Very well.'

'Thank you.' She turned to the remaining canvases stacked in the room.

Langham glanced at his watch. 'I'd better be pushing off,' he said. 'I'll conceal myself along the lane, as arranged,' he said to Ralph.

'And I'll try to screw Lombard's address from the hauliers while I help them load up. You never know, they might blab when I've gained their confidence.'

Langham drove up the track from the farmhouse and turned right along the lane. A hundred yards further on, he came to a timber gate and did a three-point turn, parking in a patch of cow-churned mud. From here he could see the farmhouse to his left, and straight ahead the lane to Hereford, dipping and rising through the rolling countryside.

He settled down, wishing he'd thought to make a sandwich before leaving Kensington that morning. As he waited, he considered the Lombard brothers. One was a fascist misogynist influenced by the views of Lombard senior, while the other had been a political opportunist taking Moscow's dirty money in order to get back at his father – though, of course, Nigel's claim to have been in the pay of the Soviets might have been nothing more than a fairy tale to impress Penny Archer.

He saw movement along the lane a mile ahead. A green Vauxhall van hove into view on the crest of a rise, then disappeared as it rolled down into a dip. The vehicle came into sight again and turned down the track leading to Henderson's Farm. He looked at his watch. It was one minute to twelve. The hauliers were nothing if not punctual.

He reached into the glove compartment and pulled out a pair of field glasses. For the next half hour he watched two workmen – garbed in the camel-brown dust coats favoured by hauliers – ferry the paintings from the farmhouse to the back of the van, ably assisted by Ralph.

He focused on the numberplate of the van, and as a matter of course made a note of the registration.

At one point the men stopped for a cuppa and a smoke, and Ralph offered them his Capstans and chatted in the sunlight.

Then they returned to work, shuttling back and forth with admirable speed.

Less than an hour after arriving, the workmen loaded the final canvas into the van, slammed and locked the door, and set off. Langham watched as the van emerged from the end of the track and turned left. He waited fifteen seconds, then eased his Rover into the lane and followed at a discreet distance.

In his rear-view mirror, he made out Ralph's Morris Minor turn on to the lane after him.

He'd thought to load his pipe with tobacco while he waited, and as he followed the van along a straight stretch of lane, he steered with his knees while he lit up.

The van turned south on to a main road, maintaining an average speed of just over forty miles an hour. Langham had no trouble keeping the vehicle in sight. The traffic was light, the day getting warmer by the minute. He rolled down the side window and found himself drifting mentally, considering the novel he was working on.

A couple of hours into the journey, the van pulled into a roadside café on the London road. Langham did the same, grateful for the break and the opportunity to buy some lunch. The workmen entered the café and Langham duly followed; as he did so, he saw Ralph turn in and pull up beside the building.

The hauliers were sitting down with sandwiches and mugs of tea, and Langham ordered a couple of bacon butties and two small bottles of dandelion and burdock to take with him.

He left the café and rounded the building; Ralph saw him coming and climbed from his car.

Langham passed him a butty and a bottle of pop.

'You're a gent, sir. I'm starving.'

Langham stretched, enjoying the sun. 'Learn anything?'

'Nah.' Ralph took a great bite of sandwich and chewed. 'All I got out of 'em is that they're heading for King's Cross. I said I had an aunt who lived on Collier Street, and asked if they were going anywhere near.' He laughed. 'They got all tight-lipped and clammed up.'

'King's Cross,' Langham said. 'Well, I suppose that narrows it down a bit.'

He chewed on his butty and swilled the mouthful down with a draught of dandelion and burdock. 'I feel like a twelve-year-old again, bunking off school and nipping round to the corner shop.'

'Can't imagine you playing hooky, Don.'

'I detested Latin and I'd do anything to get out of lessons.'

'Hark at him. Latin? I weren't even teached proper English.'

'And look where it got you – best gumshoe in Earl's Court.' He finished his butty. 'Oh, by the way. Back at the farm, I found out something very interesting about Nigel Lombard.' He went on to relay Penny Archer's claim that Nigel Lombard had been in the pay of the KGB.

'Blimey!' Ralph laughed. 'What a bloody family. Two of 'em are Blackshirts and the other's a commie. Ain't there a decent Tory among 'em?'

Langham cocked a playful eye at him. 'Is there such a thing?' he asked.

Ralph pointed. 'Hey-up, Don. There they go.'

The workmen left the café and crossed to the van. Langham watched them pull out on to the main road, then hurried across to the Rover and followed.

The traffic became heavier as they approached London, and Langham moved closer to the van. Ralph was right behind him. They came to the ring road, cut along the A40 for a few miles, then turned south and headed for central London.

For the next half hour, progress was stop-and-start, and at one point a grumbling Leyland bus interposed itself between Langham and the van. When it stopped to disgorge passengers, he overtook it and caught sight of the van passing through a set of traffic lights. He accelerated and nipped across just as the lights were about to change to red.

Ralph had been caught, but five minutes later he saw the Morris Minor in his rear-view mirror a couple of hundred yards behind.

They came to King's Cross, passed the station and turned down Cardigan Street, which was lined with small red-brick Victorian terraced houses.

Ahead, the van came to a stop behind a parked car. Langham continued along the street and found a parking space twenty yards further on. Ralph's Morris Minor passed him and pulled into the kerb.

Ralph jumped out and ran back along the street. Langham opened the passenger door and Ralph slipped in beside him. 'Number fifty,' he said.

'Good work.'

'The workmen had the keys to the place and were letting themselves in,' Ralph said, 'so Lombard obviously isn't at home.' He lit a Capstan. 'So now it's a matter of waiting till they've offloaded the pictures, then kicking our heels until Lombard shows himself. Only . . .'

Langham looked at him. 'What?'

'Don't know about you, but I don't fancy spending God-knows-how-long waiting out here.'

'What do you suggest?'

Ralph reached into his jacket and produced a scuffed leather wallet: skeleton keys.

'We'll get in there and see if there's any sign of recent occupancy. If there is, we'll settle down and wait for him. He's wanted for questioning by the rozzers, after all, so he can't rightly complain.'

'Well, he can – but we'll ignore him.'

Langham lit his pipe and Ralph sat back and smoked his cigarette, glancing in the side mirror to keep an eye on the workmen carrying the canvases into number fifty.

'What if Lombard doesn't show up?' Ralph asked after a while.

Langham glanced at his watch. It was almost six. 'We could give him a couple of hours, then call it a day. I'll phone Jeff Mallory and give him the address.'

'And if Lombard does turn up?'

Langham thought about it. 'First priority, haul him off to the Yard and let Jeff question him – and ask him to visit his father. Not that he'll agree, given that he's shown a marked reluctance to do so since Christmas.'

'I want to break the news to him about his brother, Don – see how he reacts.'

'We'll do that, if he turns up.'

'I think he will. Presumably, he'll want to make sure his daubs arrived safe and sound.'

Langham nodded to the side mirror. 'They still at it?'

'Back and forth like beavers. I'll give 'em their due: they're workers.' He peered into the mirror. 'Looks like they're carrying three of the bloody things at a time.'

They sat for a while, smoking in silence. Langham glanced at his friend. Yesterday afternoon in the Bull, he thought that Ralph had seemed distracted. Now, he smoked his cigarette nervously and continually jiggled his knee up and down.

He said, 'What is it?'

Ralph looked at him. 'What's what?'

'Something's on your mind.'

His friend shook his head. 'It's nothing.'

Langham removed his pipe. 'Ralph?'

'Look, if you must know . . .' Ralph stared through the window for a second or two. 'The greyhound case the other day. Grayson sent someone to follow me.'

'What on earth for?'

Ralph hesitated, avoiding Langham's gaze. 'You know I
covered for that Len Turner, told Grayson the dog'd been
nabbed by some thugs from Essex way? Well, Grayson wants
to know who they were. He sent a chap to tail me, and I forced
the story from him.'

'So Grayson thinks you know who these Essex boys are,
and is putting on the pressure?'

Ralph nodded. 'That's the long and the short of it, Don.
But don't worry, I can look after myself.'

'I hope so,' Langham said. 'From what I've heard about
Arnold Grayson, the man's a nasty piece of work.'

Ralph leaned forward suddenly, screwing up his eyes as he
peered at the mirror. 'Right-ho. Looks like they're locking up.'

Langham glanced at the side mirror and saw the van pull
out into the road and drive past. He and Ralph watched it turn
left at the end of the street, then climbed from the car and
approached number fifty.

While Ralph attended to the lock with his skeleton keys,
Langham stood by the gate and looked up and down the
street. There was no one about, and no curtains twitched
suspiciously in neighbouring houses.

'Got it, Don. In we go.'

Langham followed Ralph inside. Late-afternoon sunlight
cascaded through the pebbled transom above the door, illumin-
ating dust motes in the hallway. Ralph locked the door behind
them.

The house proved to be sparsely furnished, with brown
linoleum flooring in the hall and kitchen and threadbare carpets
in the living room and on the staircase. It was typical of the
low-quality, high-rent dwellings offered by rapacious landlords
since the end of the war.

The workmen had deposited the paintings in the living room,
having pushed the utility furnishings aside to accommodate
the artwork.

'We might as well have a nosey around while we're here,'
Ralph said, poking his head into the living room. 'Nothing in
here, beside the paintings.' He sniffed. 'Never noticed it when
we were loading up,' he went on, 'but they fair reek, don't they?'

'The heady aroma of oil paint, dope and thinners,' Langham said, following Ralph into the kitchen.

It was evident that Christopher Lombard was living here. There was a stack of groceries in the larder and a half-full bottle of milk standing on the draining board. Three cups, three saucers and three plates occupied a rack above the electric cooker.

Upstairs they found two small bedrooms and a tiny bathroom. At least the place had an inside loo, Langham thought. He recalled returning to London after the war and viewing a dozen houses and flats that had only outside lavatories.

One bedroom was empty, the second furnished with a single bed that had evidently been slept in, with a stained pillow and crumpled sheets.

They returned to the kitchen and Ralph peered into the larder. 'Doesn't even have any beers to wet our whistles,' he said. 'I don't call that very hospitable.'

They set up two chairs just inside the kitchen, out of sight of the front door.

'So why do you reckon Christopher hasn't got in touch with his old man?' Ralph asked.

'Maybe he's found out that it's his father who's been buying up all his paintings, and he resents it.'

Ralph shrugged. 'Maybe.'

'Can you imagine how he might feel if he has found out? There you are, working away and believing you have real talent, because a West End gallery is selling your stuff like hot cakes. Then you find out that your works of genius are being bought up by someone through motives of sympathy, or misplaced nepotism. It would be soul-destroying for a creative person.'

'Must be nice to have all that dosh, though.'

Langham glanced at his watch. It was just after six thirty.

'I wouldn't half mind a fag,' Ralph said. 'But if Rembrandt turns up, takes a whiff and scarpers—'

He fell silent as a key sounded in the front door. Langham tensed, climbed to his feet and pressed himself against the wall.

Ralph reached into the inside pocket of his jacket, pulled

out his revolver and slipped it into a side pocket. He remained seated and crossed his legs casually.

They heard the front door close, followed by footsteps in the hall. There was a delay, and Langham imagined Lombard looking into the living room to check that the paintings had been delivered.

Footsteps sounded on the linoleum, approaching the kitchen.

Langham pushed himself from the wall and stood facing the door.

A tall, well-built man appeared in the doorway and stopped dead when he saw Langham and Ralph.

'Christopher Lombard?' Langham asked.

The man looked from Ralph to Langham. 'That's right,' he said. 'But more to the point, who the hell are you?'

Langham showed his accreditation.

Lombard leaned against the doorpost. 'Police?'

'Private investigators,' Ralph said, still nonchalantly seated. 'We're working for your father.'

Christopher Lombard had a thin face with sunken cheeks, and black hair in a receding widow's peak. He wore a black roll-neck sweater and black trousers, and looked less like an artist than one of Mosley's black-clad thugs.

He looked from Langham to Ralph and saw the barrel of the revolver, tent-poling the material of Ralph's jacket.

'Working for my father?' he said.

'He wants to see you,' Langham said, 'and employed us to find you—'

'So you thought you'd break in and—'

'We didn't break in,' Ralph said. 'Merely let ourselves in and made ourselves comfortable until you came back.' He indicated the chair that Langham had vacated. 'Take the weight off your feet.'

'I'd rather remain standing if it's all the same,' Lombard said. 'So you've delivered your message – my father would like to see me. Received, loud and clear. Now get out.'

'Not so fast,' Ralph said. 'Like I said, sit down. I think it might be wise. I don't like delivering bad news, but I really must. So I suggest you take the weight off.'

Lombard stared at him. 'Is it my father?'

'As Mr Ryland said, take a seat.' Langham indicated the chair.

Lombard hesitated, then pulled the chair towards him and sat down.

'It's not your father,' Ralph began.

'Not Victoria?'

Ralph looked up at Langham, who said, 'Your brother, Nigel, was shot dead on Sunday. I'm sorry.'

The artist sat back, taking deep breaths. 'Nigel?'

'It would appear that he was murdered,' Langham went on.

Lombard closed his eyes. If this was an act, he thought, then the artist was convincing.

'He was discovered at Madras Wharf in Wapping,' Langham said. 'I understand you rent the loft there?'

Lombard opened his eyes. 'That's right. I worked there when I needed a break from the country.'

'When was the last time you saw Nigel?'

The artist considered the question, leaning forward and pinching the bridge of his nose. 'A few weeks ago. I can't recall. He rang me while I was at Swavesy, said he needed to see me. I was coming down to London anyway, so we arranged to meet at the Washington in Swiss Cottage.'

'What did he want?' Langham asked.

'A loan. He owed some people rather a lot of money.'

'How much?'

'Two grand, a little more.'

Ralph whistled. 'So you helped him out.'

The artist grunted. 'I told him I couldn't lay my hands on so much money—' He stopped and looked suddenly stricken. 'You don't think . . .?'

Langham said, 'Go on.'

'You don't think whoever he owed the money to . . . that they—?'

Langham interrupted, 'How did Nigel react when you said you couldn't help him out?'

Lombard rubbed his eyes, looking exhausted. 'He took it pretty well, considering. Finished his whisky and left.'

'Why do you think he went to the loft at Madras Wharf, Mr Lombard?'

'Perhaps . . . Look, it was the last London address of mine that he had. He knew I was leaving Swavesy, so he must have tried the warehouse. I gave him a spare key last year, so he could use the place when he was in London.'

Ralph asked, 'Do you own any kind of gun, Mr Lombard?'

'A gun?' He shook his head. 'No.' Then he stared at Ralph 'How was Nigel—?'

'He was shot in the head at close range with a double-barrelled shotgun,' Ralph said.

Lombard pulled a kind of slow motion, agonized grimace, then leaned forward and held his head in his hands, moaning to himself.

Langham said softly, 'We're sorry to be the bearers of such bad news. You'll understand that we need to take you in for questioning. The case is being investigated by one of the best – Detective Inspector Mallory of Scotland Yard. If you'd agree to accompany us . . .'

Lombard looked up, seeming to take an age to process what Langham had said. 'Yes, yes . . . of course. I'm sorry. This has come as a hell of a shock.'

Ralph climbed to his feet and moved into the hallway, gesturing for Lombard to follow him. Langham brought up the rear as they left the house, then waited at the gate while Lombard locked the door.

Ralph murmured, 'I'll come with you, just in case he tries to do a runner.'

Langham nodded.

They took Langham's Rover, with Lombard sitting silently in the back beside Ralph. The sun was low over the rooftops, burning orange, as they motored towards Scotland Yard.

Langham broke the silence after a couple of minutes. 'First thing tomorrow, Mr Lombard, I think it might be wise if you paid your father a visit. Quite naturally, in the circumstances, he's worried sick.'

Lombard snorted. 'I very much doubt it, Langham. Nothing worries my father – I doubt he even feels such things as normal human emotions.'

'He's just lost his younger son—'

'Whom he despised with a passion.'

'Nevertheless, he hired us because he wishes to see you.'

'He wishes to exert control over me, you mean.'

Langham glanced into the rear-view mirror: Ralph rolled his eyes.

'I think, all things considered, that it might be in your best interests to accede to your father's wishes and visit him,' Langham went on. 'He mentioned the fact of his will and the state of his health. He's not a well man, Mr Lombard. As far as I could make out, you will be his sole beneficiary.'

To his surprise, Lombard laughed. 'So he thinks he can reel me in with a sob story and the promise of wealth?' he said bitterly. 'Very well, Langham. I'll go and see him – but just so that you'll earn your filthy fee. I'll drop round first thing in the morning.'

They arrived at Scotland Yard five minutes later, and Langham and Ralph escorted Lombard to the reception desk.

Langham gave the briefest of details to the desk sergeant, then asked to see Detective Inspector Mallory. The sergeant spoke into a phone and said that Mallory would be down presently.

In due course Mallory rushed through a swing door, pushing a hand through his blond thatch and looking like a man who'd won a jackpot on the pools.

'Don, Ralph,' he said. 'And this, I take it, is Christopher Lombard?' He extended a hand. 'It's good of you to agree to drop by,' he said.

The detective and the artist shook hands, and with a gesture Mallory invited Lombard to accompany him. As Lombard moved out of earshot, Mallory said, 'Good work, boys. I owe you a few jars.'

'I'll be in touch tomorrow,' Langham said. 'I learned something about Nigel Lombard that might be of interest.'

'I'm in at nine in the morning,' Mallory said. 'I'll give you a bell.'

They left the building, and, after dropping Ralph off at King's Cross to pick up his Morris Minor, Langham drove west to Kensington, congratulating himself on a good day's work.

THIRTEEN

When Langham entered the office at nine thirty the following morning, Pamela looked up from her typewriter. 'How do you spell "Nebuchadnezzar"', Donald?'

He told her. 'Why on earth are you typing "Nebuchadnezzar"?'

'I'm typing up Ralph's notes on the greyhound case. It was the name of the dog.'

'How did Ralph spell it?'

She referred to Ralph's handwritten notes. 'N-E-B-U-C-A-N-E-Z-A. I thought it didn't look right.'

'Not far off. Jeff Mallory hasn't called, has he?'

'No. Would you like a cuppa?'

'I'll make it. One for you?'

He made two cups of tea and sat on the corner of her desk. 'How was your date the other night with Dennis?'

'Lovely,' she said. 'After the film we went for supper at the Tivoli on Leicester Square. He's such a gentleman, unlike some of the others I've known.'

'So wedding bells are in the offing?'

She scowled at him. 'I've only known him four months, Donald!' She sighed. 'But I wish my mum and dad were still alive to meet him. They'd've got on like a house on fire.'

'So it *is* serious,' he said.

The phone shrilled, saving her blushes.

'If that's Jeff, put him through.'

He waited till she took the call; she looked up and nodded.

He moved to the inner office and picked up the receiver. 'Jeff?'

'Don, good work in locating Christopher Lombard last night. We had a nice little chat.'

'I sense a "but" coming.'

'He has an alibi. He was with a reputable citizen all Sunday afternoon and evening.' He hesitated. 'However, there's something a bit odd about all of it.'

'In what way?'

'That's what I'm trying to work out. Look, are you free later? You said you wanted to see me about something to do with Nigel Lombard.'

'Name a time.'

'How about eleven at the caff just along from the Yard? I've got a lot of paperwork to catch up with before then.'

'I'll see you then,' Langham said, and rang off.

He was finishing his tea when Ralph breezed in, sat down and lodged his winklepickers on the desk.

'I've just got off the blower to Jeff,' Langham said, and told Ralph about Christopher Lombard's alibi. 'There's always the possibility that this "reputable citizen" is lying, of course. I don't think we can't discount Christopher quite yet.'

'Things are never cut and dried, are they?' Ralph said. 'Why couldn't Lombard just've broken down and confessed to blowing his brother's brains out?'

'And leave us with nothing to do?' Langham said.

'I think I'll mosey on down to the wharf and have a poke around,' Ralph said. 'People might've seen Nigel coming and going – and you never know, he might not've been alone.'

'Good luck,' Langham said. 'We might make some progress on the case if we could locate Nigel's contacts. He seems to have led a somewhat peripatetic life.'

'In plain English, Don.'

'He moved about a bit, never in one place for long.'

Ralph swung his feet from the table. 'Right, I'd better get to it.' He moved to the door. 'Be seeing you, Cap'n.'

'Be careful of Grayson and his thugs, OK?'

Ralph scowled. 'Can it, Don,' he said, and slipped from the office.

Langham leaned back and read the latest edition of the *Daily Herald* before heading out into the sunshine. He drove south, then turned along the Embankment, passing Scotland Yard and pulling up outside the run-down café patronized by Jeff Mallory and other detectives from the Yard. He'd frequented the café perhaps half a dozen times over the past few years and surmised that its popularity had more to do with its close-ness to the Yard than the quality of its fare. It was the kind of place that served all-day breakfasts and managed to burn at least one item on the plate with every serving.

Langham arrived early and ordered a black tea. He sat at a window table and read the sports pages of the *Herald* until Mallory bustled in.

'Your usual, Mr Mallory?' the grizzled old Italian called from behind the counter.

'With coffee today, Giuseppe,' he said, joining Langham. 'I've been on the go since six, Don. I need something to wake me up.'

Langham gestured to his tea. 'I'm amazed that every time I've been here, they manage to stew the ruddy brew.'

'But you must admit, Don – it's cheap.'

Langham smiled. 'It certainly is.'

Giuseppe deposited a plate of tinned spaghetti on toast on the table and Mallory dug in.

Langham watched him. 'Doesn't Carrie feed you these days?'

Mallory gestured with his fork. 'She does, and she's a fine cook. How did I get so lucky? The woman has talent, looks, and she's a genius in the kitchen.'

Langham sipped his tea and pulled a face.

'While I remember,' Mallory said, 'I've just been on the blower to the passport office, checking their records against Nigel Lombard's passport we found the other day.'

'And?'

'They confirmed that they issued it six months ago.'

'That's good to know,' Langham said. 'So, about Christopher Lombard's alibi.'

Mallory swallowed a mouthful of carbohydrates and pointed at Langham with his fork. 'Smooth-talking customer, Mr Lombard, with friends in high places.'

'How high?'

'Have you heard of Manville Carrington?'

'Didn't he hold some post in Churchill's coalition cabinet during the war? I thought he died years ago.'

'That's the chap. He's in his eighties now, an old Labour radical. Word was, just after the war, he was one of Stalin's "useful idiots".'

Langham grunted. 'The party's riddled with 'em.'

'He was up for a knighthood for his wartime services, but the kibosh was put on that when his cosying up to Uncle Joe came to light. He retired from parliament five years ago, but still writes a weekly opinion piece for the *Tribune*.'

'A die-hard Stalinist, four years after the monster's demise,' Langham said. 'You're not telling me that Christopher Lombard and he are acquainted?'

'Lombard was at Carrington's Belgravia place from around four on Sunday afternoon until after midnight.'

Langham stared at the detective. 'Now I've heard everything. So tell me: why would a radical old leftie hobnob with the fascist son of a well-known arms dealer? You've interviewed Carrington, I take it?'

'I sent Venables round this morning, and Carrington confirmed everything that Lombard told me. He said he and Lombard discussed politics all evening, and Lombard left by cab just after midnight.'

'Did Venables ask Carrington how he came to know Christopher Lombard?'

'Apparently, through his father – Carrington and Lombard senior are acquainted.'

'Perhaps Carrington admires Christopher Lombard's paintings – almost exclusively of naked women, by the way.' Langham picked up his tea, had second thoughts and replaced it on the table.

Mallory said, 'You mentioned something about the other brother, Nigel?'

'That's right. I've had some interesting gen on him. This came from a woman up at the farm in Herefordshire, where Nigel stayed from time to time. According to her, Nigel had dealings with agents from the Russian embassy.' He went on to recount Penny Archer's claims in more detail.

'Christ,' Mallory said. 'Well, if it's true, it's the sweetest damned trick I've ever heard – setting his father up to sell arms to the Reds. Whatever gripe Nigel held against his father for alleged childhood mistreatment, he's certainly avenged himself. I wonder if Lombard found out and got the heavies in?'

Langham shrugged. 'That had occurred to me,' he said. 'Or maybe MI5 found out and decided to silence Nigel?'

Mallory rocked his head from side to side. 'I very much doubt it.'

'What, do you think our boys are beyond getting their hands dirty like that?' Langham asked.

'Not at all. I'm sure that MI5, like every other government security agency world-wide, often puts political expediency before moral and ethical niceties.'

'Then why rule it out in this case?'

'Because I'm pretty sure I would have been asked into the superintendent's office for a quiet word. He would have mentioned things like "the powers that be" and "decisions made at the top level", and told me to drop the investigation, "there's a good man".'

Langham grunted. 'There's time for that yet, Jeff.'

'All this is assuming that Nigel Lombard wasn't telling Penny Archer a tale to impress her,' Mallory pointed out. 'I'll look into it. If Nigel was in the pocket of the Soviets, one of my colleagues – or a contact of theirs – might know something about it.'

Langham nodded and pushed aside his unfinished mug of tea.

'While I remember,' Mallory said, 'Victoria Lombard was asking after you. Our surgeon dropped by the hospital to check up on her yesterday, and she said she wanted to talk to you. She was being discharged this morning, so she should be back at her place by now.'

'I'll pop round and see her. I wonder if she's recalled something about Nigel or his acquaintances.'

Mallory pointed at him. 'Oh, and on that front, we traced one of Nigel Lombard's chums yesterday. A civil servant called Cedric Evans. Shifty character. He certainly didn't like it when I showed up and wanted a word. He claimed he hadn't seen Nigel Lombard for a couple of years but he was sweating buckets, and as far as I was concerned, he was lying through his teeth. We're keeping an eye on him.'

Mallory polished off his spaghetti on toast and finished his tea. 'I bet you'd love another cuppa?'

'I'd rather drink battery acid. I was wondering . . . As Victoria and Nigel were close, might she know something about Nigel's political leanings and whether he did approach his father about an arms deal with the Africans?'

'It's certainly worth asking her about it,' Mallory said. 'Right, that paperwork won't get done by itself. Give me a bell if you learn anything.' He pointed to Langham's cup. 'I'll get this.'

'You're generous to a fault, sir. Give my love to Carrie.'

'Will do.' Mallory paid at the counter and hurried off.

Langham sat for a few minutes, considering the implications of Christopher Lombard's alibi, then left the café and drove to Highgate.

FOURTEEN

Ralph Ryland rolled his Morris Minor along the cobbled road and pulled up outside Madras Wharf. The warehouse loomed to his right, with a mechanics' workshop occupying part of the building. The sound of hammering issued from the shadows.

He climbed out, stretched and read the sign above the shutter: *Cohen Brothers, Vehicle Repairs.*

Christ, reminders were everywhere. Since his chance meeting with Alf Bentley had stirred up all those unpleasant memories, not an hour had gone by when he wasn't confronted by something that brought back the guilt like a knife twisting in his gut.

He made his way to the alley between the warehouses and stared at the staircase zigzagging up the side of the building. He moved down the alley and negotiated the steps with care, remembering what Don had told him about the state of the treads and the handholds.

When he came to the top, he paused and inspected the door, which the police had made secure with a padlock. He moved to the dusty window beside the door and peered through. All

he could see was a cavernous loft space and the sofa where
Nigel Lombard had died at the far end, and to the right a
mattress on the bare boards. It beat him how anyone could
fashion to live in a place like this, without creature comforts
like a hot bath from time to time.

He sat down on the top step and lit up a Capstan.

He considered Alf Bentley, and what he'd let slip about the
twentieth – which was precious little. Something about it
kicking off again, and the good old days, and Cable Street.
Was Arnold Grayson planning to cause a bit of trouble in the
East End? The idea made him sick.

Involuntarily, his thoughts went back to his father, and
the mid-thirties, and what had occurred then.

He'd looked up to his dad, an unemployed six-foot-four docker
with arms like girders and hands the size of coal scuttles. Ralph
had always been puny, the runt of a litter of four boys – even
though he'd been the eldest – and he supposed that had made
him respect his dad even more. He'd wanted to be like him, to
grow up to be as big and strong as his old man. He remembered
the thrill of seeing his dad dressed up when he went out to his
weekly BUF meetings: all in black, with a big black belt, a trim
moustache, and his hair slicked back with brilliantine.

He recalled how excited he'd been when his old man said
Ralph was old enough, at sixteen, to attend the meetings. His
younger brothers had envied him, and he'd felt proud enough
to burst when he marched out with his dad, past the watching
neighbours, to the meeting at the Bow assembly rooms.

He'd experienced a comforting feeling of belonging, which
he'd never enjoyed before – especially not at school where,
small for his age, he'd been picked on by bigger kids.
He remembered taking the pledge, and joining the union, and
the first day he'd donned his uniform in front of the bedroom
mirror. He was part of something bigger than himself, an army
of like-minded men. For too long, his dad had told him, the
working classes had been oppressed from both sides: from
the top by the aristocrats who hoarded wealth and power, and
from the bottom by the immigrants who came and took the
jobs that rightfully belonged to people like him and the others
who met every week in Bow.

Marching down the street next to his towering old man, he'd felt suddenly empowered.

And the day he'd seen Oswald Mosley speak at Hackney . . . He remembered the excitement, the stomach-churning thrill of seeing the man in the flesh. He recalled the power of Mosley's oratory and the wisdom of his words as he strode the stage, gesticulating.

It had all seemed so *right*, at the time.

He removed his cigarette and spat at the wall. If only he could go back and meet the stupid, impressionable fool he'd been, puny and farcical in his black trousers and roll-neck sweater, playing at being the big man. But what could he have said to persuade his younger self that what he was doing, what he was being led into, was no more than a charade to compensate for his inferiority? The cocky young Ralph Ryland would've laughed in his face and told him to eff off.

He finished his cigarette, then made his way down the treacherous stairway and back along the alley.

An overweight, balding man in an oil-stained boiler suit was in the process of jacking up a car when Ryland stepped into the garage. The mechanic stopped his cranking and straightened up. 'Can I help?'

'You Mr Cohen?'

'That's right. I'm Norman.'

'Ralph Ryland,' he said. 'Own this place, do you?'

'Rent the premises, own the business with my brother.'

Ryland flashed his accreditation. 'I'm looking into the murder on Sunday,' he said.

Norman Cohen wiped his hands on his boiler suit. 'Police've been crawling all over the place for the past day or so. Gangland killing, so I've heard.'

'Is that so?'

'And not the first. Police should do something about 'em.'

'What've you heard, exactly?'

Cohen shrugged. 'Rumours, down the pub. Young bloke selling drugs, apparently. Lord of the manor don't like it, gives him a warning, which the bloke ignores. And what happens next? He gets his block blown off.'

'And who might do a thing like that?' Ryland asked.

Cohen opened the bonnet of the car and peered down at the engine. 'If you're from round here, you'd know.'

'Let me hazard a guess,' Ryland said. 'The big fish round these parts is a geezer called Grayson. Ring any bells?'

Cohen affected interest in the head gasket. 'I'm saying nothing, mate.'

'Probably wise. I take it you pay protection money to this Mr Grayson?'

'Like I said, I'm saying nothing.'

Ryland lit another cigarette. 'You were working here on Sunday?'

'That's right.'

'Did you happen to see anyone near the alley at any time that day?'

'Matter of fact, I did. A couple of people. Youngsters.'

'Get a good look at 'em?'

Cohen shrugged. 'Can't say I took much notice, though the girl was a looker.'

'Could you describe her?'

'Small, pretty, blonde – but an artificial blonde. What do you call it?'

'Peroxide?'

'That's it. Peroxide, but it suited her.'

'How old was she?'

'Late twenties, maybe thirty.'

'What was she doing?'

Cohen scratched his balding head. 'She was just standing at the end of the alley, looking up at the loft.'

'Are you sure about that? She was looking up at the loft, where the body was discovered later that day?'

'That's right, just standing there, looking up.'

'And what did she do then?'

Cohen shrugged. 'She just watched for a minute or two, then turned and hurried off.'

'Watched what?'

'A bit earlier, a young man turned up and went down the alley. I got the impression she was following him.'

'A young man?' Ryland said. 'Can you describe him?'

'I only got a glimpse, but he was wearing one of those

brown duffel coats that're fashionable with the youngsters these days.'

'How old was he?'

'Hard to say. Like I said, I only got a glimpse. Anything from mid-twenties to thirty, I'd guess.'

'And he definitely went down the alleyway?'

Cohen nodded. 'That's right. Then a few minutes later I saw the blonde.'

'Neither of 'em sound like gangland types to me, Mr Cohen,' Ryland grunted and lit another Capstan. 'What time was this?'

The mechanic shrugged. 'Early on – one-ish. I heard the guy was shot later that day, so I reckon they had nothing to do with it.'

Ryland drew on his cigarette, thinking things through. A pretty peroxide blonde? The girl up at Henderson's Farm fitted that description, and she'd known Nigel Lombard into the bargain. But then again, peroxide blondes were ten a penny in London these days. He'd mention it to Don, anyway.

'You've been very helpful, Mr Cohen,' he said. 'If you remember anything else about that Sunday, give me a bell.'

He passed the man his business card and made to go.

He hesitated. 'One other thing. I had an acquaintance, back in the thirties. Chap by the name of Manny Cohen – he had a barber's shop on Cable Street. Don't suppose he's any relation of yours?'

The man smiled and Ryland's stomach turned. 'Old Manny? Yes, I know Manny. No relation, but my old man knew him well.'

'How . . . how's he keeping these days? We lost touch during the war, you see.'

'Manny's doing fine. Retired now, of course. After what happened in Cable Street that night . . . Well, he sold up and rented a premises up Golders Green way. It took him a long time to get over that – not so much the beating, you see, but up here.' Cohen tapped the side of his head. 'It affected his nerves really bad, it did. But you'll know that, if you knew him back then.'

Ryland nodded. 'Yes. Yes, of course.' He shrugged. 'Well, I'd better be getting along. Thanks again for your time, Mr Cohen.'

'Don't mention it,' Cohen said, and bent to examine the engine.

Ryland walked back to his car and climbed in behind the wheel. He sat for a while, staring out at the cobbled road, then started the engine and drove off. He needed a drink. He'd pop into the Bull, have two or three and a bite to eat.

In his mind's eye he saw Alf Bentley's leering face, made ugly by fresh slash marks, and he cursed the bastard.

He parked as near to the Bull as possible and hurried into the pub.

'Ralph,' the publican said. 'You're a bit early today. Pint of Fuller's?'

'Hot day, Ted,' Ryland said. 'Thirsty work. A pint and a couple of pork pies, please.'

'Coming up.'

Ryland carried the pint pot and the pies to a table by the window and sat in silence for a time, staring out.

He took a long drink of bitter and wished that he'd never accepted Len Turner's offer of a pint at the Lion and Unicorn that day. If he'd not walked into the pub and clapped eyes on Alf Bentley . . .

He remembered being shocked when he heard about young Alf getting cut up back in '36, and even more shocked when he'd visited him in hospital and seen the state he was in, his head swaddled in bandages and his right eye covered by a thick white pad.

'Got into a brawl with some yids,' Alf had told him. 'Still, I slashed a couple of the bastards, right enough.'

A month later, when Ryland turned up at a meeting at Bow assembly rooms one Thursday night, there was excitement in the air, a charge like electricity, and Alf Bentley had said, 'Heard what's goin' down, Ralph? Next week, Cable Street.' He'd punched a fist into his palm. 'Ever heard the phrase "revenge is sweet", Ralph?'

Ryland finished his pint and went to the bar for a second and a double whisky chaser.

'You OK, Ralph?' Ted asked. 'You look a bit rough.'

'Early start,' he muttered. He took the whisky and beer back to his table and knocked the spirit back in one, then took a drink of ale.

Christ, that was better.

He stared through the window at the sunlit street. Pedestrians passed back and forth, laughing and smiling. He wondered what Annie was doing now. It was her day for the laundrette, so no doubt she'd be gassing with the other mums, and the boys would be safe in school.

He'd gone along with Alf and a dozen others that night, armed with a cricket bat and knuckledusters, fired up with adrenaline and encouragement from his old man. He recalled marching along the street, feeling so bloody big, proud and powerful at the same time, part of an army, a *cause*. He remembered taking the bat to the barber's shop window and smashing it with one blow, and he recalled wading in and trashing the place, and then coming across the proprietor cowering in a back room.

He squeezed shut his eyes in a bid to stop the tears. He took a long drink of beer, then gasped.

He remembered attacking the proprietor, hitting Manny Cohen across the head with the bat, and all these years later he could still hear the poor man's cries for mercy.

And the worst of it was that, at the time, he'd gained an undeniable animal thrill from the attack, and had felt not the slightest sympathy for his victim.

He returned to the bar for a third pint and another double whisky.

FIFTEEN

Langham climbed the steps to Victoria Lombard's flat and found the door wedged open with a cast-iron doorstop in the shape of a duck.

'Hello?' he called. 'Victoria?'

'Mr Langham, is that you?' Her voice sounded tremulous. 'Do come in.'

He entered the flat and found her seated in an armchair in the open-plan living room. She was wearing a red dress; her dark hair was dishevelled and her face pale. Dark patches, like bruises, underlined her eyes.

Before her on the coffee table was a glass tumbler and a bottle of Gordon's gin.

Langham sat down on the sofa opposite her.

Victoria lifted a limp hand to indicate her face. 'You must forgive me, Mr Langham. I haven't had time to . . .' She gestured towards the door. 'And I left it open as it's such a nice day, and sometimes birds come in here. Some people think that having birds in the house brings bad luck, don't they? What do you think, Mr Langham?'

'Call me Donald,' he said, and shrugged. 'I'm not superstitious.'

She reached out, took the tumbler in an unsteady hand and drank.

'I've only just got back from the hospital. It was a rather nice place. The nurses were so kind. They gave me some wonderful medication.' She indicated a small brown vial of pills on the table beside the gin.

'Do you think it wise,' he said, 'drinking on top of the medication?'

She blinked at him and he wondered if this was her first glass. 'They said that a little drink wouldn't harm me, Mr Langham. Just one *little* drink.'

'Well, just as long as it is only one, and a little one,' he went on, feeling like a nursemaid. 'You wanted to see me?'

'I just wanted to ask how the investigation was proceeding, Mr Langham. I mean Donald.' She hesitated. 'I was thinking, while I was in hospital . . . Could what happened . . . could it have had anything to do with Nigel's gambling debts?'

'We considered, and pretty much discounted, that possibility,' he said.

She leaned forward and said, almost despairingly, 'I just want to know who killed my brother.'

'I'm attempting to build up a comprehensive picture of the kind of man your brother was. I'm trying to trace his friends and acquaintances. I've already spoken to people up in Herefordshire—'

'Nigel was a kind and gentle man,' she interrupted. 'Unlike Christopher. They were very, very different. Nigel wouldn't harm anybody.'

'Meaning that Christopher might?'

She shrugged. 'Given the right conditions, I wouldn't put *anything* past Christopher.'

'I understand that Nigel was married briefly. Do you happen to be in contact with his former wife, or with any of his recent girlfriends?'

She peered down at the glass in her hand, considering the question. 'I met his wife a few times. This was seven or eight years ago. A mousy little thing. Audrey, I think she was called. But they weren't together for long and I've no idea where she might be now.'

'Do you know if he was seeing anyone more recently?'

She shook her head. 'He never told me about anyone, but then he was secretive when it came to that side of his life.'

She drained her glass, then looked at the bottle on the coffee table. 'Do you think, Donald, you could hide it somewhere in the kitchen? Don't tell me where. You see, I'm tempted to drink the lot, and I think in the circumstances that might not be such a good idea.'

He agreed, picked up the bottle and moved to the kitchen. He shut the door behind him so that she couldn't see him conceal the gin in the cupboard under the sink. He looked around, saw an unopened bottle on top of the Frigidaire and secreted it in the cupboard beside the first one.

He returned to the living room and sat down. 'I know it's painful to dredge up old memories like this,' he said, 'but it really would help me if I knew a little more about Nigel.'

She sat back in the chair and crossed her legs. 'What would you like to know, Donald?'

'Did he ever speak to you of his political beliefs?'

She smiled at the question. 'He had none.'

'None at all?'

'He was – what's the word? – apolitical. He despised politicians of all stripes, Left, Right and in between.'

'When did you last speak to him about politics?'

She hesitated. 'I can't recall. Years ago, perhaps. It was not something we discussed, as such.'

Langham sat back and considered his next question. 'What would you say if I were to tell you that Nigel had in fact held trenchant political beliefs?'

'What on earth makes you think . . .?'

'Someone I spoke to claimed that not only was he committed to a certain cause but he was active in furthering it—'

'It was Christopher who was the fascist. Nigel would have nothing to do with them.'

'Nigel's sympathies were not fascist. Quite the contrary, in fact.'

His words appeared to sober her. 'Communist?' She laughed. 'I think you're very much mistaken. My brother, Nigel, a communist? The very thought!'

'Moreover,' he went on, 'I'm given to understand that he was in contact with agents of the Soviet Union.'

She stared at him, her expression frozen. Very deliberately, she said, 'Are you claiming that Nigel was a spy?'

'Not so much a spy, merely . . . an informant, let's say.'

'Do go on. I'm finding this fascinating beyond belief.'

He turned his palms upright in a candid gesture. 'I can only relay what I've been told. I was informed that your brother was paid by the Kremlin to facilitate an introduction between your father and an intermediary working for communist rebels in Africa.'

'But this gets better and better.' She laughed. 'Next you'll be claiming that my father, whose political beliefs would make Franco seem a moderate, was willingly working for the Soviets!'

'Not willingly,' Langham said. 'According to my information, he knew nothing of the deception. He was lured into it, unknowingly, by Nigel, and your father fell for it and sold arms to the facilitator of a leftist insurrection in a certain African state. As far as he was concerned, it was just another arms deal carried out for profit.'

'This is absurd.'

'I was wondering,' Langham continued, 'if there might be any way you could confirm the deal?'

'What makes you think I might know anything about it?' She paused, staring at him. 'And if you think I'd agree to asking my father—'

'It occurred to me that, in your position as his daughter, you might have access to company records. All that would be needed is confirmation that your father's firm did a deal with a company in Africa a couple of years ago.'

She shook her head in disbelief. 'That would be impossible. My father still has a controlling interest in the company. He holds a majority of the shares but he rarely ventures into the office these days. And I certainly don't have access to company records. Indeed, I don't even know precisely where the company has its head office. The idea is preposterous.'

'Might there be another way for you to obtain the information? Does your father keep documents at home? Does he have a safe on the premises?'

'I have absolutely no idea, and I refuse to go creeping around the house in search of such documentation. I know . . . I *knew* Nigel well enough to be sure he'd never work for the Russians.'

'Very well,' he said, smiling. 'I'll drop it.'

'But you won't, will you? You're just saying that. You'll just try to find out from a different source.'

He sighed. 'In this line of work you must keep your options open. Nothing is impossible, no matter how unlikely it might seem. What I meant is that I'll stop questioning you about it now.'

She smiled primly. 'I appreciate that.'

He looked at his watch, preparatory to taking his leave. 'There is one more thing. I traced Christopher last night and spoke to him.'

She leaned forward, staring at him. 'Christopher?' she said, surprised. 'Did you tell him about Nigel? I hope you weren't taken in by his crocodile tears?'

'As I recall, he shed none.'

'Of course not,' she said. 'He would be too cynical and cold-hearted even to dissimulate.'

'The police wanted to question him, of course, so I dropped him off at Scotland Yard. I also said that his father wanted to see him. He seemed reluctant, but finally agreed and said he'd call round here this morning. I don't suppose you know if he did so?'

She shrugged. 'I saw my father when I arrived home at eleven, and he said nothing about having seen Christopher.'

'I wonder if you could mention to your father that Christopher is safe and well?'

She nodded. 'I'll do that, Mr Langham. Thank you.'

'I don't think there's anything else I need to know for the time being. I'll be in contact if anything comes up.' He climbed to his feet and crossed to the open door.

Victoria rose hurriedly, swaying. 'Donald . . .' She reached out. 'I wonder if you'd be so kind as to assist me . . . I feel more than a little woozy. I think I need to lie down.'

He returned to her and took her arm. As she leaned against him, he placed an arm around her shoulders and steered her across the room. She clung to him, exuding the aroma of gin and stale perfume, and indicated the bedroom door. He opened the door and half carried her towards the double bed.

As he tried to ease her on to the bed, she turned to face him.

'Donald . . . you could stay if you wished.'

He disengaged her fingers from his lapel. 'If I were you,' he said, 'I'd get some rest.'

As he moved to the door, she stared at him from the bed and said, 'I never asked you, Donald. Are you married?'

He ignored the question and closed the bedroom door after him. As he left the apartment, something flashed past his shoulder. He flinched automatically and turned. A sparrow made a circuit of the living room, chirruping in alarm as it went.

Leaving the front door wedged open, he hurried down the steps.

He dropped in at the office on his way back to Kensington.

'Ralph back yet?' he asked Pamela.

'No, and he hasn't rung in, either.'

'When he does return, tell him I'm calling it a day. I'll be at the flat if he wants to discuss anything.'

'I'll do that.'

He made for the door.

'Oh,' Pamela called after him. 'One thing. A woman named Dorothea Marston telephoned, wanting to speak with you. She asked if you'd managed to trace Christopher Lombard.'

He recalled the promise he'd made to her. 'Could you call her on this number' – he found the farm's telephone number in his notebook – 'and tell her that Lombard is staying at fifty, Cardigan Street, King's Cross.'

She made a note of the telephone number and the address. 'Will do, Donald. Have a pleasant day.'

'You, too. Are you seeing Dennis tonight?'

'How did you guess? He's taking me for a meal up the West End.'

'Very posh,' he said. 'See you in the morning.'

He drove to Kensington and let himself into the apartment. He found Maria curled up on the sofa with a manuscript and flopped down beside her.

'Hard day, Donald?'

'Exhausting. A terrible cup of tea with Jeff in the morning, and this afternoon a drunken woman tried to lure me into bed.'

She sat up. 'Intriguing. Do tell!'

'Well, the tea managed to be both weak *and* stewed, and it came in a big blue-and-white china mug—'

She hit him over the head with a cushion. 'About the inebriated vamp, you awful man!'

Laughing, he described his meeting with Victoria Lombard.

A little later, Maria declared that she had a surprise for him and slipped an envelope from between the pages of the manuscript. 'Two tickets for tonight's performance of Priestley's *Time and the Conways*, courtesy of Charles.'

'My word, these are rarer than hen's teeth after the rave reviews last week.' He kissed her. 'You wonderful woman.'

'Thank Charles; he knew we wanted to see the play.'

'It'll take my mind off the damned Lombards,' he said. 'Now, how about a drink?'

SIXTEEN

Langham found Ralph in the office when he arrived at nine thirty the following morning. He was sitting back in his chair, his feet lodged on the desk as he flipped through an early edition of the *Express*.

'You're late,' Ralph said, peering at him. 'And you look like something the cat's dragged in.'

'Feel like it,' Langham said, slumping into a chair. 'Bit of a session last night. We went to a play, and who should we bump into in the bar afterwards but Jeff and Caroline.'

'So one drink turned to five, eh?'

'They were with a bunch of Carrie's theatre friends. We made the mistake of joining them and didn't get back till well after one.'

'How's the head?'

Langham touched his temple. 'Delicate. I might take it easy today.' He sat back in his chair and peered at the front page of the newspaper Ralph was holding. A headline proclaimed *Right Wing Violence in Whitechapel* on Sunday.

'I see the fascists have been at it again,' he commented.

Ralph grunted something inaudible.

'Speaking of which,' Langham went on, 'I take it Grayson's thugs haven't been in touch?'

Ralph affected interest in the sports page. 'All quiet on that front, Don.'

'That's good to know,' Langham said. 'How did it go at the wharf?'

Ralph lowered the paper. 'I spoke to the mechanic who was working on Sunday,' he said. 'Around one o'clock that afternoon he saw a young man in a duffel coat approach the warehouse, followed a bit later by a young woman. She didn't enter the warehouse, just stared up at it from the end of the alley before walking off.'

'Could the mechanic describe her?'

Ralph nodded. 'She was a peroxide blonde,' he said. 'Ring any bells?'

'Well, Penny Archer dyes her hair with the stuff. But peroxide blondes aren't exactly uncommon.'

'Just what I thought.'

'By the way,' Langham said, 'concerning Christopher Lombard's alibi for the Sunday Nigel was shot.' He recounted what Jeff Mallory had told him about Lombard spending Sunday evening with Manville Carrington.

Ralph frowned. 'So why was Lombard hobnobbing with an old Labourite like Carrington?'

'Exactly what I wondered,' Langham said.

Pamela came in with two mugs of tea. 'You're a darling,' Langham said, taking his mug. 'How was your dinner date last night?'

Pamela moved to the door and turned, smiling. 'Tickety-boo,' she said. 'Dennis proposed to me.' With which, she returned to the outer office and closed the door behind her.

Exchanging a glance with Ralph, Langham tipped back his chair. 'And?' he called out.

'I said thank you very much and I'd think about it,' she called back.

'Well, I suppose congratulations are in order.'

'Thank you!'

Ralph laughed. 'I should have a quiet word with young Dennis and warn him about what he's letting himself in for.'

'Spoken like a true cynic,' Langham said.

Ralph slurped his tea. 'But this Manville Carrington,' he said. 'You'd think he'd have more in common with Nigel Lombard. Maybe he did know Nigel and might be able to tell us a bit more about him. It's a long shot, but worth trying perhaps.'

'Why not?'

'I'll nip along and have a quiet natter with old Carrington. Pam!' he shouted. 'Could you be a dear and fetch the Debrett's?'

The sound of typing stopped in the outer office and Pamela appeared, groaning theatrically under the weight of the fat volume.

While Ralph leafed through the pages for Manville Carrington's address, Langham stopped Pamela before she disappeared.

'So this proposal . . . Tell me more.'

She leaned against the door frame and smiled dreamily. 'Well, at the end of the meal he got all gooey-eyed, took my hand and said he loved me. Then asked me to marry him.'

'You didn't see it coming?'

'I did wonder. I'd seen him eyeing up married couples with kids, and he'd talked about being a dad once or twice in the past.'

'So you damped the poor chap's ardour with a curmudgeonly "I'll think about it"?'

'A girl can't simply rush into these things,' Pamela said. 'Anyway, I don't want kids just yet. I'm not even twenty-five, Donald.'

'When will you put him out of his misery?'

She bit her lip. 'I don't know. I need to talk it over with Maria.'

'She'll love that,' he said. 'Of course, going on her own experience of marriage, she'll unequivocally advise you to tie the knot.'

'Hark at him!' she sang, and returned to her desk.

Langham looked at Ralph. 'Found it?'

Ralph copied the address into his notebook and slammed the Debrett's shut. 'A big place in Belgravia, sounds like. Everett House.' He stood up and tucked his folded *Express* into his back pocket. 'Odd, ain't it?'

'What is?'

'This Carrington geezer – he was all lovey-dovey with Stalin, right? All for workers' rights and more power to the trade unions – and there he is, lording it in a palatial pad in Belgravia. Makes you think, Don. Right, I'll go have a natter with the old leftie. Toodle-pip.'

Langham smiled as he watched Ralph leave the office.

He got up and poked his head through the door. 'Pamela, anything on the books?'

'Nothing, Donald.'

He returned to his desk and finished his tea. He thought he might call it a day at the office, pop along to the British Library and do a bit of research for the Sam Brooke book he was working on.

The phone shrilled in the outer office and Pamela answered. His intercom flashed and she said, 'It's Detective Inspector Mallory. Putting you through.'

Langham picked up the phone. 'Jeff?'

'Don,' Mallory said, against the background noise of what sounded like a passing train. 'The other day you mentioned a woman called Dorothea Marston.'

'That's right. What about her?'

'She was involved with Christopher Lombard, right?'

'*Was* involved, yes.' His stomach turned. 'Why?'

At the far end of the line, a train rattled past. Mallory waited it out, then went on, 'She's been found dead.'

Langham felt a hot flush rise from his chest to his face. 'Go on.'

'Strangled,' Mallory said. 'Look, could you get yourself down here for a quick word?'

He murmured, 'Of course.'

'We're on Tudor Street, a dead-end near King's Cross.'

'I'm on my way.'

He replaced the receiver. In his mind's eye he saw big, friendly Dorothea Marston in dungarees and headscarf, ripping into Christopher Lombard's painting.

He massaged his eyes, then had a thought and called out, 'Pamela, did you speak to Dorothea Marston yesterday?'

She appeared at the door. 'Well, I got through to the farm.'

'But did you speak to her?'

She shook her head. 'No. A young woman told me she was out, so I gave her the address and she said she'd pass it on to Dorothea when she returned.'

'What time was this?'

'One second.' She returned to the outer office to consult her notes. 'A little after four o'clock,' she called.

Langham picked up the phone, dialled the number he had for Henderson's Farm, then waited tensely as the dial tone rang on and on.

At last, someone picked up the receiver. 'Hello?' a woman's voice said.

'Penny? Langham here.'

'Oh, hello, Mr Langham—'

'My secretary rang yesterday afternoon with a message for Dorothea.'

'Yes, that's right,' she said. 'I gave her the message when she got back.'

'You did? I see. And did Dorothea—?'

'She was on the warpath and set off to catch the next train to London.'

Langham swallowed. 'Right.'

'Mr Langham, is something the matter?'

Unable to bring himself to tell her of Dorothea's death, he said, 'I'll be in touch, Penny. Thank you,' and replaced the receiver.

He sat for a minute, staring at the wall. If only Dorothea had not made him promise to supply her with Christopher Lombard's address; if only he'd delayed passing it on, or not supplied it at all.

He left the office and hurried along the busy street to his car.

It was a fifteen-minute drive up to King's Cross and Langham spent every second of it feeling sick and murmuring the phrase *if only* over and over.

The day was warm, and the pedestrians on the streets of the capital were dressed for the weather. Everyone today appeared to be light of heart and smiling. It was amazing – or perhaps it was entirely natural – that good weather should engender optimism in the populace, when nothing else had changed at all. There was still poverty, disease and death abroad in the world, along with the ever-present threat of atomic annihilation. A little sunlight didn't alter that.

Poor Dorothea . . .

He thought, inconsequentially, of her artwork, her sculptures up at the farm. She was a talented woman, who through her art had worked to make the world a better place.

He swore and hit the steering wheel and tried to turn his thoughts to other things.

He came to King's Cross, motored around the station and

turned down Tudor Street. It was one of those depressing dead-ends that proliferated in industrial areas, hemmed in by small factories and warehouses and loomed over by gasworks and gasometers. A few stunted sycamore trees lined the street, alternating with ugly lamp posts. It seemed even more tragic that a woman like Dorothea should have met her end in a place like this.

At the far end of the road he made out a navy-blue police van, two squad cars, the police surgeon's car and Jeff Mallory's green Humber.

Beyond the vehicles, a rope cordoned off the scene of the crime. A knot of men stood forlornly on a patch of waste ground next to a railway line curving in a long iron parabola from the station.

He climbed from the car and approached the cordon. Even the birdsong hereabouts sounded scant and ragged, having to compete with the rattle of passing trains. A young constable stopped him and asked his business. Langham showed his accreditation and asked to see Detective Inspector Mallory.

The constable hurried across to the gathered officers, spoke to Mallory, then beckoned to Langham.

Langham lifted the rope and crossed the uneven ground. A green canvas screen had been erected to shield the body from the prying eyes of passengers on the frequent trains leaving the station. A series of carriages clattered by, and Langham was aware of the passengers' fixed stares as he joined Mallory.

He didn't want to look but against his will he took one quick glance at the woman's swollen face, then looked away.

Mallory said, 'You can confirm it's Dorothea Marston?'

Swallowing, Langham nodded.

'*I'll murder the bastard! I swear, I'll murder him!*' Dorothea had cried on their very first meeting.

Mallory murmured, 'She was found by a railway worker at six this morning. We estimate she died between eight last night and the early hours.' He paused. 'The motive wasn't robbery. She still had her purse with more than ten pounds in cash, and an old ration card, which is how we put a name to her.'

Langham gestured around the waste ground. 'What was she doing here?'

'Forensics say she was killed elsewhere and dumped here.'

The thought of her dead body being transported through the streets of the capital, to be dumped at this forlorn spot, brought a lump to his throat.

'There's only one set of footprints leading from the road,' Mallory went on. 'They're patchy, but discernible. They reckon it was a male, over six feet tall judging by his stride.'

Langham said, 'Dorothea made me promise I'd give her Christopher Lombard's address if I found it. I had my receptionist contact Dorothea with it yesterday.' He shook his head. 'That's why she came down here, Jeff. She wanted to confront Lombard. If I hadn't . . .'

Mallory looked at him. 'If you hadn't forwarded the address, Don, she might have found some other way of locating him . . .'

'It points to Christopher Lombard, doesn't it?'

'Forensics have examined the finger marks on the neck. They were made by strong, male hands, which ties in with the suspect's profile drawn from the footprints.'

The surgeon, kneeling beside the body, gestured Mallory over.

Langham kept his eyes averted.

Mallory returned. 'She put up a fight, but unfortunately there's no evidence of the attacker's skin or blood under her nails.'

Langham looked around the waste ground, taking in the warehouses on the far side of the street. 'Lombard would have waited until darkness, presumably, before dumping the body. No one would have seen him do it in a place like this, after dark.'

'But did he have a vehicle?' Mallory asked.

'The people up at the farm said he had a van.'

'I'll get someone up there pronto to interview the artists,' Mallory said. 'And I'll have a team ask door to door along Cardigan Street.' He called to Detective Sergeant Venables and issued a series of orders.

'How about we take a shufti at his place on Cardigan Street?' Mallory suggested to Langham.

On the way back to their cars, the South African said, 'If Lombard did do it – the question is why?'

Langham shrugged. 'According to Penny Archer, when Dorothea left yesterday, she was "on the warpath". She resented Lombard walking out as he did, and also was pretty upset about a painting he'd done of her.' He told Mallory about the portrait that Dorothea had destroyed. 'She came down to confront him, and it turned nasty.'

'I'll say.' Mallory sighed.

Langham returned to his car and followed the detective's Humber along the road and around the railway station. They turned down Cardigan Street and pulled up outside number fifty.

Mallory thumped on the front door. 'Even money we find no one at home,' he said. 'Or maybe we'll strike lucky and Lombard invites us in, all innocence, for a cuppa?'

'In your dreams, Jeff.'

They waited a minute, then Mallory called Venables over and told him to fetch a sledgehammer. Venables returned to his car and came back wielding a long-handled hammer. Mallory and Langham stood back while the officer made short work of demolishing the lock. The door racketed open on a shadowy, silent hallway.

'Get the fingerprint boys in here, Venables,' Mallory said as he led Langham into the house.

Mallory peered into the living room off the hall and sniffed. 'Empty. Looks as if no one's lived here for ages.'

Langham peered over his shoulder. 'The room was chock-full of canvases the other day when Ralph and I dropped by.'

'So Lombard's skedaddled and taken his paintings with him,' Mallory said.

Langham thought about it. 'There are two possibilities, as I see it,' he said. 'Either he'd arranged with his gallery to have his paintings collected at some point yesterday, or he intended to store them here for an indefinite period, but what happened when Dorothea turned up altered all that and he loaded up his van and did a runner. I'll pop round to the gallery and see what they know about the paintings,' Langham said. 'Will you be here long?'

'I'm heading back to the Yard,' Mallory said. 'I'll leave Venables and the forensics boys to go over the place.'

The detective made for the front door, then turned and said, 'Talking about Venables – he dug up a bit more about this Cedric Evans character.'

'Ah, Nigel's acquaintance.'

'Venables was asking around a few pubs down Limehouse way the other day, and he ran into a cove who knew Cedric Evans and didn't like him. To cut a long story short, Evans was in his cups a few weeks ago and started bragging about this haul he'd made. Apparently, he'd stolen a lot of dosh from a solicitor's office where he worked a couple of years back and stashed it under his bedroom floorboards. Venables got a warrant and searched the gaff, and hey presto.'

'I hope you bought him a pint or two?'

'I'll say. And another thing Venables discovered. Despite Evans swearing blind that he hadn't seen Nigel Lombard for a couple of years, witnesses saw them in the Crown and Anchor in Limehouse six months back, as thick as thieves.'

Langham stared at the South African. 'You don't think Evans could have anything to do with Nigel Lombard's murder, do you?'

Mallory laughed. 'No such luck, Don. Beggar has a cast-iron alibi. Evans was in Bognor Regis all weekend!'

Langham followed Mallory from the house and returned to his car.

SEVENTEEN

Ryland took the precaution of parking half a mile away from Manville Carrington's pile in Belgravia and continuing on foot, taking a circuitous route to the square. He paused from time to time to take surreptitious glances back the way he'd come, but made out no suspicious characters in his wake. After the warning from Mr Jones, he couldn't be too careful.

He came to Belgravia Square and gazed across the road at Everett House. How the other half lived, eh? And Manville

Carrington called himself a socialist. That's what he couldn't stomach about many of these well-born lefties: the discrepancy between the ideals they spouted and the lives they led left a lot to be desired.

He crossed the road, climbed the steps and rapped on the door.

His summons was answered by a fish-faced butler, whose 'Yes?' sounded more like 'Years?' Here was another species he didn't much like: in his experience, butlers tended to take on the snobbery of their employers and look down on the common man.

He flashed his accreditation and said, 'Inspector Ryland. I'm investigating the recent murder of Nigel Lombard.' He was in no mood to pussyfoot around with jumped-up gatekeepers. 'I'd like a word with Mr Carrington, if he's around.'

To his surprise, the butler stepped back and held open the door. 'If you'd care to accompany me, sir.'

Well, perhaps this one wasn't as bad as some he'd met.

He followed the chap along a plush hallway to the back of the house and into a sweltering conservatory.

'Inspector Ryland,' the butler announced, and it was a few seconds before Ryland made out Manville Carrington sitting in a wicker chair amid the tangle of tropical shrubbery. He wore a padded smoking jacket and had a thick rug spread over his lap, despite the equatorial temperature. He looked like a shrivelled, balding garden gnome who had ceased his horticultural duties to take afternoon tea.

'Inspector, capital! How pleasant! You will join me? Tea?'

Ryland ran a finger around his collar and loosened his tie. 'Not for me, all the same. But those muffins look good.'

'Then draw up a seat and help yourself, Inspector.'

Ryland positioned a wicker chair before the small glass-topped table and picked up a muffin. He bit into it and wiped a dribble of butter from his chin.

'Delicious, aren't they? Fortnum and Mason's best,' Carrington said. 'A colleague of yours paid a call yesterday, Inspector. Not that I am for one minute complaining – I do enjoy the company. And I know how you work, Inspector.'

Ryland squinted at the man. 'You do?'

'Oh, quite. I have watched *Fabian of the Yard*, you see.'

Ryland smiled. He had come quite prepared to despise the old commie, only to find the man charming.

'You've come to interview me,' Carrington went on, 'and then you'll compare notes with the chap who was here yesterday – to see if I've contradicted myself.'

'I'm sure you won't do that, sir. This is merely a routine call to dot the i's and cross the t's.'

'Well, fire away, Inspector, and please do help yourself.'

'Thank you kindly,' Ryland said, chomping into a second muffin. He wiped his fingers on his handkerchief and consulted his notebook.

'Now, Sunday last. I understand that Christopher Lombard was here from late afternoon to after midnight?'

'You are not mistaken, Inspector.'

'He's a good friend of yours, is he?'

'I would classify him more as an acquaintance.'

'Ah, him being from the other side of the fence, like?'

The old man looked quizzical. 'Fence, Inspector?'

'The political fence, that is.'

'Oh, quite. I get your meaning. Well, yes, Mr Lombard and I do hold somewhat diametrical views on a variety of subjects.'

'How would you describe Mr Lombard's politics, sir?'

Carrington smiled benignly. 'Reactionary, bourgeois, ill-informed . . . I could go on.'

'No need. I get the picture,' Ryland said. 'Can you recall what you talked about?'

'The world, current affairs – the debacle of the Suez affair – Lombard was pro-intervention, you will not be surprised to learn. Oh, and cricket.'

'Cricket?'

'The chances of Surrey winning the championship this season. We both adore the game, despite our many other differences.'

Ryland nodded. 'It's these differences that perplex me,' he said.

'Perplex, in what way?'

Ryland scratched his head. 'Call me naive, but what puzzles me is why a man of your political leanings should hobnob with the likes of Christopher Lombard – or do you like his paintings?'

Carrington laughed. 'As a matter of fact, Inspector, I can't abide his artwork. Most vulgar, in my opinion. Our views on art clash as much as our politics.'

'Then – forgive the question, sir – why did you invite him here if you have so little in common?'

The old man peered at Ryland like an inquisitive tortoise. 'You doubt that I did? Is that it, Inspector? Do you think I am lying?'

'Perish the thought!' Ryland exclaimed. 'Not at all. I've no doubt Lombard was here on Sunday. It's just that I can't see why you'd go to the bother of entertaining him, that's all.'

Carrington leaned forward and tapped Ryland's knee with an arthritic forefinger. 'Ah, but you see, Inspector, it is through associating with those with differing views to one's own that one learns what the opposition is thinking – and, at the same time, one hones one's own ideas and opinions.'

'Ah, I see.'

'Christopher Lombard put forward some views I found offensive, and I countered with my own long-held beliefs and arguments. Alas, I did not manage to change his views on a single subject. Not that I thought for a second that I might – once a fascist, I have found, always a—'

Ryland interrupted. 'Don't know about that, sir,' he said quickly. 'I knew a few, back in the thirties.'

Carrington smiled. 'Is that so?'

Ryland nodded, reddening. 'I mean to say, you're right enough about most of 'em, sir. Leopards don't often change their spots. In the course of my investigations lately, I've met a few of 'em, and they're nasty thugs, no mistake. But,' he went on, smiling at the old man, 'believe me that now and again they do look back and regret what they did.'

Carrington smiled. 'I'll take your word for it, Inspector.'

'Now other than Suez and cricket,' Ryland went on, 'can you recall what else you discussed?'

Carrington smiled. 'I answered the very same question posed by your colleague yesterday, Inspector – you won't catch me like that! We spoke of the merry hash Thorneycroft is making of the economy; we discussed the Cold War, and American propaganda in Asia, among other topics which, I must admit, have slipped my mind.'

Ryland scribbled in his notebook. 'I take it you're all for banning the bomb, sir?'

'Indubitably. Great Britain does not need the atomic bomb. Our arming ourselves with nuclear weapons is an open act of hostility towards the Russians.'

'But some would say,' Ryland said, 'that if we didn't have it, then the Russians would take that as a sign of weakness and walk all over us.'

'Poppycock, if you don't mind my saying. All this talk of Soviet world domination is propaganda of the basest sort.'

'I take it that Mr Lombard disagreed with you on this matter?'

'He was rather of the opinion that America should bomb Moscow and wipe the scourge of communism from the face of the earth.'

'I see. It's a wonder you didn't throw him out on his ear.'

'Oh, the debate was heated, Inspector, but civil.'

'And you say he left around midnight?'

'Just after, yes, as I recall.'

'Was your butler working that evening?'

'He was, and he will confirm the fact of Mr Lombard's presence.'

Ryland swallowed a mouthful of muffin, then said, 'Now, turning to Lombard's brother, Nigel—'

'Such a tragedy!' Carrington declared.

'I take it you were acquainted with Nigel Lombard?'

'I had met him on one or two occasions, Inspector, but I didn't know him as well as I knew Christopher.'

'That is interesting, given Nigel Lombard's politics.'

'His politics?'

'I understand the young man was a . . . what's the word? . . . a "fellow traveller", I believe they're called.'

'I really have no idea, though I find the notion that a son of Vernon Lombard's might have leftist sympathies somewhat far-fetched, to say the least.'

'Do you know if Christopher and Nigel had friends and

acquaintances in common? You see, we're trying to trace Nigel's contacts, and it's proving more than a little tricky.'

Carrington caressed his wattled neck. 'I'm afraid I can't help you there, Inspector. As I said, I met him only once or twice.'

'Did Christopher mention his brother on Sunday?'

'Nigel Lombard did not enter our conversation,' the old man said.

Ryland closed his notebook. 'Well, I think that's quite enough to be going on with, sir. Thank you.'

'It has been my pleasure entirely, Inspector. Do call again.'

'Do you know,' Ryland laughed, getting to his feet, 'those muffins were so good that I might just do that.'

'Fortnum and Mason's!' Carrington called out as Ryland moved towards the conservatory door.

The butler showed him along the hallway. At the door, Ryland paused. 'I understand you were working on Sunday night, when Mr Carrington entertained a Mr Lombard?'

'That is correct, sir.'

'And you can confirm what time Lombard came and went?'

'He arrived a little after four, sir, and left at ten minutes past midnight. I recall because I rang for his taxi at the stroke of midnight.'

Ryland thanked him and stepped from the house.

He paused on the bottom step and looked out across the sunlit square. He glanced at his watch. It was just after eleven o'clock. He could nip round the corner to the Star for a quick pint and a sandwich and then make his way back to Earl's Court.

He moved to the edge of the pavement and was about to cross the road when someone came up beside him. A second figure approached him at speed from the other side. One man grabbed his arm while the other pressed something over his mouth and nose, the reek of chloroform overpowering.

Ryland struggled, attempting to elbow the first bastard in the ribs and pull his revolver. He felt his senses swim. He managed to free his right hand and reach for the gun. 'No you don't, matey!' the big, bald geezer to his right said, and knocked the gun from his grip. It clattered to the ground just as a van pulled up in the street before them.

Already he was feeling weak and nauseous. He tried to fight, but his limbs had the sudden consistency of rubber and failed to obey his commands. A door in the side of the van rattled open and he was bundled inside. As if from miles away, he heard one man say something about the revolver, and the other snap, 'Leave the bleedin' thing! C'mon!' Then the door slammed shut and he was plunged into darkness as the van accelerated.

One of the thugs was holding him face down, his right arm forced painfully halfway up his back. Someone sat on his legs, crushing his left knee. He was aware of the van turning, the sound of its engine loud, his face pressed painfully against the vehicle's gritty floorboards. Aside from the sharp chemical reek of the chloroform, he detected something else, and it was a minute before he could place it: the heady aroma of hops.

He was in the back of one of Grayson's brewery vans.

So the bastard had taken his advice and, this time, sent men to do the job.

After a while the van slowed, turned and crunched over gravel.

Someone forced a coarse sack over his head, and the smell of brewers' hops intensified.

The van stopped and the side door opened. Hands gripped his arms and legs and pulled him from the vehicle, face down. He was past struggling now: he felt immensely tired, and the chloroform had even had the effect of dulling his fear about what might happen next.

He was carried down a flight of steps, his abductors grunting as they forced him around tight corners.

He heard a lock click, and something grate open – a gate or a door? Then he was dropped unceremoniously on to a hard floor and the breath rushed from his chest in a painful, involuntary exhalation.

'Well, well, Mr Ryland,' said a familiar voice. 'Welcome to my little dungeon.'

He rolled over, grunting, and forced himself on to all fours. He reached up and pulled the sack from his head. He blinked, staring around him. He was in what looked like a cellar, with a stone floor and whitewashed brick walls.

He crawled forward, panting, then turned and sat back against the wall.

The cell was small, perhaps six feet square, with a barred door just like the kind he'd seen in cowboy films. On the other side of the bars stood the rotund, silver-haired, grey-suited figure of Arnold Grayson, smiling down at him.

On this side of the bars, standing over him, was the bald-headed thug he'd seen in the Lion and Unicorn the previous week . . . He recalled that Len had called him Horace.

It seemed a strange name for such a barbarian.

'Very well,' Grayson said. 'He's all yours.'

Horace reached out, grabbed a swatch of Ryland's jacket and hauled him to his feet.

The first blow of his meaty fist hit Ryland in the stomach, winding him. The second punch broke his nose. He cried out, the pain unbearable.

In the corridor, Grayson chuckled.

Horace lashed out again, and Ryland slammed against the wall, the back of his head making painful contact with the brickwork.

By the time he slid to the floor, he was unconscious.

EIGHTEEN

Langham stepped into the Weatherby & Lascelles show-room and examined the contemporary paintings hanging on the walls. None of them were by Christopher Lombard.

A middle-aged woman, with an unerring eye for moneyed customers, examined Langham through a pair of lorgnettes and evidently found him lacking. 'And how might we assist?' she enquired with the air of a schoolmistress addressing a delinquent schoolboy.

Langham affected an air of casual indifference as he peered at a landscape, then turned and proffered his accreditation. He moved on to the next canvas, ignoring the woman, and only when she cleared her throat for the third time, ever so genteelly, did he say, 'I understand you handle the work of Christopher Lombard.'

'Might you be interested in purchasing, sir?'

'My word, no. Of course not.' He turned and stared at the woman. 'I'd like to know if Weatherby and Lascelles collected a consignment of Lombard's paintings yesterday?'

'That would be the domain of Mr Timothy,' she said.

'Then if you'd be good enough to lead me to Mr Timothy, or Mr Timothy to me, I'd be grateful.'

'I will endeavour to ascertain if Mr Timothy is available,' she said, and moved off.

In due course, a young man with a green-and-white polka-dotted bowtie, whose round face resembled that of a choirboy, despite a receding hairline, approached Langham with a diffident smile.

'I understand you were enquiring after the Lombards?'

Langham flashed his accreditation, and Mr Timothy blinked at it and said, 'The police?' in a surprised tone.

Langham said nothing to disabuse him of the notion. 'Did Lombard arrange for the gallery to collect some of his paintings yesterday?'

'I don't specifically deal with that side of transactions, sir, but if you would care to come this way . . .'

He led Langham down the long room, through a door and along a narrow corridor to a capacious warehouse area with a high glass ceiling. The chamber was full of paintings in various stages of packaging, and a dozen men in overalls moved back and forth with canvases loaded on trolleys.

The young man crossed to a desk behind which a harried-looking clerk with a green visor at his brow, and a Biro pen lodged behind his right ear, bent over piles of paperwork. They conferred, and the clerk gestured vaguely towards the rear of the warehouse.

'This way, please,' Mr Timothy said, and led Langham down an aisle between paintings wrapped in brown paper.

They came to another door and passed into a courtyard. Half a dozen royal-blue vans, emblazoned with the gold livery of Weatherby & Lascelles Fine Arts, were parked on the cobbles.

The young man hurried across the courtyard to a long

outbuilding which proved to be yet another warehouse, this one stacked with mostly unpackaged paintings. Langham made out a few Christopher Lombards leaning against the wall.

Mr Timothy spoke to another clerk behind a desk, who pushed a fat ledger towards him. Langham watched as he opened the book and ran an impeccably manicured little finger down a long list.

'Ah, here we are. Consignment thirty-two.' He read out the previous day's date and smiled at Langham.

'Do you know what time it was collected?'

The young man peered at the list. 'At five minutes past eleven, sir.'

'Do you know when the collection was arranged?'

The man smiled. 'That would be a little over three weeks ago,' he said. 'I handled the transaction myself.'

'With the artist personally?'

'Over the phone, sir.'

'Is that usual – for the gallery to take so many paintings in one go?'

'Highly unusual, but then we were dealing with Christopher Lombard, sir.'

Langham smiled. 'I take it his work sells for huge sums?'

'I am not in a position to discuss private financial details, you understand, but between you and me, sir, I can say that Mr Lombard is one of our most popular artists.'

Langham strolled across to the stacked Lombards and regarded the outermost painting. The young man joined him and they stared down at the blotchy, jaundiced body of a naked young woman.

'Tell me,' Langham said, 'what do you make of this one?'

Mr Timothy cleared his throat. 'Well, sir, I must say that it isn't to my liking.'

I bet it isn't, Langham thought, smiling to himself. 'I meant as a work of art,' he said. 'The technique . . .?'

'Personally, I find Lombard's technique somewhat primitivist, shall we say?'

'Crude?'

'In a manner of speaking, yes. Both from an aesthetic and a technical point of view.'

'And yet,' Langham went on, 'they sell for more money than your average working punter would make in months – am I right?'

'You are certainly not wrong, sir.'

Langham glanced at the neighbouring canvas and found it singularly unpleasant. The subject looked as if she'd been strangled.

'Do you know who buys them?' Langham asked. 'Now, let me hazard a guess – a single purchaser, by any chance?'

'A collector began buying our Lombards a number of years ago,' the young man said, 'and, as is the way of things, his interest generated increased sales.'

Not for the first time, Langham wondered if Christopher Lombard had discovered his father's singular patronage, which might account for their rift.

'Have you ever met the artist?' Langham asked. 'Do you know what kind of person—'

'I have never had the pleasure of meeting him, sir, though I have often spoken with him over the phone. I am given to understand that he is pleasant and personable.'

'One more thing. Do you know if Lombard was present when the paintings were collected?'

'I'm not at all sure, but I can check.'

They returned to the desk, and the young man enquired about the collection of consignment number thirty-two.

The clerk referred to the ledger. 'Wilf and Benjamin made the pick-up, Mr T.'

Langham asked, 'I wonder if I might have a word with one or the other?'

'Wilf's taking a tea break out back,' the clerk said, indicating a door.

Langham thanked him and moved to the door, the young man by his side. They returned to the courtyard and approached a lean-to where a balding man in his sixties was reading the *Daily Mail*.

'Mr Langham is from the police,' Mr Timothy said with a rather proprietorial air. 'If you would be so good as to answer a few questions, Wilfred.'

Wilf jumped to his feet and smoothed down the front of his overalls in a reflex gesture.

'It's about consignment thirty-two,' Langham said. 'I understand you collected it from a King's Cross address around eleven yesterday morning?'

'That's right,' Wilf said, grinning. 'Lombard's naked women.'

'Did the artist meet you at the premises?'

'No, he didn't. We were met at the gate by a woman who had a key and let us in.'

'A woman?' Langham was unable to disguise his surprise. 'Could you describe her?'

Wilf frowned. 'Small, blonde, in her thirties. She hardly said a word, just let us in, watched us while we carted the pictures out to the van, and collected the receipt when we'd done.'

'Blonde?' Langham said. 'Natural, or—?'

'Peroxide, I think they call it.'

The peroxide blonde, again. But surely, he thought, not Penny Archer?

'Do you recall if she was driving a car?'

Wilf scratched his head. 'Now that's a poser, sir. No, I'm sorry. I never noticed.'

Langham thanked him and joined Mr Timothy, making their way back through the gallery.

At the front door, he turned to the young man. 'You've been more than helpful, thank you.'

'Any time, sir.'

Langham returned to the street and found a phone box. He fished out his notebook and dialled Victoria Lombard's Highgate number.

She answered almost immediately.

'Victoria? Donald Langham here. I wonder if I could drop by for a quick word?'

'Ah.' She sounded more than a little irked. 'It's rather inconvenient. I was about to pop out.'

'It is rather important,' he said, not at all relishing the prospect of informing her that her brother was the prime suspect in a murder investigation.

'Very well. Look, I'm due to visit a friend in Hampstead; I'll be crossing the heath. We could meet by the model boating pond. Do you know it?'

'When will you be there?'

'In fifteen minutes,' she said.

He made a rapid calculation. 'I'll see you then,' he said, and replaced the receiver.

Langham came to the crest of the rise and stared down the hillside. A little boy and his father were sailing a model boat on the water, causing a commotion amid the resident mallard and teal. The sun was warm, and men and women strolled along the curving pathway, enjoying the clement spring weather.

Victoria Lombard sat on a park bench at the far side of the pond, peering into the small mirror of her compact as she attended to her make-up. She wore a scarlet dress and a big yellow sun hat, the splash of colour startling against the green of the background vegetation.

He walked down the hill and around the pond. She looked up as he approached, smiling at him.

'Donald,' she said as he sat down beside her. 'I think I owe you an apology.'

'Don't mention it.'

'Yesterday I was . . . I think the medication adversely affected me. And what with the gin . . .'

He smiled. 'I hope you didn't find it.'

'I must say the hiding place you chose was not very original,' she said. 'Under the sink was the first place I looked yesterday afternoon. Although by then, I hasten to add, I'd stopped taking the pills.'

'I trust you're feeling better now.'

'A little, yes. I think the initial shock has worn off. I . . . I feel a little dazed, numbed. I still can't believe that Nigel . . .' She hesitated. 'I don't suppose you're any closer to working out who might have . . .'

'These things take time,' he said. 'We always seem to be getting nowhere, and then the details and facts start to come together to provide links.' He smiled at her. 'We'll get there, in time.'

'I hope so.' She looked at him steadily. 'You said you wanted to see me about something.'

'I was wondering if Christopher has contacted your father yet.'

She shook her head. 'I saw my father this morning and told him you'd succeeded in locating Christopher. Quite naturally, he was upset that Christopher hadn't had the decency to call on him.' She gestured. 'I said that he was very busy with his painting at the moment, and that I was sure he'd drop by soon. It seemed to mollify him somewhat.'

'Has Christopher been in contact with you?'

'No,' she said. 'I've heard nothing from him.'

He stared at the miniature boat on the pond. The woman sensed something in his manner. 'What is it?' she demanded.

'Dorothea Marston was found dead near King's Cross station earlier today.'

Victoria stared at him. 'Dorothea? Found dead?'

'She was strangled. She travelled down to London yesterday with the express intention of seeing Christopher. She had his address—'

'Are you implying that Christopher . . .?' She looked aghast.

'The police would like to question him in relation to the killing.'

'But Christopher wouldn't . . .'

'I recall you saying that your brother was a thug,' he said.

Anger flared in her eyes. 'There is a world of difference between being a thug, Donald, and a murderer.'

He allowed a few seconds to elapse. 'It is a rather glaring coincidence, however, that Dorothea came to London to meet your brother, and then was found dead less than a mile from where he was staying.'

'But why would Christopher . . .?'

'If Dorothea did succeed in meeting him . . .' He hesitated. 'She was angry about the way he walked out on her, and about a painting he did of her.' He described the painting and Dorothea's reaction to discovering it at Henderson's Farm. 'If they argued, and the confrontation escalated . . .' He looked at her. 'Would you say that Christopher is the type of person to lose his temper, fly into a rage and . . .?'

She was slowly shaking her head. 'He had a short fuse, yes, but he would never attack a defenceless woman. I could see him hitting out in anger, striking someone in the heat of the moment. But to . . . to strangle someone . . . it takes *intent*. No,' she finished, 'Christopher would never do a thing like that to someone he'd once loved. It's a horrible idea.'

Langham recalled Lombard's painting of Dorothea, and thought, *Professed to love* . . .

He said, 'Isn't it strange that he seems to have vacated the premises he was renting so abruptly?'

She leaned forward suddenly, her shoulders shaking as she wept.

Hesitantly, Langham reached out and touched her arm. 'I'm sorry.'

She found a small lace handkerchief in her bag and wiped her eyes. 'It's all a little too much, Donald. First Nigel, and now this business with Christopher. Yesterday I had the doctor in to see my father.'

'He's taken a turn for the worse?'

'Wilkins came rushing upstairs to say my father had had a fall and he'd called an ambulance. I was afraid my father had suffered another heart attack. As it happened, it was just a chest infection. The doctor got him to bed and prescribed some pills. So, you see, what with one thing and another . . .'

'I'm sorry to be the harbinger of more bad news,' he said inadequately.

She sniffed, then ventured a hesitant smile. 'Don't worry, Donald. I won't shoot the messenger.'

'I won't keep you any longer,' he said. 'Needless to say, if Christopher does contact either you or your father, please give me a ring. You never know,' he finished lamely, 'there might be some innocent explanation for his non-appearance.'

She regarded him evenly. 'But you think not?'

Langham shrugged. 'I honestly don't know,' he said.

Victoria replaced the handkerchief in her bag and climbed to her feet. 'I suddenly no longer feel like meeting my friend for afternoon tea,' she said, 'but I suppose one must keep up appearances. Goodbye, Donald.'

She walked around the pond and passed from sight behind

a stand of rhododendron, and Langham sat watching a toy boat bob across the water. He consulted his watch. It was almost three o'clock. He'd call in at the office, then head for home.

A quiet glass of wine with Maria this evening would be just the ticket.

He parked outside the Lyon's tea room and took the steps up to the agency two at a time.

Pamela was on the phone, nodding as she took something down in her notebook.

She thanked the caller and replaced the receiver. 'That was Inspector Mallory,' she said, and read from her notes. 'A witness saw a green Ford van turn from Cardigan Street at eleven last night, Donald, and this morning the same van was discovered burned out on waste ground in Hackney. The van belonged to Christopher Lombard.'

So much for Victoria's protestations that her brother would never do a thing like *that*.

Pamela pulled a face. 'It looks as if Lombard strangled the woman, doesn't it?'

'Everything certainly points that way,' he said. 'Has Ralph been in, or called?'

'I haven't seen him since this morning, and he hasn't phoned.'

'I'll be pushing off. If he does call in, tell him to ring me at home. I want to know how he got on with the chap he was seeing today.'

'I'll do that.'

'And could you get through to Henderson's Farm in Swavesy? Ask to speak to Penny Archer or Simon Lipscombe and tell them that I'll be calling in to talk to them tomorrow morning, around eleven.'

He made for the door. 'Oh – have you accepted Dennis's marriage proposal yet?'

Pamela pressed a pondering finger to her lips. 'I am still giving the matter my most serious consideration,' she said loftily.

Langham laughed and hurried down to the street.

Maria was still out when he arrived back at the Kensington flat. He found a joint of beef in the Frigidaire and decided to surprise her by making dinner that evening. He peeled a few potatoes and diced a couple of carrots, then slipped the beef into the oven and poured himself a beer.

He lay on the sofa with a copy of *Encounter*, read the book reviews and sipped his beer. Presently, lulled by the warmth of the day, he slept.

When he came to his senses, Maria was sitting on the floor beside the sofa, stroking his cheek. He struggled upright, befuddled, and sniffed. 'What time is it, and what's that *awful* smell?'

'It's six o'clock, my sweet, and you've cremated the joint.'

'Blast! I'm sorry. I was going to surprise you.'

She laughed. 'You have, Donald. But I appreciate the gesture. Hard day?'

'Where to begin? You?'

'I had a rather bad lunch with a dull author,' she said.

'About dinner . . .' he said.

'Yes?'

'Buono Napoli?'

She laughed. 'Ah, *oui*, Donald. Buono Napoli.'

NINETEEN

On Friday morning, Langham rolled the car down the hill and turned right along the track to Henderson's Farm.

It was not yet eleven and the sky was cloudless and blue. He'd driven all the way from London with the side window wound down, admitting a cooling breeze, and it was only when he pulled up outside the farm that he felt the warmth of the sun. He climbed out and stretched.

He suspected that the police had been in touch with Penny and Simon the previous day about Dorothea's death: if so, they would be grief-stricken. If they hadn't had the news yet, then he would have to break it to them. Either way, he was not exactly looking forward to the imminent meeting.

Then there was the business of the peroxide blonde who was seen near the warehouse on Sunday, and again in Cardigan Street on Wednesday.

Penny Archer emerged from a studio, wiping her hands on the front of her dungarees. Langham found himself wondering if some subconscious desire to identify with Dorothea had driven her to wear the dungarees and headscarf, or if it was simply a utilitarian form of dress that both women had adopted for work.

'Oh, hello there, Mr Langham.'

He waved. 'The invalid still abed?'

'He did get up this morning, but the news about Dorothea knocked him for six. Well, it did us both. So he's gone back to bed.'

'When did the police—?'

'Yesterday, late afternoon. First the local chaps, then someone from London.'

She appeared blank-faced, as if grief had sapped her facial features of the ability to exhibit any emotion.

He followed her into the big farmhouse kitchen. 'Would you like tea, or maybe something cooler? We have some homemade lemonade that—'

She stopped suddenly and slumped on to a kitchen chair. She looked up at him, her pretty face distorted. 'Dorothea made it a few days ago. Her own special recipe. It was the best. She said she'd show me how to make it.'

'Then I'll have some lemonade,' he said.

She stared across at the larder. 'I wonder . . . could you pour it, Mr Langham? It's in there.'

He crossed the kitchen, found a big earthenware jug on a stone shelf and carried it to the table. Penny found two tall glasses and he poured.

He sat down, lifted his glass and clinked it with hers. 'To Dorothea,' he murmured.

'Yes, to Dorothea.' She raised the glass to her mouth in both hands and drank like a child.

'I don't know how we're going to manage without her,' she

said. 'She held everything together. If we ever had a problem, of *any* kind, Dorothea could sort it out. And her vision, her artistic vision . . . Oh, the hours we spent chatting about our work, about other artists. She knew so much! And now she's gone. I just can't believe it . . .'

She hung her head and wept, and for the second time in as many days Langham found himself consoling a grieving woman with ineffectual words and gestures.

She sniffed and tried to pull herself together. 'I suppose she was like a mother to me, Mr Langham. She wasn't just a talented artist, she was a wonderful person. How could . . . how could someone *do* that to her?'

Langham shook his head.

Staring straight at him, she said, 'It was Christopher Lombard, wasn't it?'

He hesitated. 'We can't be certain, but it's a possibility.'

'That afternoon, when she left for London . . . You should have seen her. She was so angry.'

If it had indeed been Penny Archer who had let the gallery men into the Cardigan Street house on Wednesday morning, he wondered, would she have had time to get back to the farm and take the call from Pamela?

He asked, 'What time did you receive the message from my secretary that afternoon?'

She thought about it. 'Around four,' she said. 'And Dorothea got in about ten minutes later.' She shook her head. 'I'd been painting in my studio all day but came in here to make a cup of tea. If only . . . if only I'd kept on painting and not answered the phone, then Dorothea . . .'

Penny smiled through her tears and went on, 'When I gave her the address . . . she said she was more upset about that awful painting he did of her than about him leaving her. You see, he did that painting years ago, so it showed what he really thought of her, even then. She told me that it made all the time she spent with him somehow . . . somehow invalid. Can you understand that?'

'Yes,' he murmured. 'Yes, of course I can.'

'Dorothea said she was going to have it out with him. Ask him why he'd painted her like that, what he meant by all that awful symbolism, and if he'd ever really felt anything for her. Do you want to know what I think happened?'

'Go on.'

'I think she confronted him about the painting, about his *supposed* feelings for her . . . I think she said something like he'd never felt anything for her because he was a shallow, egotistical *user.* And I think that's what made him . . . made him do what he did. He couldn't face the truth coming from a woman who was better than him, and the only thing he could do to deny it was to . . . to *destroy* her.'

She fell silent, staring down at the glass with an odd look of defiance on her face, then suddenly raised the lemonade to her mouth and drank.

He matched her and took a mouthful.

She was silent for a while, then said, 'I couldn't sleep last night, Mr Langham. I was lying awake for hours, just thinking. And it came to me – the two deaths. It can't have been a coincidence, can it? Dorothea's death and Nigel Lombard's? Do you think Christopher Lombard killed them both?'

'It's a possibility that the police are looking into,' he said.

She looked at him, suddenly red-faced as if unaccountably embarrassed.

'What is it?' he asked.

She swallowed and looked down at her fingers. 'I didn't tell Sergeant Venables this yesterday,' she murmured.

Langham leaned forward. 'You didn't tell him what?'

She rotated her glass in its circle of condensation and watched the operation in silence. At last, she said, 'The other day. Sunday. When Simon went down to London . . .'

'Go on,' he said, wondering if she was about to admit that she too had travelled to London that day. 'What about it?'

Avoiding his gaze, and in a voice so quiet he could hardly make out the words, she said, 'I followed him.'

'Right. Do you mind telling me why, Penny?'

'Because I was jealous,' she said. She looked up at him. 'Jealous of a woman.'

'Would you care to explain?'

'Last year, last summer . . . An artist came to stay here for a month or so. A young woman called Samantha. She was

. . . well, she was beautiful and she knew it. One of those women who have everything. Talent, looks, money. And because she had everything, she thought she could take *anything* she wanted. Even men.'

'I see.'

'She was all over Simon. I couldn't believe it – she was so open about it. I think that was part of the thrill for her – not only the thrill of chasing Simon, but of showing me that she could do it so flagrantly and knowing that she could succeed.'

'And?'

'I . . . I don't think she did – succeed, that is. I had it out with Simon, and he swore that there was nothing between them, that nothing had happened. And soon after that, Samantha just upped and left. Gone, just like that! Imagine my relief.'

'But that wasn't the end of it?'

'I thought it was at the time. Then a few weeks later a letter came for Simon, and the name and address on the back was Samantha's, and a few days later Simon said he had to see someone in London. And, well, how do you think that made me feel – even though when I asked him if he was going to see her, he denied it? He said he was seeing someone on business, but I didn't believe him. I . . . I was distraught. I really thought it was over between us.'

She fell silent, smiling to herself. 'Then he came back from London and showed me a contract he'd signed with a small gallery in Camden Town.'

'So why did you follow Simon this time?'

'A couple of weeks ago he received another letter. From her. He didn't know I'd seen the letter, and this time I didn't mention it to him. And then last week Simon told me he was going down to London on Sunday to visit friends.' She looked up at him. 'I felt sick, Mr Langham. Sick to my stomach. I said I'd come with him, but he fobbed me off.'

She took a long drink of lemonade, replaced her glass on the table without letting go of it, and slowly shook her head. 'On the Sunday morning, when he borrowed Dorothea's car and set off for the station, I called a taxi from the village and followed him. I was just in time to catch the London train. I boarded it after him, in a carriage further along from his. When we arrived in London, he took the train to Wapping and headed for the river. I followed him. I . . . I was beginning to feel a little silly by now, because . . .' She shrugged.

'Because? Let me guess. This Samantha lived in an entirely different part of London, right?'

She smiled. 'She lived in North Finchley – and Simon went to Madras Wharf in Wapping.'

'Madras Wharf,' he repeated. 'Where Nigel Lombard was murdered?'

The young man in the duffel coat that Ralph had mentioned yesterday . . .

Penny gave a quick, tense nod, not looking at him. 'I saw him turn into the alleyway and climb the stairs to the loft. At the top, Nigel came out and I saw them go inside together.'

'What time was this?'

'A little before one, I think.'

'And a few hours later,' Langham said, more to himself, 'Nigel Lombard was shot dead.'

Penny said, 'All I could feel at the time, though, was relief. You see, because I knew about Nigel Lombard's politics, I just assumed that Simon had found out, too, and decided to put aside his personal differences.' She smiled and shrugged. 'So I went back home, feeling three parts foolish to seven parts relieved. I heard about the fascist march on the radio news that evening, and when Simon came home on the Monday with a broken arm . . . well, I guessed what had happened, and Simon admitted he'd been on the counter demonstration.'

She was silent for a time and then looked up at him. 'Imagine my shock when you turned up the other day, Mr Langham, and with news of Nigel Lombard's murder.'

'Did you suspect Simon—?'

'No. I . . . I mean, I was shocked, of course – but no, I knew he'd never do a thing like that. But naturally I was worried. He was there, on the scene, just hours before Nigel was murdered. What if the police found out?'

'And that's why you didn't tell me the truth on my last visit?'

She looked down at her hands and murmured, 'Yes. I'm sorry . . .'

'Did you tell Simon you'd followed him, seen him at Madras Wharf? Did you ask what he'd been doing there?'

She nodded. 'After you left that day, I told him all about my jealousy of Samantha, and that I'd followed him, seen him meet Nigel.'

'What did he say?'

'He told me that he'd found out about Nigel's political leanings from a contact in the Socialist Action Front. This contact thought that Nigel might have some inside knowledge about the fascists, and Simon wanted to pick his brain.'

'I see,' Langham said.

'I begged Simon to tell the police that he'd been there on Sunday. I said they were bound to find out sooner or later, and if they did discover his lies, then it wouldn't look good for him.'

'What did he say?'

'He said he had no intention of coming clean. He claimed no one had seen him near Madras Wharf, so the police had no reason to suspect him.' She hesitated, looking fearful. 'You . . . you don't think Simon had anything to do with it, do you?'

For her sake, he said, 'No, I don't.'

He finished his lemonade, left her sitting at the kitchen table and made his way upstairs.

TWENTY

He knocked on the door and ducked into the bedroom. Lipscombe was sitting up in bed, drenched in the sunlight falling through the open window. A warm breeze stirred the lace curtains and birdsong sounded in the ivy outside.

Langham drew up a chair and sat down.

A pile of books was stacked on the bedside table: a few detective novels and Trotsky's autobiography.

'I see your shiner's on the mend.'

The young man absently fingered his eye. 'The swelling's gone down. I can hardly feel it.' He hesitated. 'Have you come about Dorothea?'

'Among other things.'

Lipscombe shook his head, a hank of dark hair falling over his black eye. He swept it back. 'They had an odd relationship, Dorothea and Lombard.' He stopped, then said, 'I take it that it was Lombard who . . .?'

'As I've just told Penny, the police suspect so. In what way was their relationship odd?'

'They were so different in attitude, for one thing. Dorothea was liberal, open-minded. She had true aesthetic vision, real talent and a tolerance of the views of others.'

'And Christopher Lombard was the very opposite?'

'He could only see the obvious; everything was funnelled through his own narrow, selfish perception of the world. He had no real talent and could never see the other man's point of view. I failed to see what Dorothea saw in him.'

'Well, you did say she was tolerant,' Langham said. 'And quite often love is blind. Though, no – in Dorothea's case, I think she was aware of Lombard's shortcomings and thought she might be able to change him, or at least influence him for the better.'

'Do you think Christopher killed both Dorothea and his brother?'

He looked at the young man. 'Do you?'

'It certainly seems that he murdered Dorothea. She went down there expressly to see him.'

'But what makes you think that Christopher might have killed his brother?'

The artist shrugged. 'Well, they didn't particularly like each other. They were forever arguing.'

'That's hardly enough to suspect someone of murder.' He hesitated, watching Lipscombe as he asked, 'Did you see anything, the day Nigel was shot?'

The young man looked up quickly. 'What?'

'When you were down there on Sunday, at Madras Wharf, did Nigel say anything to make you suspect that Christopher might have had a motive for killing him?'

The young man's expression froze. 'What makes you think . . .?'

'A witness saw you walking down the alleyway – a mechanic working nearby. You met Nigel at the top of the steps and entered the loft at around one o'clock on Sunday afternoon, just hours before Nigel died.'

Lipscombe looked down at the counterpane, then nodded. 'Yes,' he said. 'I was there.'

'Why? I thought you detested the man.'

'I did.'

'Then why did you meet him on Sunday afternoon?' Langham pressed.

'It was about what was happening later that day.'

'The counter demonstration?'

'That's right. I heard from a friend in the Socialist Action Front that the fascists were planning something – that the Stepney march was just a cover for something bigger. This friend said he knew someone who could tell me more – someone I'd had dealings with in the past.'

'Nigel Lombard?'

'That's right. Imagine my surprise when my contact told me that Nigel was on our side. I must admit, I was floored. I'd always had him down as someone of the Right, like his brother. But according to my friend, he was nothing of the kind. Word was that he knew what the fascists were planning that Sunday, and my friend wanted me to sound him out. A few days before the demonstration, he gave me Nigel's address at the wharf. On Sunday I took the train to London and met him.'

'Did you arrange this beforehand—?' Langham began.

Lipscombe shook his head. 'No. There was no way I could contact him. The loft didn't have a phone. I turned up cold.'

'He must have been surprised to see you.'

The young man smiled. 'Oh, he was. I think he thought I'd come to finish what I'd started, that time when I said I'd knock his block off if he ever went near Penny again. Anyway, I explained why I was there and asked him what the thugs were up to.'

'How did Nigel know what the fascists were planning on the Sunday?' Langham asked.

'He knew people on the Right, through his father and brother. He said he kept his eyes and ears open.'

'So, what were they planning?'

'The march was just a cover. While the Socialist Action Front were at the counter demonstration in Stepney, a gang of fascist thugs planned to wreck premises in Whitechapel owned by Jews and West Indians. They reckoned the police would have their hands full with the Stepney march and the counter demonstration, and would be thin on the ground in Whitechapel.'

'Useful bit of inside information,' Langham said.

'Very. I left the warehouse and made for a pub where friends in the SAF were gathering and gave them the gen.'

'What time was it when you left Nigel?'

Lipscombe shrugged. 'About one thirty.'

'So you and your friends changed your plans and made sure you were in Whitechapel when the trouble kicked off?'

He smiled ruefully and nodded to his broken arm. 'And that's where I got this.'

'To go back to your meeting with Nigel,' Langham said. 'How did he seem at the time?'

'Well, he was a bit surprised at my turning up out of the blue like that. And . . .' Lipscombe hesitated.

'Go on.'

'He seemed edgy, nervous. As if he didn't want me there.'

'As if he might have been due to meet someone and didn't want you around at the time?'

'Yes, that's exactly it. I recall, he kept glancing at his watch – a big, square, fancy-looking thing. He kept looking at it as if he had an appointment and wanted to get rid of me.'

'Did he mention that he was due to meet anyone later?'

'No, nothing like that.'

'Did you see anyone in the area, either when you arrived or when you left at one thirty?'

'No, not a soul – other than a mechanic, that is.'

'Is there anything you noticed, either about Nigel himself or the loft, anything that struck you as odd, not quite right?'

Lipscombe shrugged and gave a lopsided smile. 'Well, the whole set-up was a bit odd. There I was, meeting someone

who I'd had down as a fascist, but who was actually on our
side . . .'

Langham watched the artist as he said, 'You must have been
shocked when I told you that Nigel had been shot dead on
the very day you met him?'

The young man swallowed. 'Well, shocked doesn't quite
describe it.'

'Frightened? Terrified that the police might find out you
were there on Sunday?'

Lipscombe looked down at his hands. 'Yes, that's right.'

'Is that why you lied to me the other day when you claimed
you didn't know about Nigel's communist sympathies?'
Langham asked.

Silently, avoiding Langham's gaze, the young man nodded.

'Did you really think the police wouldn't find out that you'd
been in the area?'

'I suppose I wasn't thinking straight. Nigel and I hadn't
seen eye to eye in the past. I didn't want the police to think
that I'd gone there to renew hostilities. And anyway, as far as
I saw things, there was nothing I could tell them that might
help the investigation. It wasn't as if I saw anyone that afternoon, or he'd said anything out of the ordinary.'

Langham pursed his lips. 'Oh, I don't know. I think I've
learned something from speaking to you.'

'You have?'

'The fact that Nigel Lombard was expecting someone. He'd
arranged a meeting at the loft and he wanted you out of the
way.'

'You think he'd arranged to meet the person who killed
him?'

'That's the obvious inference.'

The young man looked nervous. 'Will you tell the police?
I mean, about my being there?'

Langham sighed. 'I'm afraid I'll have to,' he said. 'Detective
Inspector Mallory must know about this.'

Lipscombe laid his head back against the pillow. 'Oh, God!'
He stared at Langham. 'What will happen? Will they . . .?'

'A slap on the wrist and a reprimand,' Langham said. 'I'll
tell Jeff to go easy.'

'Do you think they'll . . . they'll suspect me?' A panicked note entered his voice. 'Will they suspect that I killed Nigel?'

Langham climbed to his feet and made for the door. 'Well, *I* don't think you killed him, for what that's worth.'

The young man let out a relieved breath. 'Thank you, Donald.'

Langham opened the door, then hesitated. 'Oh, there is one other thing. Has Penny been here for the past couple of days?'

'Yes, we both have – working.'

'She didn't take the train to London on Wednesday morning?'

Lipscombe shook his head. 'No. No, she was here, with me, all day.'

The artist opened his mouth to ask the obvious question, but Langham quickly thanked him and slipped from the room.

Penny Archer was still sitting at the table when he entered the kitchen. She looked up quickly, her eyes wide. 'What did he say?'

Langham gave her a precis of their conversation.

'And you believe him?' she asked. 'Simon didn't . . .?'

'He was telling the truth, or I'm not a private detective.'

'What now?'

'The police will be back to interview him. He'll receive a reprimand, as I told him.'

Penny nodded and pointed to the larder. 'Would you like another glass of lemonade?'

'I should be pushing off,' he said, moving to the door.

'Goodbye, Donald,' she murmured.

'Keep painting,' he said.

As he left the kitchen and crossed to his car, he realized that both Penny and Simon might be lying about her presence at the farm on Wednesday afternoon. However, intuition – or was it wishful thinking? – made him believe otherwise.

On the way back to London, it came to him that he wanted nothing more than to wash his hands of the case. He'd had enough of the Lombards, fascist thugs, communist fellow travellers and murder. He'd drop into the office when he reached London, phone Jeff with what he'd learned, then ask Ralph if he could take a week off. He needed a break with nothing more to occupy his mind than the rewrite of his novel and conversation in the evenings with Maria.

He parked outside the Lyon's tea room and was crossing the pavement when the window display of cakes and buns reminded him that he'd had nothing to eat since breakfast. He popped in and bought a ham sandwich and a vanilla slice, and was chewing on the sandwich as he hurried up the steps and pushed through the door to the agency.

Pamela looked up when he entered. 'Thank God you're here!' she cried.

His stomach turned. 'What?'

'It's Ralph.'

He dropped the half-eaten sandwich and the cake on the desk. 'What's happened?'

She made a feeble gesture. 'I had Annie on the phone first thing. She was in a right state. It was a while before I could get anything from her—'

'For Christ's sake, Pamela – is Ralph OK?' He pulled up a chair and slumped into it.

'Annie said Ralph didn't come home last night, and he didn't ring to say he'd be late. She thought he might have gone straight down the pub from work – but normally he'd phone to tell her. She said she'd rung your place last night, but there was no reply.'

'No,' he said, 'we went out for a meal and didn't get back till late.'

'Annie was beside herself. She asked if he'd rung in yesterday, but he hadn't. Last I saw of him, he was leaving the office just after ten.'

Langham nodded, trying to concentrate. He thought back a day, trying to recall where Ralph had said he was going.

Manville Carrington, he thought. Ralph had looked up Carrington's address in Debrett's, then said he was going to have a 'natter with the old leftie'.

Pamela said, 'Maria rang. She wanted you to call her as soon as you got back. She's worried sick about Ralph – Annie rang your place again this morning and spoke to her.'

Langham picked up the phone and got through to the flat.

'Donald! Any news about Ralph?'

'Nothing. I've just got back to the office.'

'Annie rang. She was distraught. Donald, do you think I should go down and stay with her?'

He thought about it. 'Would you? Reassure her that I'm going to see someone. I know where he was going yesterday, so I'll . . . Look, take a taxi, Maria. That'll be quicker.'

'Donald, what do you think has happened?'

'I honestly don't know,' he said, recalling Ralph's mention of Arnold Grayson's thugs and feeling sick.

'Be careful, darling,' Maria said, and rang off.

He got through to Scotland Yard, gave Mallory the details of his conversation with Simon Lipscombe, then told him about Ralph. Mallory promised to get someone on the case.

Langham thanked him and braced himself to phone Annie.

He dialled Ralph's number and Annie answered immediately. 'Hello?'

'Annie, Donald here.'

'Any news?'

'No, but I'm working on it, Annie.'

She began to sob. 'I thought he was down the pub, but he never rang . . . He always does if he's going straight to the Duck and Drake. So when he didn't get in at eleven, I went down there myself and had a word with Bill, but he said Ralphy hadn't been in that night. Oh, Donald, what's happened to him?'

'Annie, I know for a fact that he's armed. He can look after himself. I think he's probably following a lead, and . . . and he's found himself somewhere without a phone . . . down the marshes or at the docks . . .' He babbled on, hoping she didn't detect that he was clutching at straws.

'It's not like him, Donald. If he's going to be late, he phones. And he said . . . the other day he said there'd been some murder or other. Is he in danger, Donald?'

'I'm sure he's fine, Annie. Look, I'm working on it. I have a lead and I'm setting off right now. Oh' – he went on – 'Maria's on her way. She should be with you in half an hour.'

'She needn't go to the bother—' Annie began.

'It's no bother, Annie. She wants to be with you.'

'Bless her!'

'I'll get off now, Annie, and I'll be in touch as soon as I find him, I promise.'

He replaced the receiver and stared at Pamela; she was chewing her knuckle and looking petrified.

'If he's got his shooter with him,' she said in a tiny voice, 'then why hasn't he used it to get himself out of trouble and get back here?'

With her question still ringing in his ears, he left the office and made his way down to the street.

TWENTY-ONE

R yland opened his eyes and stared at the ceiling.
He lay on his back, all his weight resting on his arms. He rolled on to his side, relieving the agony in his wrists, and gasped as a new pain lanced through his ribcage. He tried to move his arms. Not only were they numb from a lack of circulation, but his wrists were tied behind his back.

He reckoned Horace must have laid into him good and proper after he'd passed out, because he felt a throbbing in his groin, his left shoulder ached, and his right knee felt as if it'd been hit with a sledgehammer.

He recalled the bald-headed bastard smashing his fist into his face. He knew his nose was broken from the lancing pain, and his top lip was thick with dried blood.

He lay very still for a few minutes, taking deep breaths of warm, fetid air.

He was surprised at how difficult it was to move into a sitting position with his hands tied behind his back. It didn't help, either, that even the slightest movement sent electric jolts of pain around his ribcage.

At last, after five minutes of slow, careful movement, he sat with his back against the whitewashed wall and examined his prison.

Immediately before him was the barred door, with a darkened corridor beyond. To his left, high in the wall, was a semi-circular window made up of small squares of glass, fronted by thick iron bars. The glass was dusty and covered with old spiderwebs, and daylight cast a pale illumination into the cell.

He wondered how long he'd been there. He'd been bundled into the back of the van around eleven o'clock and thrown into the cell not long after that. Was it still the same day, or had he been unconscious for a full night?

He thought of Annie. If he'd been here all night, then she'd be frantic with worry.

The cell was bare. There was nothing he might use as a weapon, even if he could free his hands, and nothing he might use to slice the cords that bound his wrists.

At least his ankles hadn't been tied. He could stand – if he was able to – and walk around the cell.

He took a breath, wincing at the pain in his ribs, and pushed himself slowly up the wall until he was standing upright.

Taking another shallow breath, he pushed himself from the wall and crossed to the barred door. He pressed his face between the bars, relishing the sensation of the cool iron on his cheeks. A flag-stoned corridor stretched away to the right. To his left, the corridor terminated in a stone wall a few feet away. The cell door was secured by a thick iron bar and a padlock.

He moved his wrists behind his back, attempting to assess the tightness of the cord. There was no give.

He wondered if Don was aware that he was missing. If a day had passed, then Annie would have been in touch with him, and Don would be on the case. His only hope, he thought, was if someone had witnessed his abduction.

The bloke who'd followed him the other day, Jones, had said that Grayson wanted to know what Alf Bentley had told him that day in the pub.

What had Bentley said? Something about the good old days, and did Ralph want to join them again? Grayson had it all planned. The twentieth. That night they were going to teach a few bastards what was what.

He moved back to the wall and manoeuvred himself until he was sitting on the floor with his legs stretched out before him. He took a deep breath, but the air was warm and humid. He was sweating and he needed to relieve himself.

Maybe he could make something up, say that Bentley told him about some robbery or other. But he knew Grayson would see through the lie.

As the minutes ticked by, he recalled some of the stories he'd heard about Arnold Grayson. A few years ago a couple of up-and-coming local gang bosses had mysteriously vanished, and word was that Grayson had had his boys abduct these men as a warning to any others who might have been thinking of muscling in on his territory. Apparently, Grayson had sealed the gang bosses in barrels which he'd half filled with concrete. When the concrete had set, he'd had the barrels rolled into the river at the back of his brewery while his victims were alive and screaming. Not that anything had been proven.

To all intents and purposes, Arnold Grayson was a successful local businessman, a pillar of the community who contributed to charities and to the annual police ball.

He heard a sound. Voices, followed by footsteps along the corridor.

He swallowed and attempted to control his breathing.

Grayson ambled into view, his hands in the pockets of his grey trousers. He was smoking a fat cigar and smiling.

Next to him was a man Ryland had not seen before.

If Ryland had found Horace intimidating, then something about this bastard filled him with dread.

He wore black boots, black trousers, a black roll-neck sweater and a thick leather belt. He sported a small black moustache and his hair was slicked back with brilliantine.

He looks, Ryland thought, like the spitting image of my father.

And there was something psychopathic in the immobility of his features and the deadness of his eyes.

Grayson leaned casually against the brickwork of the door and removed his cigar. 'I've been conducting a little bit of research, Ryland,' he said, 'after what Alf Bentley told me about you.'

'What do you want?'

Clearly part of a rehearsed routine, the man in black asked

his boss, 'And what did Bentley tell you, Mr Grayson?' His voice, like his eyes, lacked all emotion.

'When I asked Bentley what he'd told you, Ryland, he claimed you were a good man. One of us. He blabbered on about the good old days, back in the thirties. Remember that far back?'

Ryland said nothing.

'Apparently, you were one of the boys. A good man to rely on in a scrap. But that was to be expected, wasn't it, with a father like Dennis Ryland? I've spoken to a few people recently, people who knew your father back then, and they had nothing but praise for him. He was as tough as nails and committed to the cause. He'd do anything for Mr Mosley. Anything.'

Ryland swallowed, unable to meet Grayson's eyes.

'And he did a good job in raising his eldest son, a veritable chip off the old block. Little Ralphy Ryland might have looked like a runt but he was as fanatical as his father.' Grayson chuckled. 'Oh, Bentley was singing like a songbird about how you and him and a few others turned over a few places on Cable Street that night and roughed up a few Jew-boys.'

'What do you want from me?'

'In the course of my research,' Grayson went on, 'I found out a little more about you, Mr Ryland. How, back in '46 when you were demobbed, you were approached by an associate of mine, someone high up in the union. He was recruiting and wanted to enlist a few good men. And what did you tell him?'

When Ryland failed to reply, Grayson directed the same question to the man beside him. 'What did he tell him, Razor?'

Razor? Ryland didn't know whether to laugh or piss himself.

'Ryland told him to go screw himself, Mr Grayson.'

Both men fell silent, staring at him.

Ryland was aware of his drumming heartbeat, the throbbing pain in his torso.

When he looked up and met Grayson's eyes, the man was no longer smiling.

'But when Bentley asked you to join us the other day, he didn't know you'd turned your back on the cause, did he? He didn't know you were a traitor. I asked Bentley again and again what he'd told you about our little plans, but he claimed he was so pissed he couldn't remember a thing. And that's what he went on repeating, right up until he died.'

Ryland swallowed. 'You killed him?'

Grayson smiled. 'To teach Bentley a lesson, I had Razor here slit his tongue.' He shrugged, affectedly casual. 'How did I know that he'd drown on his own blood?'

'It was an accident, Mr Grayson,' Razor said. 'Like you said, how were we to know?'

Grayson leaned forward, staring through the bars at Ryland. 'We don't like traitors, do we, Razor?'

'We don't like them at all, Mr Grayson. Scum of the earth, they are.'

'Traitors,' Grayson said, 'do not deserve to live.'

He nodded to Razor, who withdrew a key from his pocket and unfastened the padlock.

Grayson swung the barred door open and gestured for Razor to enter.

Smiling at the thought of the task ahead of him, the man in black stepped into the cell.

Grayson pulled the door shut and clutched the bars. Sweat covered his face and his porcine eyes gleamed, and there was something appalling in his anticipation of what was about to happen.

'Now, what did Bentley tell you, Ryland?' he murmured.

'He . . . he asked me to join him. He said you had something planned. He didn't say what. Something down the East End, on the twentieth.' He shrugged. 'I presumed it was just a bit of argy-bargy—'

'What else did he tell you?'

'Nothing, not a word. That was it.'

Grayson nodded to the man in black. 'Razor.'

The man pulled a pair of knuckledusters from his trouser pocket and fitted them with exaggerated care on to the fingers of his big right hand. Then he reached into the same pocket and produced a cut-throat razor which he opened with a nonchalant flick.

'No,' Grayson purred. 'Save that for later.'

With obvious disappointment, Razor folded the cut-throat and returned it to his pocket.

'Now, Mr Ryland,' Grayson said, 'what else did Bentley tell you?'

'Like I said, he told me nothing—'

'Razor,' Grayson said, nodding.

The man in black reached down, picked Ryland up by his throat and drove the knuckledusters into his stomach. Ryland doubled up, winded, and Razor smashed him across the side of the head. He hit the ground, dazed, and Razor kicked him in the stomach.

Ryland looked up, expecting another kick. Grayson gripped the bars, staring down at him. Sweat dripped from the fat man's face. His eyes were wide, like a child's at a sweetshop window.

'What did Bentley tell you!'

Ryland fought for breath. He thought, then, that words were beyond him, and surprised himself by saying, 'Nothing. Nothing more. A riot. The twentieth. The good old days—'

'You're lying, Ryland!'

'I'm not! I swear . . .'

Razor glanced at Grayson. 'You want me to cut him up a bit, boss?'

Grayson thought about it. 'Did you hear that, Ryland? Razor would like to cut you up.' He smiled. 'Where would you cut him, Razor?'

'Thought I might start on his belly, boss. He'll bleed a lot, and it'll be painful, but it wouldn't be fatal.'

'And then?'

'Then I thought I might slice his face a bit, maybe take an eye out, boss.'

'Did you hear that, Ryland?' Grayson asked.

Ryland groaned.

'Now,' Grayson said, '*what did Bentley tell you?*'

'Join him . . . a riot . . . rough up a few . . .'

Grayson said, 'You're lying. Bentley told you a lot more than that, Ryland. That's why you went squealing to that commie bastard Manville Carrington, isn't it?'

Ryland blinked, confused. 'What?' He focused on Grayson, his fat face pressed into the bars. 'No . . . No, that was something else. An investigation, a murder. Nothing to do with Alf Bentley.'

Grayson sighed. 'Not only are you a traitor, Mr Ryland, but you're a liar into the bargain. All you have to do is tell me the simple truth. What did you tell Carrington?'

Ryland tried to laugh. 'Sod off!' he spat.

'Razor . . .'

With evident relish, and smiling now, the man in black pulled the cut-throat razor from his pocket.

Ryland had a sudden vision of his boys, laughing at him as he played the goat, pretending to die when they shot him during a game of cowboys and Indians in the back garden . . .

Defiantly, he pushed himself up the wall and stood, staring at the thug.

'*What did you tell Carrington?*' Grayson screeched.

'Go to hell,' Ryland spat.

Razor smashed him across the face, first one way and then the other. He looked back at Grayson. 'You want me to cut him up good now, boss?'

Grayson thought about it. 'Perhaps,' he said, 'we'll leave that for later. But you can hit him – hard.'

Razor did so, striking Ryland in the face with his knuckledusters.

He felt his vision swimming and toppled to the floor.

The last thing he heard before he lost consciousness was Grayson saying, 'We don't like traitors, Mr Ryland.'

TWENTY-TWO

Langham pulled into the kerb and stared up at the immaculate white frontage of the Georgian terraced house which looked out over the square.

Try as he might, he couldn't imagine a scenario in which Ralph had come to harm at the hands of the octogenarian politician. He'd quiz the old man, try to ascertain if Ralph had mentioned where he might have been heading after he left the premises. He climbed from his car, mounted the steps and brought down the knocker in three thunderous tattoos.

Within half a minute a butler opened the door and regarded Langham with vocational disdain.

'Inspector Langham, Scotland Yard.' He was in no mood to risk being turned away. 'I need to see Mr Carrington on a matter of extreme importance.'

The butler hesitated. 'Mr Carrington is taking tea at—'

Langham eased past him. 'Then I'll join him,' he said. 'Or if you'd rather I insist that Mr Carrington accompany me down to the Yard . . .?'

'This way, Inspector,' the butler responded without allowing his face to register the displeasure he was no doubt feeling.

He led the way along a hallway fitted with a carpet that felt as thick as a pelt. Scenic watercolours hung on the walls, and on a Queen Anne occasional table stood an ivory-handled telephone.

The butler came to a door and knocked. A thin croak sounded in reply. Langham was ushered into a luxurious drawing room with a maroon carpet and deep leather armchairs.

'Inspector Langham,' the butler announced, 'of Scotland Yard. Inspector, Mr Carrington.'

Despite the warmth of the day, he was amazed to see that a fire was blazing. Before it sat a tiny, shrunken figure in a huge armchair.

The old man smiled up at Langham and said in a high, whinnying voice, 'Why, Inspector, what a delight! An honour indeed. Join me, do! I am taking tea. Harrison, another cup for our guest. The muffins are excellent, Inspector. Please, be seated.'

The butler ghosted away.

Langham pulled up a chair and sat down, loosening his tie as he did so.

So this was the famous Manville Carrington, the bane of the House, the thorn in the side of the Tories, and the notorious defender of the crimes perpetrated by Stalin in the name of revolutionary Bolshevism.

He was entirely bald, and his peculiarly pale, waxen flesh was drawn tightly over the prominent bones of his skull: the effect was as if the old man had been embalmed.

Harrison returned with a second cup and poured Langham a black tea.

'Now, Inspector, how might I assist you?' Carrington blinked, slowly, rather like the lizard he so resembled.

Langham apologized for barging in, and went on, 'I understand you spoke with my colleague yesterday, one Ralph Ryland?'

'Indeed, the Cockney fellow. Rather partial to my muffins, I recall. A man of good taste.' He waved a palsied hand towards the plate of buttered muffins. 'You will partake?'

'If it's all the same, I'll decline.'

As if to compensate for Langham's refusal, Carrington snatched a muffin and munched contentedly. 'Yes, the fellow stayed awhile, and we had a rather pleasant chat. Perplexed, he was.'

'Perplexed?' Langham moved his chair a little further away from the fire.

'About the apparent – as he saw it – contradiction between one's political beliefs and the acquaintances one might entertain.'

'Ah, Christopher Lombard?'

'Precisely,' Carrington said, chewing vigorously. 'Mr Ryland seemed to think it odd that a man of my political persuasion should have discourse with those in the opposite camp. On the contrary, I responded, it was through engaging with the enemy – and I use the term in its loosest sense – that we come to understand the minds of others, and so hone our own ideologies. Do you follow?'

'Quite.'

'But I think Inspector Ryland failed to comprehend – and I rather received the impression that he thought I was lying.'

'About the Sunday you entertained Christopher Lombard?'

'Quite so,' Carrington said.

'Did Inspector Ryland mention where he might be going after he'd finished interviewing you?'

'Where he was going? What an odd question! It sounds rather as if he's vanished.'

Langham stared at the wizened goblin. 'He has.'

Carrington blinked. 'My word. Do you mean he hasn't been seen since leaving the premises?'

'That's right. So, if you'd be so kind as to cast your mind back to the interview. Did he say anything at all to indicate where he might have gone, or whom he might have intended to interview after leaving here?'

Carrington lowered his tissue-thin eyelids over the prominent orbs of his eyes and sat for ten seconds in silent consideration. A trickle of butter dribbled down his chin.

He opened his eyes. 'He mentioned that he'd seen some old acquaintances recently, men he had known in the thirties. Fascists.'

Langham leaned forward. 'Did he say whether he was meeting them after seeing you?' He tried to keep the desperation from his tone.

Carrington screwed his reptilian eyes half shut in concentration. 'I'm afraid he didn't say, Inspector. I recall his saying that his investigations had brought him into contact with these people, but he said nothing about renewing the contacts.'

'Did he say *where* he'd met them? A public house, a club, anywhere?'

'He mentioned this only in passing, almost incidentally. He didn't go into detail. I'm sorry.'

Langham finished his tea and climbed to his feet, more than a little frustrated. 'Thank you for your time, Mr Carrington.'

'I do hope you find the little man, Inspector.' He rang a bell, and the butler appeared. 'Harrison, Inspector Langham is leaving.'

Langham thanked the politician again and followed the butler from the room.

He recalled his promise to Annie and wondered what the hell he was going to do next.

They came to the front door and the butler hesitated, clearing his throat.

'Inspector, I could not help but overhear a little of your conversation. I understand that you were enquiring after the whereabouts of a certain Inspector Ryland?'

'That's right. You must have shown him in yesterday morning?'

'At approximately half past ten, sir – and I escorted him from the premises just after eleven.'

Langham regarded the imperturbable Harrison. 'And?' he asked, his pulse quickening.

'I was in the drawing room a minute or so later, adjusting the curtains, and I happened to look out into the street and notice Mr Ryland in conversation with two rather disreputable-looking gentlemen.'

'In conversation?'

'*Heated* conversation, sir.'

'What happened?'

'I'm afraid that's all I saw, sir. I left the room and thought no more of it, until I overheard you just now.'

'Could you describe these men?'

'One stood with his back to me, and I was unable to get a clear view of the individual. The other man was large, thickset, with a bald head and ears which I understand are termed "cauliflower".'

'And you saw nothing more? There wasn't a vehicle nearby, perhaps?'

The butler shook his head. 'Not that I noticed, sir. But I did happen to see some children out in the street, playing hopscotch. Perhaps they might have seen more than I did.'

Harrison opened the door, and Langham thanked him and stepped into the sunlight. He paused on the top of the steps and looked up and down the street.

A young girl in a torn light-blue summer dress sat on the kerb nearby, doodling on the pavement with a nubbin of chalk. Langham tapped down the steps and approached her casually.

The girl, perhaps eight years old, looked up at him, shielding her eyes from the sun.

Langham nodded at the faint outline of hopscotch squares and numbers on the flagstones. 'Playing hopscotch yesterday?' he asked.

'What if we were?' the urchin retorted. 'Got Missus Fletcher's say-so, we have.'

He smiled. 'I wonder . . .' He reached into his pocket and pulled out a half-crown, flicking the silver coin into the air and catching it. 'Did you happen to notice anything yesterday morning, around eleven? Three men, arguing?'

The girl jumped to her feet and stared at him. 'I'll say! A right scrap, it were!'

Langham's stomach turned. 'Can you tell me what happened?'

The girl became suddenly unsure of herself and murmured, 'Is it about the gun?'

'The gun?' he echoed, alarmed.

'Two big blokes, they got hold of a littler fellah, only he didn't want to go with 'em, see? And he tried to pull out a shooter, but it fell on the ground.'

'And what happened then?'

'The big blokes, they shoved the little fellah into the back of a waggon, didn't they?'

'A waggon? Can you describe it? What colour was it, and did it have any writing on the side?'

She screwed up her face in thought. 'Can't remember the colour, but it had animals on it.'

'Animals?'

She nodded earnestly. 'A what-do-you-call-it? A horse with a horn, here?' She touched the middle of her forehead. 'And the other animal was a lion. And there were somethink else – a big cup.'

'Grayson's Ales!' Langham said to himself.

Their trade emblem was of a pint of foaming ale with a lion and unicorn rampant. The brewery had its premises in Shadwell overlooking the Thames, with a small pub attached to the brewery exclusively serving Grayson's ales.

'And then what happened?'

The girl shrugged. 'Then they drove off, didn't they, and Tommy picked up the gun.'

Langham nodded. 'And what did he do with the gun?'

'Why you want to know?' she asked. 'You a copper?'

'I'm a friend of the man who was taken,' he said. 'Now tell me, what did Tommy do with the gun?'

The girl bit her lip, clearly pondering the wisdom of imparting this information. She stared at the coin in Langham's hand.

'This is yours,' he said, 'if you tell me.'

That decided her. She nodded and said, 'Tommy hid it, he did!'

'Hid it? Can you show me—?'

She dashed across the road and dodged through the gates of the park in the centre of the square. Langham crossed the road and followed her. She was already on her hands and knees and scrambling into the enveloping leaves of a rhododendron bush.

She emerged with soiled knees and a big grin on her face. Incongruous in her small right hand was Ralph's silver revolver. She waved it at him and Langham flinched, then reached out. 'Now, give it to me, please.'

'The half-crown first, mister.'

He complied, smiling, and the exchange was completed. The girl skipped off, singing to herself, and Langham hurried back to his car.

He drove south to the river, sickened by the thought that Grayson's thugs had abducted Ralph.

TWENTY-THREE

L angham pulled up in the cobbled street fifty yards before the big red-brick building that housed Grayson's brewery. A high wall enclosed the premises, and set into the wall was a timber gate painted with the legend *Grayson's Ales*.

A public house was attached to the brewery, and the pub sign above the door showed a foaming flagon between a lion and a unicorn. Three cloth-capped workmen stood on the pavement outside the premises, enjoying pints of ale in the sun.

He pulled out the revolver and checked its chamber. It was fully loaded. He returned the weapon to his inside pocket.

He considered what Ralph had told him about Grayson, that the gang boss wanted to know the identity of the outfit that had supposedly kidnapped his greyhound. But try as he might, Langham couldn't see why Grayson should resort to snatching Ralph off the street just to find out.

He mopped the sweat from his face with his handkerchief, then wiped his palms.

He stared along the road at the public house.

He had to be very careful. It would be a mistake to rush straight in and enquire after Ralph's whereabouts. The best course of action would be to trace the driver of the van, the thug with the cauliflower ears.

He was about to make his way to the public house when the gates of the brewery swung open and a waggon, in the maroon-and-cream livery of the company, pulled out on to the road. He was unable to make out, beyond the dazzle of sunlight on the windscreen, whether the driver was bald-headed.

He had a sudden change of plan.

He watched the vehicle trundle along for fifty yards, then started the engine and followed.

He allowed the waggon to pull ahead by another fifty yards. It turned left, away from the river towards Stepney, and Langham followed. They passed down a cobbled street between small red-brick back-to-backs, with occasional gaps in the terraces where buildings had been taken out by German bombs.

A hundred yards ahead, the waggon pulled up outside a public house. Langham slowed and drew to a halt behind the vehicle.

Two men jumped down from the cab. Neither of them was the bald-headed thug with cauliflower ears. One was a strapping blond youth in his early twenties, the other a wiry, whippet-thin older man.

While the youth opened up a timber trapdoor giving access to the pub's cellar, the older man slid open a door in the side of the waggon and tugged a heavy hessian bolster on to the pavement. He climbed up into the van and rolled a barrel out and on to the bolster, where it landed with a padded thud. The blond youth then manhandled the barrel towards the trapdoor and rolled it down a ramp into the cellar.

They delivered half a dozen barrels in this fashion, then paused for a breather. The youth leaned against the side of the van while the older man sat on the bolster and lit a cigarette.

Langham left the car and approached the public house.

He paused on the pavement before the timber trapdoor and

stared into the Stygian gloom of the cellar, nodding to the youth. 'Hot work on a day like today.'

'Hot work every day,' the young man said.

Langham indicated the waggon. 'How many does Grayson have in his fleet?'

'That'll be two,' the older man replied in a thick Irish accent, squinting up at him.

'The driver of the other waggon – a big man with a bald head.'

'You talking about Horace?' the youth said.

'Horace?'

'Horace Fowler – he was named after some poet,' the young man said. 'His father was a bit of a scholar, see?'

'Was Horace out in his waggon yesterday?' Langham asked.

'So he was,' the Irishman said.

'Do you know where I'll find him?'

'Now, what'll you be wanting him for?'

'A little business I'd like to discuss with him.'

The men exchanged a glance.

'What kind of business?' the older man asked.

'I'm afraid that must remain confidential.'

The Irishman flicked his tab-end into the gutter and stood up. He leaned against the side of the waggon next to his mate, hooking his thumbs into his braces and staring at Langham.

He was surprised by what the Irishman said next. 'Horace doesn't come cheap, no word of a lie.'

'He doesn't?'

'No, and he don't work for just anybody. Plenty of work on for the gaffer, see?'

'The gaffer?'

'What you don't know can't be doing you no harm,' the Irishman said cryptically.

'All the same,' Langham said, 'I'd like to talk to Horace.'

The Irishman and the youth exchanged another glance, and the older man nodded. 'He knocked off at two. He'll be in the Lion.'

'Thank you.'

'But be careful, whoever you are,' the Irishman said. 'Horace can turn nasty after a few pints.'

The youth smiled. 'He can turn nasty any time,' he said. 'He don't need ale inside him to pick a fight, old Horace. Ex-boxer, he is.'

Langham smiled. 'I'll bear that in mind,' he said, thanked the men and returned to his car.

He took a right turn and another right, then drove along the road beside the Thames. He came to the Lion and Unicorn and braked.

He'd go into the pub for a quick half, make sure that Horace was still there, then drink up and return to the car. He looked at his watch. It was almost five o'clock. If Horace had been drinking since two, he would be well oiled by now. When the thug decided to wend his way home, he'd follow him at a distance and bide his time before choosing his moment. Horace might be a thug and an ex-boxer, but Langham was armed.

With the reassuring weight of the revolver in his pocket, he entered the pub.

A few drinkers were lined up along the bar, and a couple of tables were occupied at the far end of the long room. Langham ordered a half of Grayson's Mild, took a mouthful and pulled a face. It was the closest he'd come to imbibing neat vinegar in years.

He lodged the glass on the bar towel and glanced at the occupants of the closest table. Half a dozen workmen from a nearby foundry, in boiler suits and overalls, were engaged in a noisy game of cards. Horace wasn't one of them.

At the second table, a bald-headed thug with cauliflower ears sat with his back to the wall, a fresh pint of bitter before him. Langham assumed that this was Horace, and he looked every bit as brutish as he'd feared. Supplementary to the mangled ears was a nose that spoke of multiple breakages.

Langham looked away, careful not to establish eye contact with someone who would be only too glad to interpret a stray glance as a challenge.

He took another sip of the vinegary ale, then glanced at Horace's two drinking partners. One was a man in his forties who looked almost as thuggish as Horace, though more suave: he was blue-jawed and dark-eyed, and wore a navy-blue suit.

The third drinker, by contrast to his strapping companions, was an undernourished youth with a thin, misaligned face, shifty eyes and acne.

The danger, of course, was that Horace would not leave by himself. If he departed with his cronies, either to frequent another pub or to continue the drinking session at home, then Langham would have to revise his plan.

He looked away quickly as Horace caught his eye.

He took another sip of beer, examining a row of whisky bottles behind the bar. Between the bottles, yellowed press cuttings had been taped to the wallpaper: one showed a grainy black-and-white photograph of Oswald Mosley, another a marching column of belligerent-looking Blackshirts.

Someone eased in beside him and a gravelly voice said, 'Half a mild?' in a mocking tone.

Langham turned. Horace stared at him, swaying. Seen close to, his face spoke of a hundred punishments in the ring and a few, more recent, in the form of bruises beneath his eyes.

'I beg your pardon?'

Horace indicated Langham's glass. 'Mild's a woman's drink, mate. Clive!' he called, passing his empty pint glass to the bartender. 'Fill her up.'

Horace stank of sweat and old ale. His eyes lacked focus. Langham wondered how many pints he'd downed since two o'clock.

'Haven't seen you round here before.'

'I was passing,' Langham said, 'and decided to stop for a drink.'

The bartender passed Horace a brimming pint. Beer slopped on the bar as he raised it to his lips. Half a pint vanished in two gulps.

Horace belched and said, staring at Langham, 'Saw you looking.'

'No offence meant,' Langham said, deciding that appeasement was the better part of valour.

'Fancy Terrence, do you?'

'I beg your pardon?' he said for the second time, and cursed himself for sounding so priggish.

Horace took another massive swallow of ale and belched

again, poisoning the air with the reek of regurgitated beer fumes. 'Terrence, in the suit. Handsome chap. One for the boys, if you know what I mean. Not that I could give a monkey's.' He leaned forward, and Langham stepped back, fearing Horace was about to lose his balance.

He said into Langham's ear, 'A fiver and you can have Terrence in the khazi.'

'Thanks all the same, but not today.'

Horace sniggered. 'Not from round here?'

'North Finchley,' Langham said, aware that to say Kensington would only risk provoking Horace's disdain. 'What about you? Local, are you?'

'Local? Very local.' He banged his empty glass on the bar and stared at the bartender.

'Another pint, Horace?'

The big man swayed and pointed. 'My key, Clive.'

The bartender unhooked a key from a board behind the bar and passed it to Horace.

'Been nice talking,' Horace said, saluted with the affability of the hopelessly inebriated and staggered off. Langham watched him open a door at the end of the bar and make his way, barrelling from side to side, up a narrow staircase.

He caught the bartender's attention. 'Do you rent rooms?'

'We do, but they're all taken. Try again next week.'

Langham thanked him, peering at the board where Horace's key had hung. There were five numbered hooks, and the keys beneath numbers three and five were missing. So Horace lodged in one of those rooms.

He turned and leaned against the bar. At the far end of the room, the blue-jawed Terrence climbed to his feet and left the pub. The scrawny youth was sitting alone. He glanced up, saw Langham looking, then quickly stared down at the dregs of his pint.

Langham took another sip of mild, made sure he was unobserved, and crossed to the door. He climbed stairs covered with a sticky floral-patterned carpet and came to a landing where he made out three numbered doors.

He hesitated, considering his options. Horace was a bruiser, up for a fight at any time – especially under the influence of a skinful – but surely the sight of the revolver would make him see sense?

A quick tap on his door, and when Horace answered, he'd thrust the shooter in his ugly mug and threaten him with a face-full of lead if he didn't keep quiet.

He drew the revolver and approached the door marked with the number three.

He leaned close and listened, but heard nothing within the room. He knocked on the door. His heart thudded and the butt of the gun was slick in his palm.

There was no reply.

Either Horace had fallen into a drunken stupor or this wasn't his room.

He moved along the landing and turned right, along a short corridor. He made out two more doors, marked respectively with the numerals four and five.

He crept up to number five and heard someone stumbling around beyond the door, then the sound of muttered curses.

He was reaching out for the door handle when he heard a sound behind him.

Before he could turn, a quiet voice said, 'I wouldn't do that if I were you.'

TWENTY-FOUR

'Put your hands up and don't do anything silly with that shooter.'

Langham did as instructed.

'Now turn around.'

He did so and regarded the thin-faced youth he'd seen downstairs with Horace. The young man looked nervous. His eyes were wide and his face was dripping with sweat as he stared at the gun above Langham's head.

The youth appeared to be unarmed, which perhaps accounted for his nervousness. Langham smiled and lowered his revolver.

'Maybe *you* can help me,' he said. 'I saw you drinking with Horace.'

The young man flinched at the mention of the name. 'What do you want with Horace?' He kept his voice low, obviously not wanting to be overheard. 'I saw you follow him up here—'

'Forget Horace,' Langham said. 'Maybe you can help me.'

The youth backed off, staring at the revolver. 'What do you want?'

'I'm looking for someone, and I think Horace knows where he might be.'

A strange expression of relief appeared on the young man's face. 'I wondered if it were you – Ralph mentioned he had a partner, see? You're looking for Ralph, right? Ralph Ryland?'

'You know Ralph?' Langham said.

'Keep it down!' the youth hissed. He looked indecisive for a second or two, then gestured to a door along the landing. 'In here!'

He fumbled with a key in the lock of number four. Langham slipped the revolver into his pocket and stepped into the tiny bedroom. The youth closed the door and leaned against it, sweating even more.

'You know Ralph?' Langham repeated, hardly daring to hope. 'Do you know where he is?'

'I said keep it down!' He nodded towards the wall, whispering urgently, 'Horace is next door.'

He indicated the narrow bed and Langham sat down. The youth lowered himself on to a straight-backed chair against the wall, placed his shaking hands on his thighs and swore to himself.

Langham tried again. 'How do you know Ralph?'

'I owe him one,' the young man said. 'I'm Len. I train greyhounds for Grayson.'

Langham nodded. 'I work with Ralph,' he said. 'He told me about Neb.'

'Ralph saved my skin, he did. If Mr Grayson had found out . . . he would've killed me, so he would. No word of a lie. Ralph saved my bacon. So, like I said, I owe him one.'

'Where is he?'

The youth looked up from his twitching hands. 'That's just

it. I don't rightly know. All I do know is that Mr Grayson's got him. He let Horace have a go at him, and now it's Razor's turn, ain't it? Horace was bragging about it just now, he was.'

Langham's stomach turned. 'What does Grayson want with Ralph?'

Len glanced nervously at the wall as if Horace might burst through at any second. 'Ralph knows something. I don't know what, exactly. Something about Grayson's mob. They're planning something big, and Ralph got wind of it and Mr Grayson don't want Ralph blabbing. So he had Horace pick him up yesterday and now he's having his fun with him, ain't he?'

Langham swore.

'Horace were fair shouting his mouth off about it,' Len said. 'He said he laid into Ralph while Mr Grayson just watched.' The youth shook his head. 'He gets off on it, Grayson does. He likes watching two blokes lamming into each other – or a thug like Horace beating the living daylights out of some poor sod.'

Langham felt his pulse quicken. 'But you don't know where Ralph is? Please – I must find him.'

Len regarded his hands, then looked up and said almost pleadingly, 'If Mr Grayson found out I've been talking to you . . .' He shook his head. 'That'd be curtains for me, it would.'

'I'm on your side, Len. All I want to do is save Ralph, OK? Do you have any idea where he might be?'

Len scratched at a patch of acne on his jaw, muttering to himself. 'I don't know for sure. He could be in one of a few places.'

'Go on.'

'Sometimes Mr Grayson takes 'em to his place next to the track along the road. Young lads he picks up on the heath. He gets a couple of 'em, gives 'em a fiver each to fight. He has a room at this place, see, all sound-proofed, and these lads go at it hammer and bleedin' tongs. And if one of 'em happens to snuff it, well, as far as Mr Grayson's concerned, that's all the better. He's had his money's worth, ain't he?'

'Christ Almighty,' Langham said.

'Then he has this place up near Clapham Common, where he takes his rent boys for other things, like. Disgusting things.'

'And the third place?'

'A swank pile in Hampstead, near the heath. A mansion, it is.'

'So where might Ralph be? In the house near the track?'

Len looked unsure. 'I don't think so. I haven't seen Grayson's car at the track for a couple of days, and it'd be there if Ralph were in the room along the road. And I don't think Mr Grayson'd take Ralph to his Clapham joint.'

'So Hampstead is the favourite?'

'Maybe. You see, he has a special place in the cellar of this mansion. I've heard Horace talk about it. It's like a prison cell. That's where he takes his enemies, blokes who've done the dirty on him, who he doesn't want to get away. And he has Horace and Razor do 'em over.'

Langham sat forward on the bed and looked across at the petrified kid. 'So if Ralph's found out about something that Grayson was planning, why hasn't he just had Ralph killed straight away?'

Len shook his head. 'Like I told you, Mr Langham. Mr Grayson likes his fun. He wants to see his enemies bleed, don't he? He likes to see 'em beg for mercy.'

Langham pulled out his handkerchief and mopped his face. 'So Grayson's had Ralph for – what? – a day and a half? Do you know how long he keeps his victims alive?'

Len lifted his hands from his thighs in a hopeless gesture. 'Really depends on how strong they are, don't it? A day or so if they're weak and give in. A few days if they hold out.'

Langham nodded, his heart racing. 'This mansion Grayson has in Hampstead?' he asked. 'Do you know where it is exactly?'

'The big place at the end of Poplar Walk. Has a unicorn on the top of one gatepost and a lion on the other.'

'Does he have staff, housekeepers, valets or a butler?'

'Not Mr Grayson – he don't want any more people hanging around than he has to. He eats out all the time in posh restaurants. He'll only have one bloke up at the mansion if he's got someone in the cell, either Horace or Razor, doing shifts, like.'

'So the place isn't guarded?'

Len shook his head. 'But it's got high walls, with glass and barbed wire on top.'

'That's good to know.' Langham stood and moved to the door.

'I . . . I'd come with you, show you exactly where the place is, but if Mr Grayson caught us . . .' He shook his head. 'We'd both be dead.'

'I'm not expecting anything more from you, Len. You've done all you can to help Ralph.'

He reached for the door handle, but Len stopped him. 'If Mr Grayson nabs you, please don't tell 'im it were me who blabbed, will you?'

'I won't say a word,' Langham promised.

He thanked the youth, opened the door and slipped from the room.

Back at the car, he sat for a minute and thought things through.

He set off, found a telephone box and hauled open the door.

Fumbling with the dial, he got through to Scotland Yard and asked to speak to Detective Inspector Mallory, praying that Jeff would be in his office.

The desk sergeant put him through, and Mallory said, 'Don? Any word on Ralph?'

'I think I've found him,' Langham said, and recounted what Len had told him without divulging his informant's identity.

'The problem is,' he went on, 'I can't be sure where exactly Grayson's keeping him. My informant thinks it's the Hampstead place, but then again it might be the terraced house next to the greyhound track. Can you get teams to raid both places?'

'I could sound out the superintendent about it, Don. But . . . look, are you sure your informant's legit? It'll look bad for us if we barge into the premises of an innocent businessman—'

'Grayson's a murdering thug!' Langham spat.

'*We* know that, Don, but these people are clever. They're rich enough to have the best lawyers, and if we slip up in this instance—'

'For crying out loud, Jeff. Ralph's life's at stake and we're worrying about the force's reputation?' He calmed himself. 'Look, if you're not willing, then I'm going into the Hampstead place by myself—'

'Don't do that. I'm on my way. I'll put it to the super and I'm sure he'll let me get a team to the racetrack and another up to Hampstead. I'll coordinate the raids at the respective houses at seven o'clock on the dot.'

'Thanks, Jeff.' He looked at his watch. It was a little after six. 'I'll be up at the Hampstead place. See you there.'

He cut the connection and dialled Ralph Ryland's Lewisham number.

Maria answered. 'Hello?'

'Maria. Donald here.'

'Donald! *Mon Dieu!* I've been worried sick! Is Ralph—?'

'I don't know yet. I think I've found where he's been kept . . . Look, just tell Annie that we're doing all we can.'

In the background, he heard Annie's questioning voice.

Maria spoke to Annie, and Langham heard the woman's sobs.

'Donald,' Maria said, close to tears. 'Annie says, "Bless you". Take care.'

'I will. Don't worry,' he said. 'Love you.'

He replaced the receiver and returned to the car.

He drove north, from time to time reaching into his jacket to touch the reassuring solidity of Ralph's revolver.

He wondered how much the police would be able to pin on Grayson. As Mallory had said, the bastard would have the best lawyers fighting his corner, and money talked. Langham had never believed in capital punishment, but there were certain cases that sorely tested his humanitarian ideology.

If bodies were discovered in barrels at the bottom of the Thames, then perhaps Grayson *would* swing.

And Langham wouldn't shed a tear.

He reached Hampstead and turned down Poplar Walk. He parked twenty yards from the end of the lane, climbed out and walked towards the big house partially obscured by tall oaks and elms. To his left, on the heath, couples strolled arm in arm or lay stretched out in the sun, and a group of boys played a lacklustre game of cricket.

He came to a pair of wrought-iron gates with a lion and a unicorn on the gateposts and stared up the gravelled drive that led to a four-square Georgian mansion. A car stood in the drive before the house, a silver-grey Jaguar, and an old Wolseley was parked around the side of the building. He wondered if the latter belonged to the thug Len had called Razor.

He considered his options. He could always wait here for Mallory, or take a recce and see if he could determine whether Ralph was being held in the cellar.

Set into the wall beside the gate was a push-button intercom, and he made out a black-painted metal device affixed to the hinges of the wrought-iron gate: evidently, it was operated automatically from within the house. He considered contacting Grayson via the intercom and bluffing his way in. Alternatively, he could always climb over the gate and risk being seen by the people on the heath or by someone in the house.

Far safer, he decided, to find another means of entry.

The house was the last in the lane and was flanked by parkland. A high stone wall surrounded the building. Langham made out vicious shards of glass running along the top of the wall, embedded in concrete.

He walked on past the house, stepped off the path, and strolled through the trees. The wall was perhaps ten feet high, and its surface uneven; here and there stones projected from the concrete infill. He could probably climb the wall, at a pinch. The problem was the glass on the top.

He returned to the car and took a thick picnic blanket from the boot, folding it and slinging it over his shoulder. He returned to the parkland and walked beside the wall. He found a section which he thought afforded sufficient handholds and footholds; on the far side was a stand of elm which would conceal his entry from anyone in the house.

He looked back the way he had come; there was no one in sight.

He re-folded the blanket, looped it around his neck and found the first foothold. He reached up, gripped a jutting edge of stone and pulled himself up.

The ascent was easier than he'd imagined, even though he skinned his palms and banged his right knee. The difficulty came when he reached the top of the wall. Hanging on with one hand, he pulled the blanket from around his neck and slung it across the top, then pulled himself up after it. He flung his right leg over the top of the wall, gripped a projecting stone and hauled himself on to the blanket, wincing as shards of glass penetrated the blanket and pierced his stomach.

He pushed himself into a crouching position, like a sprinter in the blocks, and peered down into the grounds of the house.

He jumped, hit the ground and rolled, then crouched and regained his breath. He peered through the trees, but from this angle the house was obscured: even if someone had been looking out from one of the many windows, his entry should have been unobserved.

He looked down at his stomach where patches of blood showed on his white shirt front, then set off through the trees towards the house.

He stopped when he reached an area of lawn and crouched behind a clump of hydrangeas.

He had a clear view across to the side of the house and the Wolseley parked on the gravel. Several windows looked out over the parking area, but he detected no movement within. Any cellar windows would be at the rear of the building. He'd make a dash for the cover of the car, pause there, then continue to the back of the house.

He fingered the revolver in his pocket. He was sweating, and his heart raced. He thought of Ralph possibly imprisoned in the mansion, at the mercy of sadistic thugs.

He took one last look at the serried windows, determined that he was unobserved, and ran, doubled up, towards the Wolseley, the crunch of gravel sounding loud in his ears.

He ducked down beside the vehicle's white-walled front wheel and marshalled his breathing, then duck-walked forward and peered round the car's boot. The way to the rear corner of the mansion was clear. He took off and sprinted, came to the corner and pressed himself against the brickwork.

Extensive lawns stretched away to a distant line of beech trees, the emerald expanse set out for croquet. He considered the great and the good of English society who had availed themselves of Grayson's weekend hospitality, little guessing at his predilections. Or did they know, as they must have known about his dubious political affiliations, and elected to turn a blind eye?

He peered along the back of the house. He was six feet from an architrave in the brickwork at ground level which housed a semi-circular window made up of several small panes. Before the window itself, set in the brick surround, were half a dozen iron bars. Crouching, he moved along the wall and peered through the glass.

He could see nothing. The glass was thick with dust and cobwebs. He looked around and found a stone twice the size of his fist. He crouched by the window, eased the stone between the bars, and hammered on the glass. The pane shattered instantly and he pitched forward, his hand slipping through the window frame. He dropped the stone and heard it fall into the cellar.

He carefully withdrew his arm, aware that he could easily have sliced his wrist on the jagged shards of glass remaining in the frame.

He pressed his cheeks against the bars and peered through the gap. All he could make out within the cellar was shadows.

'Ralph!' he hissed.

He waited, listening.

'Ralph, for pity's sake!'

He waited, then called out again, but only silence greeted his words.

He looked at his watch. It was six minutes to seven. Mallory was due to arrive outside the mansion on the hour.

Seconds later he heard the sound of voices behind a ground-floor window a few feet from where he was crouching.

He froze, breathing hard, and waited for the window to open and someone to peer out.

A minute elapsed, then two. The voices continued, interspersed with muffled laughter.

Langham scuttled along the back of the house until he reached the window. He raised himself slowly and peered into the room.

Two men sat at a table, facing each other, with glasses of whisky before them.

One was fat, fleshy and white-haired, with a big florid face which – in different circumstances – might have been described as genial. He suspected that this was Arnold Grayson.

He was talking to a much younger man in a black roll-neck sweater, with close-cropped black hair and a swarthy face. At first Langham thought it was the thug called Terrence from the Lion and Unicorn – but this man was bigger, meatier and even meaner-looking.

Razor?

If the man was Razor, then it was likely that Ralph *was* being held prisoner here.

Langham lowered himself and leaned back against the wall, his mind racing.

If Razor was the thug attending to Ralph, then proceedings had halted: did this mean that Ralph was dead or that Razor was merely taking a break?

If the latter . . .

He withdrew his revolver and stared at it.

He could break in through the window and startle the pair before they reacted – or could he? What if the thug was armed, or Grayson for that matter? And the younger man, by his very position as one of Grayson's henchmen, would undoubtedly be able to handle himself in close combat.

If Langham's assault went wrong, then he would be endangering Ralph's life as well as his own.

He retraced his steps to the corner of the house and considered his next move.

TWENTY-FIVE

Ryland heard a sound at the very edge of his consciousness.

As he slowly came to his senses, he saw his sons again. They were smiling at him; he reached out to them, and their expressions of joy turned to ones of horror. Then Annie was staring down at him, asking why he had to go and get himself killed.

He was filled with a pain far worse than the physical pain that throbbed through his body.

He opened his eyes, wincing. He was lying on his side, staring across at the barred door. There was something different about the cell, and it was a while before he could identify it. Then he knew. It was a little cooler. In fact, a breeze played refreshingly across his face. He lifted his head and looked up at the semi-circular window. One of the panes was missing, and daylight showed through the square gap.

On the flagstones across the room, he made out shards of shattered glass and a rounded stone the size of a grapefruit.

He blinked, puzzled at how it had come to be there.

He struggled into a sitting position, wincing in pain, and stared across the cell at the stone and the fragments of glass, hardly daring to hope.

He glanced at the barred door, then cocked his head and listened. He heard nothing, no sounds that would indicate the return of Grayson and the thug, Razor.

Rather than try to stand and walk across the cell, he decided it would be more efficient to shuffle across the floor on his backside. Trying to ignore the pain in his ribs, he moved from side to side and edged his way towards the wall.

Like this, little by little, he crossed the cell. When he reached where the glass lay, he turned until he sat with his back against the wall, his fingers questing across the flagstones.

At last, with a sense of triumph, his fingertips touched a length of glass.

He felt for the gap between the flagstones, then edged the shard towards it. At last the glass slipped into the gap and lodged there.

Next, he moved his bound wrists until he judged that the cord was directly above the improvised blade, then brought it down carefully. The last thing he wanted was to slash his wrists and bleed to death.

He felt the glass connect with the cord and applied pressure. The shard slipped back along the groove. He swore. He had to shuffle back slightly to reposition himself. He located the glass and tried again, and this time he felt the glass bite into the cord.

Holding his breath, he moved his wrists carefully back and forth. He felt the cord give a little as the glass cut through the braided twine, one strand after another. After a minute, he stopped and tugged his wrists apart experimentally. He felt the cords loosen a little. But, try as he might, they wouldn't snap. Cursing, he lowered his wrists again, found the glass and resumed the laborious back-and-forth motion.

He felt the braids loosen as he tugged. His arms came free suddenly, and he dragged his hands to his lap and stared down at them. An agonizing sensation of pins and needles blitzed up and down his arms, and his hands sat like dead things in his lap. Carefully, he moved the fingers, flexing them open and shut. He rolled his shoulders, easing the life back into his arms.

He climbed to his feet and took a deep breath, and then another, gasping at the pain in his ribs. He felt his face, wincing as his fingers encountered the mess of his broken nose and the caked blood on his upper lip.

The old washing line was still tight around his left hand. He unpicked the knot and pulled it free, then inspected the result. The line, about two feet long, would make a very handy garrotte. He picked up the stone, weighing it in his hand and smiling to himself.

He moved to the barred door and listened. There was no sound from along the corridor. He wondered how long it might be before Grayson and his henchman returned for a little more fun.

He walked slowly around the cell, working life into his aching arms and legs.

On the first occasion Grayson and Razor had visited him, Grayson had remained in the corridor while Razor had entered the cell – and the cell door had remained unlocked.

He looked around the cell. They might not notice that the window had been broken, except for the evidence of the shattered glass. He bent down and picked up the shards, then placed them against the wall opposite the entrance. He returned to his original position, sitting back against the wall. He placed his hands behind his back, gripping the stone in his right hand and the washing line in his left.

When Razor – or Horace, if they were taking it in turns – entered the cell, Ryland would smash the stone into the thug's face, then loop the cord around his neck and garrotte the bastard until he was unconscious.

The imponderable, however, would be Grayson's reaction to this unforeseen turn of events. Would he turn and run, or enter the cell to assist his henchman?

If he ran, Ryland would give chase and brain him with the stone – and the same if he entered the cell.

Always assuming, of course, that Grayson didn't think on his feet and quickly lock the cell door. And there was always the possibility that he would be armed.

He heard a sound from along the corridor and his stomach clenched. He waited, his heartbeat loud. He thought about his boys and Annie, and the hell she must be going through now. He gazed up at the window. It was light outside, but whether it was morning or evening he had no idea.

A door opened; he heard footsteps, boots on flagstones. He tensed himself, ready to act. His grip tightened on the stone.

Someone came into sight. It was Razor. There was no sign of Grayson.

The thug stared at him through the bars. He made no attempt to open the cell door, and Ryland cursed to himself.

He looked up and stared at Razor. 'Where's Grayson?' he asked. 'Gone suddenly squeamish, has he?'

'Squeamish? Mr Grayson?' The thug laughed. 'He loves the sight of blood, he does.'

'So where is he?'

'He'll be down presently. Just finishing off some business.' Razor smiled. 'Then we'll finish *you* off.'

'Thought you wanted to know what Bentley told me?'

Razor shrugged. 'Too late for that, now. Things'll soon be getting under way, won't they?'

Ryland peered at him. 'It's the twentieth?'

'Too right it is, Ryland. Hitler's birthday. And when we've done with you, we'll be joining the fun.'

'So that's what Bentley was going on about.'

'And you could've been part of it—'

'Sod that!' Ryland said, and spat on the flagstones.

Razor shook his head, leaning close to the bars and staring at Ryland. 'There's enemies,' he said, 'and then there's enemies. And the worst kind of enemy is a traitor. A turncoat. You were one of us, back then. One of the boys. So what happened? I heard all about Cable Street, the yids you beat up. Went bleedin' soft, did you?'

Ryland stared at the thug. His heart hammered. 'What *happened*?' he said, then asked, 'How old are you?'

'What's that got to do with anything?'

'Too young to have fought in the war, I bet? You were hiding from the doodlebugs under your mum's skirt, right?' He stared at the thug. 'I'll tell you what *happened*, you bastard. I fought in the war, fought and killed scum like you, Nazi bully boys.'

'You lousy—'

'They were just like you,' Ryland said. 'Cowardly bullies. They'd fight in numbers, but get the yellow bastards on their own—'

'Shut it, Ryland, or I'll . . .'

'Come on, then, come in here and finish the job. But you'd never do that, would you? You need the backup of the boss, don't you? You couldn't do a damned thing on your own initiative! I was right – you're just like them. Cowardly *scum*!'

He stopped, hardly daring to hope his provocation might succeed.

For a split second, Razor calculated the cost of contravening the boss's orders – then he was fumbling in his pocket for the key and turning it in the padlock.

Ryland readied himself, his heart thumping.

Razor hauled open the door and strode into the cell, reaching into a pocket for his knuckledusters.

When the thug was three feet away, Ryland leapt up and smashed the stone into the side of his head, stunning him. Razor staggered back, moaning, and Ryland hit him again, this time straight in the face, mashing his nose. Razor lurched for him, swinging a fist that caught Ryland's jaw. He fell back against the wall, then dodged as the big man came for him.

He lashed out with the stone again, catching the thug another good one on the temple. Razor fell to his knees, and Ryland dropped the stone and looped the cord over his head. With a sense of triumph and elation, he drew the cord around Razor's neck and pulled it tight, twisting. Razor gagged, his meaty fists flailing ineffectually behind him.

Ryland dodged the blows and pulled the garrotte ever tighter. Razor made a gargling, strangled sound. Ryland pushed him forward and his head smacked against the wall. Razor fell to the floor and rolled on to his back, groaning.

Ryland retrieved the stone and stood over the thug, his breath coming in elated spasms.

Razor lay on his back, his face purple as his fingers clawed at the cord embedded in his neck.

Gasping, his every breath a labour, Ryland raised the stone, ready to smash it into Razor's terrified face. His exertions had come at a cost: his ribcage blazed with pain and his vision blurred.

'You wanted to know what happened,' he panted, 'why I became a traitor?' He nodded. 'Very well, I'll tell you. I fought in Madagascar. Then . . . then I came back here for the invasion . . . the invasion of Europe, and I was in the first push, Arnhem, then on into Germany. And . . . and then we came to a town, and a camp just outside it, and what I saw there, what I saw . . .' He closed his eyes, feeling the tears tracking down his cheeks, then opened them and went on, 'The town was called Belsen, and I'll never forget . . .'

A part of him wanted to bring the stone down again and again on the fascist's ugly face until his head was no more than a bloody pulp.

Then he recalled what Razor had said and lowered the stone.

'What's happening later? You said you'd be joining the fun, you and Grayson. *Tell me!*'

The thug stared up at Ryland, wincing at the smaller man's sudden rage.

'What's he planning?' Ryland yelled.

'I . . .' Razor shook his head, petrified.

'Tell me, or so help me, I'll . . .'

The thug stared at the stone, said something too low for Ryland to hear.

He saw Razor's hand edging across the stone floor towards a shard of glass, and Ryland brought his heel down hard on the thug's fingers. He felt metacarpal bones snap under his heel, and Razor screamed.

'Tell me!' Ralph said, 'or I'll—'

'Golders Green,' Razor managed. 'A minute after midnight – the twentieth. We're gonna torch the synagogue, then kill a few yids—'

'You miserable, evil scum!'

He glanced towards the cell door. The key was in the lock.

On the floor, Razor clawed at the cord around his neck and coughed, choking.

Ryland reeled away, moved to the door and looked back. 'Christ, I really should kill you . . .'

Before he could change his mind, he stumbled from the cell and swung the door shut, brought the bar down and fumbled with the padlock. He turned the key and looked along the corridor.

There was no sign of Grayson.

He pocketed the key and reeled away from the cell. After the adrenaline rush that had seen him through the encounter with Razor, the pain hit him. He staggered against the wall, nausea rising in a sudden hot wave. He took a deep breath and steadied himself. It would be bad luck if he pegged out now, and Grayson found him and let Razor take his revenge.

The bastards were planning to torch the synagogue at Golders Green at midnight. He had to get out, warn the rozzers . . .

Spurred on by the thought, he pushed himself off the wall and along the corridor.

He came to a flight of steps and stared at them rising before him.

They seemed insurmountable in his enfeebled state. He took a breath, then another. He clutched the rail to his right and lifted a foot on to the first step, then the second, pulling himself up the stairs one by one. The pain in his ribs felt as if someone was plunging a knife between them, repeatedly.

Somehow he gained the top of the staircase and faced a door.

He clutched the stone in his right hand and pushed open the door, ready to attack whoever might be on the other side.

He was in a kitchen, a vast stone-flagged area with a big pine table and brass pans hanging on hooks on the walls. He staggered across to the table and collapsed against it, taking deep breaths. When his head cleared, he made for the far door, pulled it open and found himself in a carpeted corridor.

He stumbled forward, reaching out to steady himself against the wall. When he withdrew his hand from the wallpaper, he saw that he'd left a long smear of blood. He stumbled along the corridor.

He came to an open door to his right and was about to push on, past the door, when something caught his attention.

He moved into the room and stared down at a glass-fronted sideboard. Behind the glass was a display of German medals, iron crosses and swastikas in velvet-lined cases.

On top of the sideboard was a nine-inch-high statuette of a German eagle with a swastika embossed upon its chest, and next to it a small, framed photograph.

It showed three men: Arnold Grayson, someone he recognized as Vernon Lombard, and a much younger man. They were smiling at the camera and raising champagne glasses in a toast.

He snatched up the photograph, turned it over and read the handwritten inscription on the mounting board.

Then he stared at the photograph again, at the smiling face of the young man. There was something he didn't understand, and he wondered if his reasoning had been affected by the blows to his head.

He heard a noise from another part of the house and quickly slipped the photograph into the inside pocket of his jacket. He was about to leave the room when he stopped and looked back at the eagle. He dropped the stone and picked up the statuette, smiling as he hefted it in his palm.

The eagle would make a far more effective cosh than the stone, and the thought of bringing it down on Arnold Grayson's fat face was a delight.

Taking a breath, and attempting to ignore the pain that pulsed through his body, he pushed himself from the room and staggered along the corridor.

TWENTY-SIX

Langham pressed himself against the brickwork of the mansion and glanced at his watch. It was ten past seven and still Mallory had not shown up.

He debated hammering on the front door till someone answered, then nobbling Grayson and Razor and searching the place for Ralph.

It occurred to him that if Razor had gone back to the cellar, while he kicked his heels uselessly out here and the blasted police dragged their feet, then Ralph might very well be dead by now.

What in Christ's name was keeping them?

Hell, how long had he known Ralph? Almost twenty years, now. They'd gone through so much, in war and in peacetime – shared experiences that had brought them closer than brothers. A product of that shared experience was a profound trust in each other.

A trust that Langham was signally failing to uphold.

He pushed himself from the wall and ran along the side of the house. He would hammer on the door, see who answered and take it from there . . . At the corner, he stopped. At the far end of the drive, the iron gates swung open automatically and a squad car appeared, closely followed by Jeff Mallory's Humber. He almost cheered with relief.

The cars pulled up outside the mansion and Mallory climbed out, accompanied by Detective Sergeant Venables.

Langham ran towards them. 'Jeff!'

Mallory stared. 'Don . . . what the hell—?'

'Never mind,' Langham panted. 'What on earth took you?'

Mallory held up a hand. 'I'm sorry. This hasn't been easy – the super isn't happy at all.'

'Isn't happy? To be honest, I couldn't give a tinker's fig—'

'He doesn't like it,' Mallory interrupted. 'He said we weren't to raid the place, merely make polite enquiries.'

'But we're going in there, right? And what about the racetrack?'

'I have a team down there, awaiting my word.' Mallory nodded towards the mansion. 'Are you sure Ralph's in there?'

'Ralph was taken by two of Grayson's men. He's either here or at the house by the racetrack.'

Mallory told Venables to get in touch with the boys at the track and give them the go ahead.

'We'll go by the book,' he said to Langham. 'We're investigating a missing person and would like to enlist Grayson's help in finding him. If he gets bolshy, we turn up the heat.'

'Once we're inside, I could take a look around—'

Mallory stopped him. 'I said we'll go by the book. We don't have a warrant. Stick with us, all right?'

Frustrated, Langham nodded.

Mallory was about to climb the steps to the front door when it opened. Arnold Grayson appeared, looking flushed and prosperous, a balloon glass of brandy in one hand and a fat cigar in the other.

'Forgive the delay, gentlemen. There were one or two things I had to clear up. Now, what was it you wanted?' He gestured to the front gates with the brandy glass. 'It might be the very best intercom that money can buy,' he bragged, 'but the sound quality leaves a lot to be desired.'

'We're looking for a missing person, sir. If you could kindly spare a few minutes . . .'

Grayson made a show of examining a big gold wristwatch. 'Well, I was just about to go out – but if you'd care to come this way.' He turned and waddled down the sumptuous hallway, saying over his shoulder, 'I was dining with Superintendent Peters just last week, Inspector. Discussing the charity ball, as it happens. You will be attending, I take it?'

'I've never missed one yet, sir,' Mallory said, and Langham found himself resenting his friend's subservient tone.

Grayson led them into a living room and invited them to take a seat.

Mallory and Venables took the proffered sofa. Grayson remained on his feet before the hearth, swirling his brandy and sucking on his cigar.

Langham perched on the arm of a chair, his right hand thrust into his pocket.

He wondered if Grayson's thug was still in the room at the back of the house, or if he'd returned to the cellar. He had half a mind to ignore Mallory's order not to search the place but decided to play it by ear.

Grayson beamed at them. 'Now, how can I help, Inspector?'

'A delicate matter,' Mallory said, rubbing his chin. 'We're attempting to trace a private detective, sir. One Ralph Ryland.'

Grayson repeated the name, shaking his head as he did so. 'A dangerous profession, Inspector. Or so I've heard. I've had very little to do with them. I always prefer to deal directly with the police.'

You ingratiating, mealy-mouthed bastard, Langham thought.

'Quite,' Mallory said. 'However, in this case Mr Ryland was last seen in heated discussion with a couple of your employees.'

'Is that so?' Grayson's big, roseate face pantomimed concern. 'In that case I'll be only too happy to facilitate your inquiries. Do you have the names of the men in question?'

Mallory looked across at Langham, who said, staring Grayson in the eye, 'Horace Fowler, one of your drivers. We don't know the identity of the second man.'

Grayson drained his brandy and placed the empty glass on the mantelpiece. 'I can give you Mr Fowler's address immediately, if you'll just allow me to . . .'

Langham interrupted. 'We understand that Fowler delivered Ralph Ryland into your custody, Grayson,' he said, ignoring Mallory's irate grimace.

Grayson looked from Mallory to Langham. '*This is ridiculous*,' he said with quiet menace. 'Just what are you implying?'

Attempting to mollify the businessman, Mallory said, 'We're examining every line of enquiry, sir, no matter how tenuous—'

'And tenuous is just the word,' Grayson said. 'Absurd is another.'

'We understand,' Langham interrupted, praying that everything young Len had told him about Grayson was true, 'that you're holding Ralph Ryland on these premises.'

Grayson moved towards a side table beside the hearth and

reached for a gold-handled telephone. 'I think a few words directly in the ear of Superintendent Peters,' he said, 'will soon sort this out.'

Mallory said, 'If perhaps you'd allow us a quick look around the premises, sir, then we can be away without bothering the super.'

Grayson hesitated in reaching for the phone and turned a glassy smile on the inspector. 'I take it that you have brought a warrant with you?'

Mallory's crestfallen expression was answer enough. Grayson smiled and said, 'In that case, we'll inform Superintendent Peters of your colleague's farcical accusations, shall we?'

Langham reached down to the skirting board and yanked the twined flex from its socket. Grayson gave an incredulous snort and turned in appeal to Mallory, who had started forward as if to prevent Langham's vandalism.

'That won't be necessary,' Langham said. 'Ralph Ryland is either here or in your place by the greyhound track. We know all about the cellar down there, too.'

'This is preposterous!' Grayson cried.

'Then allow us to search the cellars,' Langham said.

'I assure you, gentlemen, that I have never set eyes on Ralph Ryland—'

'Nor ordered your bully boys to torture him?' Langham turned to Mallory. 'As I told you earlier, Jeff, Ralph isn't the first to suffer at Grayson's hands. He has quite a track record, so I've heard—'

'Inspector,' Grayson said, 'I suggest you control your underlings, or Superintendent Peters will certainly be hearing from me.'

Langham stepped forward, drawing the revolver and directing it at Grayson's ample gut.

'Where is Ralph!'

With an exhibition of rage that almost had Langham convinced, Grayson said, 'There is no one by that name in this house!'

Mallory said, 'Don, put the damned gun away.'

'Not until this bastard tells us where he's keeping Ralph.'

'I think,' Grayson said, smiling disingenuously, 'that your man has exceeded the bounds of reasonable duty, Inspector. The idea that I'm holding anyone here is preposterous.'

He stopped at a sound from the far end of the room. As one, they turned and stared.

A door swung slowly open and a ragged figure appeared, leaning against the woodwork.

Langham took in Ralph Ryland's battered face, his blood-soaked shirt.

'The bastard's lying,' Ralph said. 'You . . . you've got to stop them. Midnight tonight, Golders Green. The synagogue . . .'

He took a step into the room, then collapsed.

Langham stepped forward, reversed his grip on the revolver and struck Grayson across the face with all the force he could muster.

One hour later, Langham dialled Ralph's Lewisham number.

'Hello?' Maria said, her voice tremulous.

'Darling,' he said. 'Tell Annie that Ralph's safe and well – other than some cuts and bruises and a cracked rib or two.'

Maria let out a cry, and all Langham heard then was her muffled voice as she relayed the news, followed by Annie's sobs in the background.

'Donald!' Maria said. 'Where are you? What happened? Are you . . .?'

'I'm fine. We're at the Royal Free. They're keeping Ralph in for a couple of days. He was concussed, so they're running tests. But he'll be fine.'

'I'll call a taxi and we'll be straight up.' Maria sounded breathless. 'But who did that to him? And how did you find him? And—'

'Later, Maria. I'll tell you all about it when you get here.'

'Oh, Donald, I'm so relieved!'

'And me, too, darling. See you soon.'

He replaced the receiver and retraced his footsteps through the interminable, echoing hospital corridors to the room where Ralph lay, his head and torso swaddled in bandages.

Langham resumed his chair and sat back, staring at his friend in the half-light.

Earlier, Mallory had escorted Grayson from the mansion in handcuffs, followed by Detective Sergeant Venables with the thug named Razor.

When he'd seen the pair across to waiting squad cars, Mallory had turned to Langham.

'Venables and I didn't see you pistol-whip Grayson, Don. He fell and hit his head on the mantelpiece while resisting arrest, all right?'

Langham had thanked his friend, then climbed into the back of the ambulance with Ralph.

'But promise me you won't do that kind of thing again, OK?'

Langham had given an affirmative salute before the doors were slammed and the ambulance raced off.

Now Ralph stirred and said with sudden urgency, 'Don! Golders Green . . . the synagogue! They're planning . . .'

'Don't worry, Ralph. Jeff's got it all under control. There's a cordon of police around the place and they've already made arrests.'

Ralph collapsed back on to the pillows. 'Don, I feel . . .'

'I know. You must feel lousy. Annie's on her way—'

'No,' Ralph murmured, closing his eyes. 'I feel . . . feel wonderful.'

'Wonderful?'

'What've they given me?'

Langham smiled. 'Morphine, I suspect.'

'Feels . . . feels like the best tipple ever. Beats beer, Don.' He gave a muffled laugh. 'When I'm out of here, let's go for a pint or three.'

Langham nodded, feeling his throat constrict. 'You bet we will. Now,' he went on, 'you settle down and rest.'

Ralph said, 'I thought . . . thought it was curtains, Don. Down there. That bastard . . . the thug . . . he was *enjoying* it, Don, no word of a lie. Loving it. And Grayson . . .'

'Ralph, try to rest.'

'Grayson . . . he was watching, Don. Strange . . .' He fell silent.

Langham asked, 'What's strange, Ralph?'

'It was all the worse because Grayson was watching the

thug lay into me. They . . . they told me they were going to kill me. And I think I believed them.'

'Rest,' Langham said.

'You know what crossed my mind, when I thought I wasn't going to make it? I was thinking about Annie and the boys. I thought . . . the boys are going to grow up without a dad, and that made me . . . that made me so *angry*, Don.'

'I can imagine, Ralph. I can imagine.' He reached out and took his friend's hand as Ralph lapsed into unconsciousness.

Later he heard voices in the corridor, and a nurse escorted Maria and Annie into the room. Maria crossed to Langham and they watched as Annie stopped in her tracks and stared at her husband, took in the bandaged head, black eyes and lacerated face, and wept.

TWENTY-SEVEN

Langham awoke to sunlight slanting into the bedroom. For a second or two he thought he was back at the cottage in Suffolk, before he heard the distant background hum of London traffic.

Maria was watching him, her head propped on her hand. 'Sleep well?' she asked.

'Like a top. You?'

'I was awake for a long time in the night, thinking.'

'About?'

'You. Your job.'

He sighed. 'I know, you think I should write more literary novels.'

She pushed him. 'Not that job, you oaf. Your work with Ralph.'

'Ah.' He turned his head on the pillow and looked at her.

She bit her bottom lip, considering her words. 'Perhaps it's time you thought about—'

'I couldn't jack in the agency work, Maria.'

'Because of Ralph?'

'We're a team. We work well together. If I quit, he'd take it badly.'

'Would he?'

'He'd see my reasons, but he'd be upset.'

'Your "reasons"?' she said. 'And what are they, Donald?'

'I could write more, spend less time in London. More time with you.'

'And the danger? Have you considered that? You would no longer be in constant danger, sitting behind your desk.'

'"Constant" is laying it on a bit thick, my girl.'

'Very well. Point taken. Not constant, then, but occasional. Donald,' she went on before he could stop her, 'I was worried sick last night, waiting for you to phone. And then when I found out what had happened to Ralph . . .' She shook her head. 'He might have *died*. It was pure luck that those vile people didn't kill him. And . . . and that could have been you, Donald. That's the awful thing about your job. There's not a day goes by when I don't worry that you've got yourself into some kind of trouble—'

He took her hand. 'Maria, trust me.'

'No! It's not about simple *trust*. Can't you see that? I *do* trust you. Implicitly. I know you don't go looking for trouble, and you take care. But it's the sheer unpredictability of the dangers of the job that makes me so sick with worry. This present case started out as a simple missing person incident and ended up as murder.'

She fell silent, staring at him.

He reached out and stroked a strand of jet-black hair from her forehead. 'I'm sorry, Maria. I didn't know you felt like that.'

'I didn't feel that way,' she murmured, 'until last night.'

He was silent for a time, considering her words.

'There's something else,' he said.

She stared at him. 'What do you mean?'

'Quite apart from upsetting Ralph . . .' he said. 'Look, I don't expect you to understand, for one minute, and I don't know whether it's a male thing. But a part of me relishes the job, the . . . not so much the danger, but the thrill – the thrill of the challenge. It's the perfect antidote to writing. And to be honest, I think I'd miss it if I did pack it in.'

She nodded, staring at him. 'So you won't even consider it, not even for me?'

He reached out and cupped her cheek. 'I love you, Maria. Of course I'll consider it.'

'Really? You're not just saying that?'

'If it makes you happy, I'll do more than consider it. I'll talk it over with Ralph. Maybe I'll give it a few more months, until he's found a suitable replacement.'

'Now you've made me feel guilty!'

'Don't,' he said, and kissed her.

The telephone shrilled in the hall. 'Damn!' he said. 'I'll get it.'

He rolled out of bed and pulled on his dressing gown, then made his way to the hall and picked up the phone.

'Hello?'

'Donald, Pamela here—'

'Pamela, I'm sorry. I should have phoned last night but it was all rather hectic. Ralph's fine – a little beaten up, but he'll pull through.'

'My word!' she gasped. 'What happened?'

He gave her a brief outline, then went on, 'He's in the Royal, nursing a couple of cracked ribs and a sore head.'

'Is it all right if I knock off work and go to see him? We're quiet at the moment. I could take him some flowers.'

'I think he'd prefer a couple of bottles of beer, Pamela.'

'Beer it is, then,' she said. 'But actually I'm ringing about something else. Jeff Mallory's just phoned—'

Langham swore to himself. 'What is it?'

'He said to tell you that a body's been discovered in the woods near Eltham Common.'

'A body? Did he say whose?'

'Christopher Lombard,' she said.

'*Christopher Lombard?*' he echoed. 'Well, I wasn't expecting that. Did he say how he died?'

'He said he'd been shot, but didn't go into details. He told me he was setting off – this was about five minutes ago – if you wanted to meet him.' She gave him the directions.

'I'm on my way.' He thanked her and rang off.

Maria was leaning against the wall, watching him. 'A body?'

He gave her the details. 'I'll grab some toast and get off.'

'I'll put some coffee on.'

Before he left, ten minutes later, she stopped him and grabbed his lapel. 'Be careful, Donald – and . . .'

'What?'

'Donald, come back early and we'll go for a drink this afternoon, then a meal somewhere, OK?'

He kissed her. 'Sounds wonderful.'

Langham wondered, as he drove east to Eltham Common, if Christopher Lombard had suffered remorse at strangling Dorothea Marston and taken his own life. But had he also killed his own brother? Perhaps Manville Carrington had lied to provide Christopher with an alibi, and perhaps Christopher had left a note, confessing to both killings – and in so doing nicely closed the case. He snorted at the chances of that. *Too neat*, he thought. *Too neat by half.*

He came to the common, found the road leading into woodland and slowed down.

Ahead, he made out a navy-blue police van, two squad cars and Jeff Mallory's Humber. It was another warm day and a cacophony of birdsong rang out from the trees on either side. A rope spanned the lane like the finish line of a marathon.

He ducked beneath it and approached Mallory, who was standing at the side of the lane with Detective Sergeant Venables. Both men were staring down at something in the ditch.

Mallory looked up at his approach. 'Don.' He pointed to the body that sprawled face-up in the ditch. 'Found first thing this morning by a woman walking her dog.'

Langham peered down at the corpse. So much, he thought, for the idea that Christopher Lombard had taken his own life.

Lombard had been shot once in the head – the bullet having entered his skull at the right temple and exited messily above his left ear – and once again in the chest. His light-blue shirt was stained with dried blood.

'How long has he been dead?'

'Surgeon reckons he was shot between ten o'clock last night and four this morning.'

Langham stared down at the man whom he'd last seen four nights ago when he and Ralph had escorted Lombard to Scotland Yard.

'We found a driving licence in his back pocket – and a wallet containing a few pounds in cash.' Mallory gestured across the lane to a squad car. The back door was open and an old man with a walking stick sat on the seat; a constable knelt beside the car, a notepad on his lap as he took down what the man said.

'The old chap happened along not long after we arrived, eager to talk to us,' Mallory went on. 'He says he was out for a stroll last night at ten and passed a couple a little further along the lane.'

'A couple?' Langham said. 'Lombard and . . .?'

'The chap thinks it might have been Lombard, though he can't be definite, and he described the woman as small and blonde. Peroxide blonde.'

'A peroxide blonde let the delivery men into Christopher Lombard's place.'

'And,' Mallory said, 'a woman answering to the same description was seen by the mechanic near the warehouse on the Sunday that Nigel Lombard was killed.'

'Penny Archer,' Langham said.

'Well, she was involved with Christopher Lombard a few years ago, according to my notes.'

'That's all very well,' Langham said, 'but why would Penny Archer shoot him?'

Mallory rubbed his chin. 'If Archer did let the delivery men into the house on Cardigan Street, then she was obviously involved with him again. How about,' he speculated, 'she killed Christopher Lombard for the money he'd received from the gallery?'

'And her motive for shooting Nigel Lombard in the warehouse?'

Mallory shrugged. 'What if Nigel had got wind of Penny's plan to steal Christopher's proceeds from the gallery?'

Langham shook his head. 'I don't buy it. I've spoken to Penny Archer a couple of times now, and take my word for it, she's not the kind of person to go around shooting ex-lovers.

And anyway, how do you account for Dorothea Marston's death? Do you still think the killer was Christopher Lombard?'

'Yes, I do – and perhaps . . .' Mallory thought about it. 'Perhaps that's why Penny shot him last night – not only to get her hands on Christopher's cash, but to avenge Dorothea's killing into the bargain?'

Langham smiled. 'So now Penny Archer has *two* motives for killing Christopher Lombard,' he said with thinly veiled scepticism.

Mallory sighed. 'I know, I'm firing off blanks in the dark here.'

'I just can't see Penny doing something like this.' He paused. 'Has Vernon Lombard been informed about . . .?' He gestured to the corpse.

'Not yet.'

'Bloody hell.' Langham shook his head. 'As far as I know, Christopher Lombard never went to see his father – and now someone's got to break the news to him that his favourite son is dead.'

He fell silent, considering the old man. 'Strange, isn't it?' he went on. 'Vernon Lombard stands for everything I find repellent, and yet I could ruddy well weep for the old duffer.'

Mallory grunted. 'You're too soft for this job, pal.'

He stared into the cloudless sky above London. 'I wonder.'

'Come again?'

Langham shrugged. 'Just something Maria said this morning. After what happened to Ralph last night, she wants me to jack it in at the agency. Said she was worried sick most days.'

'A bit of an overreaction, surely?'

'That's really beside the point,' Langham said. 'She feels it, so it's valid. Perhaps I should be thinking of her.'

'You really have gone soft in your old age,' Mallory said. 'And speaking of Ralph, how is he?'

'Quite merry on morphine last night and liking it more than a skinful of ale. I'll drop by and see him on the way back.'

'Give him my very best, Don.'

'Will do,' he said. 'Give me a call if you make any progress.'

*   *   *

He returned to his car and drove back into London, pulling into the hospital car park half an hour later.

Ralph was lying back on piled pillows, staring at the ceiling when Langham entered and pulled up a chair. He sported two black eyes and a line of stitches down the side of his nose.

'Wotcha, Cap'n.'

'No Annie?' Langham asked.

'Just popped out for a cuppa.'

'How are you feeling?'

'I'm tickety-boo. Pain's not too bad. Just a dull throbbing. Last night the old ribs ached a bit.'

'How did you sleep?'

'I was awake for hours, Don, considering the case. Mulling things over.'

Langham held up a hand. 'There's more,' he said. 'Christopher Lombard was found shot dead this morning in the woods near Eltham.' He went on to give Ralph the details.

When he'd finished, Ralph smiled at him. 'That makes sense, Don.'

Langham stared at his friend. 'What do you mean?'

'Last night, while I was lying awake . . . I was thinking about it – the killings, the Lombard brothers. It was going round and round in my head, and I worked it all out.'

Langham blinked. 'You did?'

'Everything. Who killed who, and why, and even who strangled poor Dorothea Marston, and why he did it.'

'I thought we'd decided that was Christopher Lombard?'

Ralph shook his head. 'No, Don, it wasn't Christopher. She was killed by Nigel Lombard.'

Langham smiled. 'I think they've been giving you a bit too much of that morphine, Ralph. Nigel was dead by the time Dorothea came to London, remember? Shot to death in the warehouse on Sunday.'

Ralph returned his smile. 'No, he wasn't,' he said.

'But—'

Ralph interrupted. 'Where's my stuff?'

'What stuff?'

'The clothes I came in, and the other things . . .' He waved. 'Do me a favour, Don, and press the buzzer, would you?'

'Never mind that,' Langham said. 'What do you mean, Nigel Lombard killed Dorothea?'

'I'll show you – but first I need my stuff. Press the ruddy buzzer!'

Sighing, Langham did so.

A little later a West Indian nurse breezed in, all smiles. 'And what are you wanting now, Mr Ryland?'

'My stuff,' Ralph said. 'My clothes and the rest of the stuff. A nurse took it away last night.'

'It's all safely stored away in a locker, Mr Ryland.'

'Could you be a darling and bring it to me, love?'

The nurse glanced unsurely at Langham. 'Mr Ryland can't be discharging himself.'

'He just wants to show me something,' Langham explained.

She nodded. 'Very well, I'll be back in a minute.'

Langham turned and frowned at Ralph. 'This had better be good.'

Ralph closed his eyes, in superior fashion, until the nurse returned carrying a big brown-paper parcel. 'My word,' she said. 'What have you got in here, Mr Ryland? It weighs a ton!'

Langham took the bundle and the nurse withdrew. He stared down at the weighty parcel on his lap, then looked at Ralph.

'Go on, open it.'

Langham pulled at the knotted twine and peeled back the paper. The parcel contained Ralph's neatly folded clothing, a small photograph in a frame, and a heavy bronze statuette of an eagle with the emblem of a Nazi swastika embossed on its chest.

Langham took the statuette. 'What on earth,' he asked, 'are you doing with this?'

Ralph grinned. 'Picked it up at Grayson's last night,' he said. 'Thought I'd cosh the bastard over the head with it. Thought that'd be . . . what's the word, Don?'

'Appropriate?'

'That's it. Appropriate. Brained with his own Nazi memorabilia. But that's not what I wanted to show you. Take the picture out.'

Langham placed the eagle on the bedside cabinet and picked

up the framed photograph. It showed three people, Grayson, Vernon Lombard and a young man, beaming out at the photographer and raising their glasses in an obvious toast.

'Turn it over, Don.'

He did so and read the handwriting – presumably Arnold Grayson's – on the mounting board: *With Vernon and Christopher, 20th April 1954, toasting the great man's birthday.*

He looked up at Ralph. 'April the twentieth,' he said. 'Hitler's birthday.'

'That's not what's interesting, Don. Take a closer look at the young bloke in the photo.'

Langham turned the photograph over and looked at the youngest of the trio.

Ralph said, '*That's* Christopher Lombard, Don.'

'But . . .' He shook his head. 'He looks nothing like . . .'

The young man who stood between Grayson and Lombard senior was more thickset than the man he and Ralph had taken into Scotland Yard the other evening.

'I found this last night,' Ralph said, 'when I got out of the ruddy cell. When I had a closer look, I thought I was going mad. Thought the battering had sent me round the bend. Then I started thinking about it last night while I lay awake, and I went over and over the case, and then all the pieces fell into place.'

'If this is Christopher Lombard,' Langham said slowly, indicating the photograph, 'then the chap we took into Scotland Yard that day . . .'

'That was Nigel,' Ralph said, 'masquerading as his brother, Christopher.'

'And the body in the warehouse on Sunday . . .?'

'Was Christopher Lombard,' Ralph said.

'But . . .' Langham began, 'but what about the passport we found in the warehouse?'

Ralph shrugged. 'Must've been a forgery, Don.'

Langham looked up from the photograph. 'Good God . . .'

'That explains why poor Dorothea was killed, doesn't it?' Ralph went on. 'When she came down to London to give what-for to her ex-lover, Christopher, and she knocked on the door at Cardigan Street – it was opened by *Nigel* Lombard.

Well, he couldn't have her getting away and blabbing that he wasn't dead, as we all supposed, could he? So he strangled her and dumped her body on the waste ground.'

Langham swallowed. 'But that means . . .' He tried to marshal his thoughts. 'When Victoria Lombard identified the corpse in the morgue as Nigel's, she was mistaken.'

Ralph was shaking his head. 'No, Don – she was lying.'

'Lying?'

'She knew who the body belonged to all along, because she'd planned the killing with Nigel. They lured Christopher to the warehouse on some pretext or other, got him drunk, and then one of them shot the painter dead, making sure there was nothing left of his face, or his dentistry, that might identify him. Nigel then removed his watch and slipped it on to the corpse's wrist and planted the passport in the valise.'

Langham stared at him. 'That night when Victoria phoned me about her father's address book, saying it might contain Christopher's address . . .'

'I suspect she added it to the book, making it look like her father's handwriting – she *wanted* you to find the body. You told me that she was rather insistent that she come along with you. She wanted to be on hand to identify the corpse as Nigel, not Christopher.'

'Of course,' Langham said, 'and I put her off. As it turned out, she was the only person available who could have identified the body, so Mallory had her taken to the morgue. It worked out for her in the end.' He paused, going over the details. 'Very well,' he went on, 'but why? Why did Nigel and Victoria want their older brother out of the way?'

'Why else?' Ralph said. 'Why did Vernon Lombard want us to find Christopher? He told you he intended to leave everything he had to his oldest son. Of course, Victoria and Nigel didn't like the idea of that, so they came up with a plan of bumping off the hated Christopher and having Nigel take his place.'

'Which is why Christopher – or rather Nigel – never went to see his father, because even though Vernon was blind, he'd be able to tell that Nigel wasn't Christopher from the sound of his voice.'

Ralph nodded. 'Nigel no doubt planned to lie low until such time as Vernon Lombard shuffled off and he could claim Christopher's inheritance, splitting it with Victoria as pre-arranged.'

'And they had Christopher's artwork collected by the gallery. Victoria was the woman who let them into the terraced house, disguised in a blonde wig.'

'And she was the blonde who was seen with Nigel in the woods last night.'

Langham shook his head. 'OK, so far so good. I buy everything you've said. But why did Victoria shoot Nigel?' He stopped. 'Christ,' he said, 'don't tell me she'd planned it all along? She wasn't satisfied with a half share of Nigel's inheritance – she wanted it all? So Nigel had to die.'

'I wonder . . .' Ralph said, frowning. 'With both her brothers dead, would Vernon Lombard's fortune go to Victoria on his death? Wouldn't she have to contest the will, if it still stipulated that the beneficiary was Christopher? Then again, Vernon might have changed it in some way so that she didn't receive a thing.'

'I don't get it,' Langham said. 'She was taking a bloody great risk, then, killing Nigel. If he remained alive, then presumably she'd receive half of what came to him anyway – but with him dead, she risked getting nothing if her father had decided to cut her out of his will.'

'In her greed,' Ralph said, 'perhaps she was willing to take the risk?'

Langham stared at his friend. 'There's only one way to find out. I'll drive across to Highgate now.'

'Wish I could come with you and see the look on her face when you tell her we've rumbled her little game,' Ralph said. 'But I don't think nursey will let me out.'

'I'll tell you all about it,' Langham promised.

'Hold on, Don. Put this bloody thing back before the staff see it!'

Langham took the Nazi eagle and wrapped it in the parcel, along with the photograph, and stowed the package in the bedside cabinet beside two bottles of Guinness. He smiled. 'I see Pamela paid a visit.'

'Diamond girl,' Ralph said.

Langham climbed to his feet. 'Be seeing you.'

Ralph reached out a hand. 'Before you go . . . When I'm out of here, there's something I need to tell you.'

'Go on.'

'Not now. When I've thought it through, OK?'

'Very well.' Langham nodded. 'Catch you later – and good detective work, by the way. You ought to be on morphine more often.'

He left the hospital and drove west to Highgate.

TWENTY-EIGHT

Langham came to number twelve, Saddler's Lane and made his way along the garden path, pushing aside over-grown shrubs. As he approached the house, it came to him that Victoria might still be armed. She had killed twice and he was in no doubt that she would do so again if provoked.

He slipped his hand into his jacket pocket, touching Ralph's revolver as if it were a talisman.

At the house, he climbed the steps to Victoria Lombard's flat.

The door was shut. He knocked and waited. When she answered, he would explain his presence with the pretext of bringing her, and her father, the news about her brother's shooting in Eltham.

There was no reply. He knocked again and waited a minute, then gave up and made his way back down the steps.

The chances were that Vernon Lombard would be at home, listening to Wagner in the darkness of his living room. The French windows were open, the curtains partially drawn, but no music was playing.

'Hello?' he called. 'Mr Lombard?' He backhanded the curtain aside and stepped into the room.

He peered into the shadows and made out the upright figure of Vernon Lombard seated in his customary chair. He approached. 'Mr Lombard, I hope you don't mind my . . .'

He stopped in his tracks.

Lombard's head was angled stiffly on one side, a neat bullet hole marking his right temple. A revolver lay on the carpet beside the chair.

Langham reached out and touched the back of the man's right hand, hanging over the arm of the chair. His skin was cold.

Only then did he see the notepaper on the coffee table before the chair. He moved to the French window and opened the curtains further, flooding the room with sunlight.

He returned to the coffee table, knelt and read the looping, spidery scrawl.

There comes a time when all things must end, and the end is nigh – Vernon Lombard.

He stood and crossed to the door at the far end of the room, walked along the corridor and climbed the stairs to Victoria's flat.

He came to the top of the steps and pushed open the door. 'Hello? Victoria?'

He stepped into the living room and looked around.

Victoria Lombard sat in an armchair at the far end of the room, gripping a cut-glass tumbler in her right hand. A bottle of gin stood on the coffee table before her.

She looked up suddenly, and he saw that she was more than a little drunk. 'Oh, Donald. It's you. Sorry; I did hear you knocking earlier, but . . .'

He crossed the room, pulled up an armchair and sat down.

She wore a yellow summer frock which contrasted with her fall of dark hair, and she looked, he thought, quite beautiful in the sunlight slanting in through the window.

'I heard you' – she shrugged – 'but I really couldn't be bothered. I take it you found my father?'

'I did.'

'I suppose I shouldn't be surprised he decided to end it all,' she said, speaking with the exaggerated care of the very drunk. 'But when I found him . . . it did come as something of a shock.'

He watched her as he said, 'Have you heard about—?'

'Christopher?' she interrupted. 'Yes. The police came and

told me this morning.' She raised the glass to her rouged lips and took a drink.

'Do you think news of his son's death is what made your father . . .?'

She shook her head. 'No, he didn't know. I thought it best that *I* should break the news to my father, so I told the police that he was still sleeping. A little while after they left, I heard a gunshot and went down and . . . and found him.'

He looked around the room. There was no evidence of a gun in the vicinity and, as her dress was a tight fit, it was obvious that she wasn't concealing a weapon on her person.

'What were you doing last night?' he asked.

She frowned as she considered the question. 'I was out.'

'Where did you go?'

She waved, as if she thought the question unimportant. 'A drink with . . . with a friend—'

'Were you with Nigel?'

'Nigel?' She had been in the process of lifting the glass to her lips, but she paused and stared at him.

'I know what happened,' Langham said. 'I know that you and Nigel planned to kill Christopher and carried it out last Sunday at the warehouse. Then you identified Christopher's body as Nigel's—'

She attempted to laugh. 'And why would we do that, Donald?'

'So that Nigel could take his brother's place when your father died,' he said, 'and claim the inheritance.'

He detected no discernible reaction to his words, at first. She looked at him above her glass, which she held up before her lips. Then she smiled, tipsily, and surprised him by saying, 'Very clever of you, Donald.'

'Not me,' he said. 'It was my partner, Ralph Ryland, who worked it all out.'

'Ryland – that little runt?'

'Appearances can be deceptive,' he said, staring across at the suave, elegant woman who was also a killer.

'And the passport?' he went on. 'Somehow you or Nigel managed to obtain a forgery—'

'Oh, how perspicacious you are today!'

He shook his head. 'But its issue was confirmed by the passport office,' he said. 'How on earth . . .?'

'Nigel knew someone who worked in the department,' she said. 'Nigel had something on him – the little chap had embezzled funds from his previous employer—'

'Cedric Evans?' Langham said.

She nodded. 'Nigel threatened to go to the police if Evans wouldn't agree to obtain a forged passport and certify it through his department at the passport office.'

'You and Nigel thought of everything,' he said. 'But tell me, who pulled the trigger? You, or was it Nigel?'

She regarded him levelly. 'That,' she said, 'was me.'

'And Manville Carrington?'

'What about him?'

'How did you persuade Carrington to provide Nigel with an alibi?'

'Manville and I . . . Following my fiancé's death, just after the war, we became close. In fact, we were lovers for a time. Through me, he and Nigel became friends. I told Manville that Nigel needed an alibi.'

'And he didn't think it odd that you wanted him to lie and pretend that Nigel was Christopher that night?'

Victoria smiled. 'I don't know if you've met Manville, but he's quite gaga these days. He was all for our killing fascist Christopher and thought it amusing that we should put one over on the police.'

She reached out and poured herself another gin, the bottle clinking on the glass as her hand trembled.

'Your father's inheritance,' Langham said. 'I take it you planned to share the proceeds with Nigel?'

Anger flared in her eyes. 'It was never about the money, Donald. Do you think I'm *that* shallow?'

'Then . . . why? Why did you kill Christopher?'

She leaned forward, and for the first time he discerned some animation in her demeanour.

'Who was it who wrote, "*It was not I, but rage, did this . . .*"?' She waved. 'I can't recall the rest.'

'Thomas Heywood,' he said, and quoted, '"*It was not I, but rage, did this vile murder . . .'''* He paused. 'But you aren't trying to claim you killed Christopher in rage, are you?'

'Not in the heat of the moment, no. It was a slow-burning rage, a rage that took years to reach its culmination.' She took another drink before continuing. 'Christopher, like my father, was a fascist. To hear him speak, to hear him exalt Nazi ideology . . . He was behind what Grayson and his thugs were planning. He funded them, and he had to be stopped.'

'And so you stopped him and planned to have Nigel take Christopher's place and claim his father's inheritance?'

'That was Nigel's idea – how ironic it would have been for him to inherit his father's ill-gotten millions, and then to fund causes of the Left. *That* is why we wanted the money, Donald.'

'Very well. I can understand that. I can see why you planned to kill Christopher – a cowardly act, by the way, no matter how much you might excuse it by claiming rage. What I can't bring myself to understand is why you shot Nigel last night – if you claim that you weren't motivated by the money.'

She was silent for a long time, staring at the glass in her hand.

'The inheritance had nothing to do with it, Donald. And anyway, I wasn't mentioned in the will, and had no certainty of getting anything even if I were to have contested it. No, it was rage again, Donald. I shot Nigel in *rage.*'

Langham shook his head, and she went on.

'We met last night and I confronted him about . . . about Dorothea. He told me that she'd turned up at the house and seen him – Nigel, who she'd assumed was dead. So in panic he attacked her; she fought back and . . . and Nigel strangled her.'

'And in your rage at this, you shot him,' he said, more to himself.

'I realized something last night, Donald. Speaking with Nigel, listening to him rationalizing his actions, it came to me that he was every bit as driven, as *misguided,* as his brother. The end justifies the means, he once told me.' She shook her head, and tears rolled down her cheeks. 'Have you thought through the terrible implications of that absolute diktat? *The end justifies the means* . . . It justifies *anything,* any degree of evil, if you think that the end result is worthwhile. That's when I became enraged with Nigel. We argued, and he went for me, hit me . . .'

'But why were you armed?'

'Because Nigel wanted Father's service revolver,' she said. 'He was planning to kill Arnold Grayson, Christopher's fascist crony, and he thought it poetic justice that he should do it with Father's revolver.'

'And you had no qualms about the proposed killing?' he said.

She shrugged drunkenly. 'Grayson is evil. He deserves to die.'

'The end,' he said, 'justifies the means?'

'No!' she snapped. 'Grayson's death would have been in *payment* for all those he'd injured and killed across the years – and it would prevent further deaths in future.'

'So last night Nigel went for you, and you pulled the gun and shot him dead?'

She wiped her eyes quickly and drained her glass. She reached out, unsteadily, and plucked the bottle from the table. He watched her pour the gin and take a drink.

'I don't think Nigel was as . . . as corrupt as Christopher, and I regret . . . I regret what I did, Donald. But the *rage* I felt when he hit me, when he thought that because he was a man, and stronger . . . So I pulled out the gun and shot him in the chest, and then in the head.' She screwed her eyes shut. 'Oh, the expression on his face before the second shot, the incredulity, and then the horror . . .' She leaned forward, pressed the heel of her right hand to her temple and wept.

'You killed him with your father's service revolver,' he said. 'Then this morning you shot your father and forged the suicide note.'

She looked up and stared at him, her beauty marred by tears.

He went on, 'You shot your father in . . . in revenge, for treating you as he had over the years?' He shook his head. 'I suppose you'll claim rage, again?'

'No, not rage,' she said. 'Compassion.'

'Compassion?' he said incredulously.

'Human beings are complex, contradictory animals, aren't they?' she said.

He nodded. 'I suppose they are. But . . . *compassion?*'

'I hated my father. I hated his ideals. I hated how he treated people. But last night, when I came back and found him sitting alone down there, listening to his music, he asked me to lower the volume and come and sit with him. He spoke about Christopher, how he missed his son and how it pained him that he hadn't been in touch. And do you know something, Donald?'

Silent, he watched her.

'When he said that, said how it pained him – and because I knew what we had done to Christopher, and that my father would never again see his favourite son . . . I felt such a strange compassion for him. I reviled him and at the same time I wept for him. And,' she went on, '*that* is why I killed him. I hated him and I pitied him, but I killed him from *compassion*. Not that I expect you to believe me.'

Langham sighed and made a non-committal gesture.

She laid her head back and closed her eyes, and he stared at the woman in silence.

She said, her eyes still closed, 'What will happen to me, Donald?' Her enquiry sounded frightened, pathetic.

'You will be arrested and charged with three murders.'

'And I'll be hanged by the neck until dead.'

'"*It was not I, but rage, did this vile murder . . .*"' he replied, and completed the quote, '"*Yet I, and not my rage, must answer it.*"'

She said, quietly, 'But I don't want that to happen, Donald.'

He made no reply.

'If you leave me here . . .' she faltered.

'Yes?'

'If you leave me, I promise I'll go downstairs, take my father's revolver, and . . . and do the court's job for them.'

'I can't do that, Victoria.'

'No,' she said, smiling with her eyes still closed, 'I knew you'd say that.'

The silence in the sunlit room was absolute.

Langham sat for a while, watching the woman, then crossed the room and phoned for the police.

EPILOGUE

L angham and Ryland walked along Millbank beside the Thames, their jackets slung over their shoulders. As it had been quiet at the agency that morning, Ralph had suggested a stroll along the river. Langham recalled Ralph saying, when laid up in hospital, that he had something to tell him.

Well, Langham had something to tell Ralph, too, and he wasn't exactly looking forward to it.

Ralph was still limping, a week after his discharge from hospital. His ribs were still tender and his black eyes had turned a lovely shade of yellow. The surgeon had done a good job of resetting his nose. With luck, there'd be no visible evidence that it had been broken.

Langham glanced at his friend. Ralph had been quiet all week, clearly troubled by something. Ralph's preoccupation had affected Langham in turn, making him reluctant to tell his partner that he was seriously thinking about leaving the agency.

Ralph was quiet, smoking his Capstan abstractedly.

'What is it?' Langham asked.

Ralph was silent for a time as they strolled. On the river, a lighter chugged past, churning the water.

'What happened last week,' Ralph said at last, 'brought back a lot of memories.'

'Ah . . .' Langham said. 'Your father.'

Ralph shook his head. 'No, not just my father. I've never told you this, Don. Only Annie knows.'

Langham glanced at his friend, guessing at what was coming. 'Go on.'

'In the thirties my father was involved with the fascists – and so was I.' He shrugged. 'I was young, impressionable. I'm not making excuses. Well, perhaps I am. It's just . . . I looked up to my father. I wanted to be just like him, and the

way he talked about Mosley and all his mates at the union
. . . It seemed so *right*. So when I could join them, I did.'

He fell silent again as they walked. Langham watched a
seagull swoop over the river. A woman passed, pushing a baby
in a big pram.

When she'd passed, Ralph went on, 'I wanted to be part of
something . . . something that would change things, make
things better for the working classes, which is what my dad
said the Union promised.'

Langham smiled to himself as he recalled what his father
had told him, back in his youth: that the British Communist
Party promised the very same thing.

He said, 'You've nothing to be ashamed about, Ralph. As
you said, you were young, impressionable.'

'That's just it, Don,' Ralph interrupted. 'I have got something
to be ashamed of, very ashamed . . . Something that's haunted
me for bloody years.'

Langham glanced at his friend and was shocked to see tears
pooling in his eyes. 'Ralph?'

'That night, in '36, Cable Street. I was there. All fired up.
I . . . I took part in what happened, Don, God help me . . .'

Langham nodded, then swallowed. 'I see.'

'I was with some mates, all around my own age, and we
wrecked a few shops. And then . . . then I put in the window
of this barber's shop and trashed the place, and I saw this chap
in the back, trying to get away.' He stopped walking and closed
his eyes as it all came back to him. 'So I waded in and set
about the poor old bastard with a cricket bat.'

Langham pointed to a bench and they sat down.

Staring sightlessly at the river, Ralph said, 'I look back and
can't believe what I did that night, Don – and what's even
worse, I can't believe that it seemed so *right*, then. I got a
real kick out of laying into the old geezer, hearing his cries.
It was only later, much later, and what I saw . . .'

He stopped talking, tears tracking down his cheeks. He
fumbled with a handkerchief and quickly mopped his face as
if ashamed of the tears.

'What was that, Ralph?'

Langham listened as his friend told him about the push

across Europe towards the end of the war, the advance into Germany, and what they discovered at Belsen.

'Christ, what I saw there almost did for me. I saw men, women, kids . . . And just because they were Jewish. I thought back, thought of my dad, and I hated him for what he told me, what he'd made me believe.'

He smiled bleakly at Langham, then went on, 'But that wasn't right, was it? I was only hating my old man because I couldn't hate myself, at the time. That came later, years later.'

They sat side by side in silence for long minutes, staring out across the Thames.

'So what happened last week, in the cell in Grayson's mansion . . . I knew then just what it was like to be beaten to a bloody pulp by a fascist who thought he was right. And when I cut myself free, and Razor came in to finish me off . . . you know, a part of me wanted to kill him with that bloody rock.'

'I'm glad you didn't,' Langham said.

Ralph smiled. 'Me, too, Don . . .'

He lit another Capstan. His hand shook as he raised the cigarette to his lips and inhaled. 'Anyway, I had to tell you this. I had to tell you so that you'd know what I did.' He hesitated. 'I just hope you don't think I'm still the same person I was back then. I'm not, Don. I've changed. Changed a lot.'

'I know you have,' Langham murmured.

Ralph couldn't bring himself to meet Langham's eyes as he asked, 'And it won't alter things between us?'

Langham shook his head. 'No. No, of course not.'

Ralph exhaled, relieved, then said in hushed tones, 'I value what we have, you know that? You and me, the agency. We make a good team, and I couldn't imagine working without you.'

Langham wondered, then, if Maria had said something to Ralph over the course of the past week – but he thought not. It was just that his friend had more intuition than he, Langham, had ever given him credit for.

He said, 'And I value it, too, Ralph.'

Now, he thought, to go home and explain to Maria that he wasn't leaving the agency, at least not for a while yet.

Ralph smiled. 'But that's not the only reason I wanted to come down here today.'

'It isn't?'

Ralph pointed to Lambeth Bridge. 'There's something I want to do. Come on.'

Intrigued, Langham followed him from the bench. They climbed the steps and made their way to the middle of the bridge, where they stopped.

Ralph unslung his jacket from his shoulder and laid it across the stone parapet, then pulled something from its pocket.

Langham laughed. 'I thought you had something heavy in there.'

'The thing weighs a ruddy ton.'

Ralph set the Nazi eagle on the parapet and stared at it.

'What now?' Langham asked.

Ralph pulled something else from another pocket of his jacket and set it beside the eagle – a wad of crimson material folded up like a tablecloth.

'Got it from that theatrical supply shop off Wardour Street,' he said. 'A snip at fifteen bob.'

He unfolded the material on the stonework, its crimson background and yellow hammer and sickle resplendent in the sunlight.

'A Soviet flag,' Langham said.

'I had time to think, while I was laid up in hospital,' Ralph said. 'About Christopher Lombard and Arnold Grayson, and what they believed in, and about Victoria and Nigel. Then I got to thinking about Hitler and Stalin. And you know what?'

'Tell me.'

Ralph shrugged his bony shoulders. 'What does it lead to, what they all believed in so passionately? I'll tell you: it leads to what I did back in '36, and what Victoria and Nigel did to their brother, doesn't it?'

Langham smiled. 'You're not wrong,' he said.

'So I thought, *Stuff 'em, Right* and *Left*.'

Ralph lifted the heavy bronze eagle and placed it in the centre of the spread flag, then gathered it up so that it resembled a burglar's swag bag. He took a length of twine from his trouser pocket and secured the bundle.

Then he peered over the parapet, ensured there were no passing boats down below, lifted the flag-shrouded eagle and dropped it into the river.

They leaned over, like schoolboys, and watched it plummet towards the water and hit with a splash.

'And good riddance!' Ralph said.

In seconds the bundle was lost to sight amid a swirl of bubbles.

'I don't know about you,' Ralph said, 'but I could do with a pint.'

Langham smiled. 'This one's on me.'

They walked from the bridge and made their way to the Windmill on Lambeth High Street.